WHEN THE CAT'S AWAY

ALSO BY LOUISE CLARK

The Nine Lives Cozy Mystery Series

The Cat Came Back

The Cat's Paw

Cat Got Your Tongue

Let Sleeping Cats Lie

Cat Among The Fishes

Cat in the Limelight

Fleece the Cat

Listen to the Cat!

When The Cat's Away

Death of a Crooked Cat

Forward in Time Series

Make Time For Love

Discover Time For Love

Hearts of Rebellion Series

Pretender's Game

Lover's Knot

Dangerous Desires

WHEN THE CAT'S AWAY

THE 9 LIVES COZY MYSTERY SERIES
BOOK NINE

LOUISE CLARK

Without limiting the rights under copyright(s) reserved below, no part of this publication may be reproduced, stored in, or introduced into a retrieval system or transmitted in any form or by any means (electronic, mechanical, photocopying, recording, or otherwise) without the prior permission of the publisher and the copyright owner.

This is a work of fiction. Names, characters, places, and incidents either are the product of the author's imagination or are used fictitiously, and any resemblance to actual persons, living or dead, business establishments, events or locales is entirely coincidental.

The content of this book is provided "AS IS." The publisher and the author make no guarantees or warranties as to the accuracy, adequacy, or completeness of or results to be obtained from using the content of this book, including any information that can be accessed through hyperlinks or otherwise, and expressly disclaim any warranty expressed or implied, including but not limited to implied warranties of merchantability or fitness for a particular purpose. This limitation of liability shall apply to any claim or cause whatsoever, whether such claim or cause arises in contract, tort, or otherwise. In short, you, the reader, are responsible for your choices and the results they bring.

NO AI TRAINING: Without in any way limiting the author's [and publisher's] exclusive rights under copyright, any use of this publication to "train" generative artificial intelligence (AI) technologies to generate text is expressly prohibited. The author reserves all rights to license uses of this work for generative AI training and development of machine learning language models.

The scanning, uploading, and distributing of this book via the internet or any other means without the permission of the publisher and copyright owner is illegal and punishable by law. Please purchase only authorized copies, and do not participate in or encourage piracy of copyrighted materials. Your support of the author's rights is appreciated.

Copyright © 2024 by Louise Clark. All rights reserved.

Released: July 2024
ISBN: 978-1-64457-633-5 (Paperback)
ISBN: 978-1-64457-634-2 (Hardcover)

ePublishing Works!
644 Shrewsbury Commons Ave
Ste 249
Shrewsbury PA 17361
United States of America
www.epublishingworks.com
Phone: 866-846-5123

CHAPTER 1

The day was overcast and on the cool side, a typical Vancouver June day. It wasn't raining, though, and that was a good thing because the thirty preteens attending Noelle Jamieson's tenth birthday party were busy enjoying the benefits of the open spaces and animal exhibits available at The Birthday Hobby Farm in North Vancouver.

It was two-thirty in the afternoon. The party had begun at one and Noelle's mother, Christy, was amazed none of the children had yet started to flag. There was plenty to do. Good-natured horses lazed in their corral, their heads hanging over the rails waiting for little hands to offer carrots or a pat. A shaggy Highland cow, happily browsing beside a Texas Longhorn in another paddock, was of great interest, while a mother pig, nursing her litter of six was fascinating. So were the chickens scratching around in their enclosure, especially the pretty cochin, marked in a lacy silver pattern, and the black silkie whose loose feathers made it look more like a fluffy rabbit than a bird.

"The pony ride is a hit." Quinn Armstrong, tall, dark-haired and the man Christy was falling in love with, leaned against the corral rails as Christy patted the nose of an affectionate brown horse. Unsatisfied with just Christy's attention, it butted Quinn's shoulder. He laughed and scratched it behind its ear.

Christy watched him with considerable pleasure. Like her, he was dressed casually in jeans and a long-sleeved sweater. The heather-blue color accentuated the deep blue of his eyes as they smiled at her. She'd paired her jeans with a dark green V-necked top that hugged her body and made the most of her red-brown hair and fair skin. It gave her a quiet confidence as she smiled back at him.

After that intimate moment, she shifted back to mom mode to monitor the party. She looked past Quinn to the small track where handlers led two ponies and two donkeys around the circuit at a plodding pace. When they'd first arrived, every child at the party wanted to ride the ponies, creating a huge lineup and leaving the donkeys free. As the birthday girl, Noelle was first in line for the ponies, but to Christy's great pride, she looked at the donkeys, lonely and unwanted, then stepped across to snag the first ride on one of them. Naturally, other children followed her, though the line for the ponies was still double the one for the donkeys. After her turn ended, she'd rushed to the end of the lineup for the pony ride. Once she'd ridden both, she collected her dear friend Mary Petrofsky and several other classmates and headed off to explore the farm.

Even with the birthday girl off to other areas, the demand for the rides remained steady and one of the adults monitored the line to ensure there was no queue jumping, or excited pushing. Since Christy had been busy with the farm staff dealing with party details when they first arrived, Roy Armstrong, Quinn's dad and Noelle's honorary grandfather, had been the first to manage the line. He turned over the duty to Quinn after a half an hour.

Quinn was replaced by Ellen Jamieson, Noelle's great-aunt, who was currently managing the line. Ellen, dressed elegantly as usual in tailored slacks and a silk tunic belted with a self-tie, was sending quelling looks at one of Noelle's classmates. Devon was an energetic boy who was hopping from one foot to the other as he waited impatiently for his turn. Ellen's looks were not doing the least bit of good.

Christy laughed. "The farm's manager warned me the pony rides and the goat enclosure would be the top attractions."

Like the pony rides, the goat enclosure was interactive. Kids entered through a double-door system that ensured the goats stayed in the pen as the children wandered in and out. The good-natured goats endured excited patting from their guests, but a climbing structure had been built at the back end of the enclosure should the goats feel the need to escape. It didn't always work, however, as kids followed where the goats led, and clambered up and around with considerable agility.

Like the pony ride, an adult was stationed in the goat enclosure. At the moment, it was Sledge, legally known as Rob McCullagh, lead singer with the supergroup SledgeHammer. A childhood friend of Quinn's, Sledge was now one of the close-knit group who had become Christy and Noelle's surrogate family in Vancouver. At Noelle's last birthday party, Sledge had led the kids in a sing-along. Christy wondered if he'd do it again when they finally retired to the party room for pizza, presents, and cake in another hour or so.

Sledge, his trademark shaggy blond hair covered by a baseball cap, his long legs in jeans, and his body covered by a dark T-shirt, was leaning against the rails that made up the goat enclosure's fence. His elbows rested on the top rail and his legs were stretched out, one ankle crossed over the other. Beside him, sitting on the top rail was a large gray tabby cat.

The cat would willingly stay by the chicken coup forever. He's obsessed with the fluffy black chicken. It's taunting him, strutting around looking important.

The words echoed in Christy's mind as Sledge nodded. The speaker was her late husband, Frank Jamieson, a playboy whose life had ended abruptly when he was murdered two years before. His essence had taken up residence in Stormy, the Jamieson family cat, and he was able to mentally communicate with an ever-growing collection of people, Sledge and Christy among them. Quinn, however, was deaf to his voice.

Erin, one of the girls from Noelle's class, came by to chat and pat the horse, then she skipped off to check out the Highland cow. Stormy's tail began to lash as the goat Noelle was patting butted her hand away and trotted over to the climbing hill.

Hey goat! Come back. You're being rude!

Sledge patted Stormy soothingly. Noelle looked over at them, grinned, and shrugged. She'd been able to hear her father's voice since the beginning.

The cat's tail stilled. Crisis averted.

Christy let out a breath she didn't know she'd been holding. Quinn, who had been watching the goat enclosure too, raised one dark brow. "Frank acting up?"

"He thinks the goat snubbed his daughter."

Quinn narrowed his eyes. "Was he going to pounce on the goat?"

From the tone of Frank's mind-speak, yes, that was exactly what he had been about to do. "I hope not," Christy said.

Quinn shot her a skeptical look. She laughed and moved on to another subject. "I've decided to take Noelle to see her grandparents in July for a good long visit." Christy's parents, Rachael and Miles Yeager, lived across the country, in the province of Ontario, so visits were special occasions. They'd been out to Vancouver at Christmas and last summer Christy and Noelle had gone back east for a couple of weeks in August. Quinn had come along with them for that visit and she hoped he'd join them this time too.

"How long is 'good long'?" he asked.

"The middle of July to the third week of August."

"Most of the summer," he said lightly.

She shot him a direct look. "I'd like it if you came with us." Before he could say anything about imposing on her parents, she held up her hand. "I've already talked to my parents and they'd love to see you. They have the space. It wouldn't be a problem for them."

Quinn gazed down at her, tenderness in his eyes. "I'd love it." He smiled at the relief on her face.

"Great!" Christy flashed him a cheeky grin.

"What's great? Are you talking about this party?"

Lost in each other, neither Christy nor Quinn had noticed Roy ambling their way.

With a sigh, aware his private time with Christy was over, Quinn explained.

Clad in his usual jeans and a checked shirt, Roy brightened. "I haven't been back east in a while. Sounds like fun."

Christy shot him an amused glance as Quinn frowned. "Dad..."

Trevor McCullagh, Sledge's father and Roy's long-time friend, wandered over to see what was up.

"We're heading east for the summer," Roy announced. "Got any plans?"

Trevor wrinkled his brow. "Ellen and I talked about going to Salt Spring for a couple of weeks. I've rented out my house, though, so we'd have to find accommodation, which might be difficult." Trevor, a successful defense lawyer, had retired to Salt Spring Island off the coast of Vancouver after a cancer scare. He'd been ready for a change when he met Ellen Jamieson a year and a half ago and was now once again a permanent resident of Vancouver. "I'll talk to her about it."

Before Christy could say anything to change his mind, he hurried off to the pony rides where Ellen was stationed. For a moment, the pair were deep in conversation, then Ellen looked Christy's way, smiled, waved, and nodded. After more conversation, Trevor took over Ellen's spot monitoring the still lengthy line of riders. Ellen headed over to the goat enclosure to relieve Sledge. He and the cat sauntered over to the horse corral. Noelle danced along behind, until she was hailed by Devon, who had just finished his turn on one of the ponies.

"Ellen says we're going on vacation again and I'm supposed to get the details from you," Sledge said. "Where to this time?"

Last summer, before she and Noelle and Quinn had traveled to Ontario, the Jamiesons and Armstrongs had gone camping on Vancouver Island. During that memorable vacation they'd solved a murder and the cat had gone swimming in a giant fish tank, capturing (and eating) a young salmon fry, much to the annoyance of the tank's curator. "We're visiting my parents in Kingston," Christy said, suppressing a sigh.

Sledge grinned his lazy rock star grin. He'd met Christy's parents at Christmas and her mother had been dazzled, to say the least. "Sounds like fun." The smile dimmed a little. "Justina has been after me to do some promo work back east." Justina Strong was SledgeHammer's new manager and Sledge wasn't sure how well they'd be able to work together long-term. "This gives me a chance to mix business and pleasure. What are the plans?"

"There aren't any plans," Quinn said with some asperity.

Sledge looked surprised. "Really? Ellen said it was all set."

Roy waved away Quinn's comment. "Christy and Noelle will be staying with her parents, so we'll have to rent a house. Shouldn't be hard. Kingston's a university town. The kids all leave in May so there are lots of empty places."

Quinn shook his head. "Student digs, Dad. Not exactly what most of us are used to."

Undaunted, Roy shrugged. "I'll get on it. There'll be something available."

Christy laughed. "I'll talk to my parents and see what they think."

What about me, old man? I'll be staying with Christy's parents too. They like me. Her dad thought I had promise.

Stricken, Christy looked at the cat, who had jumped up to the top rail and was eyeballing the horse, who was eyeballing him right back. She'd met Frank Jamieson when he was a student at the university where her parents taught. They'd fallen in love and married at the end of his senior year. Frank was right, her parents had liked him. And they liked Stormy the Cat too. But neither of them heard Frank's voice when they visited. When it had just been her, Noelle, and Quinn heading east, Christy had planned to leave Stormy at home in Ellen's care. Now, though, with all of them involved, that was no longer possible.

So, she said, "Yes, they do."

How will we get there? I don't want to travel in the hold of a plane.

"We could drive," Roy suggested, rubbing his chin. "Rent a bus. See the country." He looked hopeful. "Camp along the way."

"You're talking a week or ten days. That's too long for a kid and a cat," Sledge said, somewhat impatiently. "A plane's better."

I agree. The cat likes the car, but cooped up for a week? No, Sledge is right.

Quinn snorted and rolled his eyes, responding to his father and Sledge, Christy knew, not the cat.

Noelle bounded up, surrounded by half a dozen of her classmates. "We're going back to the goat enclosure, Mom. Devon hasn't been there yet." She skipped away, followed by the other kids and the cat. After a moment, Sledge followed.

Roy was still pondering the transportation issue. "I admit, a private plane would be more comfortable than flying commercial. Faster than driving cross country too." He rubbed his chin thoughtfully. "I've never chartered a plane. How do you go about it?"

Quinn pushed himself away from the corral rails. "It's more expensive, but essentially the process is the same as renting a car. You find a charter company, then check out availability, model, and price. When you find the deal that meets your requirements, you book it. Then you show up at the airport on the designated day and let the charter company do the rest."

His father eyed him suspiciously. "How do you know so much about plane rental?"

"Quinn chartered a plane to take us to Kamloops when we were looking for Frank." Christy too moved away from the corral, turning her footsteps in the direction of the goat enclosure. The two men followed.

Roy nodded. "I remember now." He looked past Christy to his son. "Since you have the experience, why don't you take on the task?"

"No need," Christy said. "I'll have Bonnie handle it. She and Isabelle know I'm going to spend the summer with my parents. Neither of them will be surprised that we're flying charter rather than commercial."

The Jamiesons were one of Vancouver's oldest and wealthiest families. Frank's fortune was secured in a trust that was overseen by a board of trustees. Christy was the CEO, with the day-to-day management handled by Bonnie King and Isabelle Pascoe.

For most of her marriage to Frank Jamieson, money had not been an issue, but when he disappeared two years before, so did most of the Jamieson fortune. Christy had to keep expenses to a minimum to conserve capital for Noelle's future. Then, last summer, investigators had located the bulk of the money and once again the Jamieson Trust was flush with cash. Christy no longer had to worry about pinching pennies and saving. Even if she was wildly extravagant—which she wasn't—the Trust would have no problem paying her bills. For a Jamieson, chartering a plane would be no more extreme than renting a car at the airport after a commercial flight.

By now, Noelle and her friends were inside the enclosure. The goats, for some reason, had retreated to their man-made hill and were bunched together near the top. Occasionally, one would bleat, but otherwise they stood watching the adults and children milling around in the enclosure.

Devon, full of energy, dashed to the hill and started scrambling up one side. The goat at the top of the hill let out a surprised bleat, and the others scattered. Someone shrieked. Devon tripped and rolled down the hill, laughing uproariously.

Christy, Quinn, and Roy arrived at the enclosure as the farm's animal handler helped Devon up and dusted him off. The boy was grinning hugely, not at all dismayed by his tumble. One of the little girls was, though. Probably the one who screamed. She was shrinking back against Noelle, who was trying to comfort her.

"I'd better go inside," Christy murmured. She let herself into the enclosure, aware that Quinn followed her.

She reached Noelle and the little girl, whose name she couldn't remember, at the same time as the animal handler, who seemed to be on a mission to comfort the child, as Christy was. They'd got her calmed down when Christy heard Ellen say loudly, "Stop it, you wretched beast."

She looked up to see a goat crowding Ellen against the fence. Christy froze, wide-eyed. The trailing end of the tie knotted around Ellen's waist was in the goat's mouth and he or she was chewing it in a determined way.

"Oh, that stupid creature," the animal handler muttered. She glanced at Christy. "Is the blouse polyester?"

Christy shook her head. "No, it's silk."

"Thought so," the woman said. "Muncher loves silk. He'd eat it all day if we let him."

"Muncher?"

"That's the goat's name. He tends to be single-minded." The woman started toward Ellen and the goat. Out of the corner of her eye, Christy saw Quinn headed in the same direction.

Ellen batted ineffectually at Muncher who was grinding his way steadily up the tie. "Would someone do something to stop this ridiculous animal?"

I'm on it, Aunt Ellen!

There was a blur of movement, then, with a low growl, Stormy the Cat, fully fluffed and ready for battle, landed on Muncher's head. For a moment, the goat did nothing, probably too shocked at having twenty pounds of angry cat on his head to react. Then he let out a terrified bleat, shook his head, and bucked. Stormy dug in his claws and clung on.

Ellen shrieked. Muncher dropped her tie and tried to spin. She took a step away from the battle. Christy started to run, well aware that Stormy was in grave danger of being trampled if he lost his grip on the goat.

Quinn got there first. He dove toward the goat and grabbed Stormy, plucking the cat from Muncher just as the goat threw back his head in a wild attempt to dislodge the cat. Stormy yowled as Quinn grabbed him. Muncher took off to the other end of the pen.

Raising Stormy high, Quinn looked him in the eye. "Behave or I'll give you back to that unhappy goat."

Stormy hissed. *Jerk!*

Quinn laughed.

CHAPTER 2

Christy snuggled deeper into the padded lawn chair, enjoying a feeling of deep contentment. The recliner was located in the backyard of her parents' gracious limestone home on the edge of Lake Ontario and she was surrounded by her family. Noelle, and Ellen of course, and her parents, but also those she'd come to see as future and extended family—Quinn, Roy, Trevor, and Sledge.

It was a little after five o'clock and Miles Yeager, her father, had just handed her a dry martini (shaken, not stirred, he'd said with a wink). He was presiding at his barbecue, which held pride of place on the wide patio that opened off the house, explaining to Quinn the intricacies involved in producing a perfectly cooked steak. Roy was in the kitchen chatting with Christy's mother, Rachael, about the vegetables she was growing in her garden plot. Ellen and Trevor were sitting under a giant maple, their heads together as they talked and sipped their own editions of the shaken, not stirred, martini. Sledge had disappeared somewhere deep in the house when his phone started ringing.

At the far end of the property, where the lawn sloped down toward Lake Ontario, a dark gray tabby cat surged into life, racing after a tiny creature Christy could barely see. Probably one of the chipmunks that called the Yeagers' backyard home.

Noelle screamed, "No! Stormy, stop!" but her cry did no good. Stormy kept running, until he was close enough for the capture. Noelle shouted again and for a second the cat's attention wavered. He pounced, but it was too late. The chipmunk reached his hole and dived in. Stormy stared at the cavity for a few seconds, then turned and trotted back to Noelle, tail high, as if nothing at all had happened. Noelle stroked him and he arched and rubbed against her.

Christy chuckled to herself. The chipmunks were not as quick as the squirrels Stormy regularly hunted back home. He'd already caught a few and carried them into her horrified mother's kitchen as trophies. Fortunately, none of the cute little creatures had been harmed. They played dead until he dropped them, then they took off, usually to some dark corner of her parents' house to hide until the danger was over.

They'd all become quite adept at corralling the tiny intruders, then evicting them while Stormy looked on benignly, no help at all. Frank said the cat enjoyed watching his people play and he liked bringing them the chipmunks to entertain them.

Noelle too was having a lovely time on their vacation. They'd only been here a few days, but, so far, their visit had been a combination of excursions and lazy days at home. Today, they'd piled into the van Christy had rented and her parents' SUV to visit Upper Canada Village, a historic site about an hour and a half down the St. Lawrence River toward Cornwall. At the last minute, Sledge joined them, slipping into the van to sit hunched up in the rear seat beside his father. Looking furtive, he muttered something about his new assistant, Alice, being in town, but refused to say more.

They'd spent hours wandering through the restored nineteenth century buildings gathered together to simulate a nineteenth century Ontario settlement. With Sledge wearing a ball cap and sunglasses no one at the site seemed to realize there was a rock star in their midst. They capped their tour with afternoon tea at the Willard Hotel. The menu replicated food of the historic era and was served by costumed waitresses. They all agreed it was a fun outing, but Sledge seemed to be more relieved that he didn't have to fend Alice's energetic efforts.

Sipping her drink, Christy shook her head. Sledge spent a considerable amount of his time avoiding his new assistant, apparently because she was bossy and managing. To Christy's mind, he'd be better using that energy to come to a comfortable working arrangement with the woman. And if he couldn't do that, he should replace her.

Sledge's voice interrupted her lazy woolgathering. "Hey everyone, look who's here."

Christy straightened and glanced toward his voice. Sledge was standing on her parents' flagstone patio just beyond the doorway that led to the kitchen. Behind him were her mother, looking curious, and Roy, whose expression was grim as he stood with his hands on his hips. Beside Sledge was Tamara Ahern, her dark hair tied back in a knot at her nape, wearing midnight blue trousers and a long-sleeved shirt.

What the hell was she doing here?

Christy dragged her gaze away from the group by the door to check out Quinn to see how he was reacting to Tamara's unexpected appearance. Several years before, he and Tamara had been an item. That was over now and he was with Christy, but.... She was always wary of Tamara's motives and could never quite believe the woman had accepted the end of her relationship with Quinn. Now Quinn's expression told her little. His brows were raised in surprise, though he was smiling warmly, but if Christy judged correctly, it was a friendly smile, nothing more.

He stepped away from the barbecue. "Tamara, hi. What are you doing here?"

Sledge ushered her further onto the patio. Gazing at Quinn with what Christy could only describe as a beseeching expression, Tamara said, "Quinn..." She looked around, making eye contact with Christy, then Ellen and Trevor, who had abandoned their private corner under the maple tree and were advancing toward the patio. "All of you. I need your help."

Christy stood, gesturing to her father. "Tamara, these are my parents, Miles and Rachael Yeager. Dad, Mom, this is Tamara Ahern, a friend of Quinn's. Last year, Tamara was accused of Fredrick Jarvis's murder and we," she gestured to the others, "found the actual killer and solved the crime. I think I told you about it."

Her father nodded. "Nice to meet you, Tamara."

Rachael said, "Sledge introduced us."

Christy nodded.

Tamara acknowledged the introductions with a tentative smile. By this time, Quinn had reached her. He took both her hands, squeezed them, then leaned in to kiss her cheek.

Tamara quivered, then grabbed him in a hug. "Oh, Quinn! I'm so scared!"

He wrapped his arms around her waist, tentatively, Christy thought—hoped!—and muttered, "It's okay. You're here now. We've got it."

Christy climbed the two low steps up to the patio. She put her glass onto the dining table, and her hands in her pockets. She wasn't sure what she'd do with them otherwise. Use them to pry Tamara's arms from around Quinn's neck? Shove her away from him before she demanded the woman leave?

Instead, she said, "How did you find us, Tamara?"

Sniffing, wiping a stray tear from her cheek, she pulled away from Quinn. He looked over at Christy and smiled reassuringly. Did he seem relieved, she wondered? She certainly hoped so.

"I contacted the Jamieson Trust. They told me where you were."

Christy decided she would have to talk to Isabelle Pascoe, the Trust's manager. She should know better than to hand out personal details to random people. Though, to be fair, Isabelle probably saw Tamara as a family friend, since Tamara had been part of the camping trip last summer.

"Why not just call me?" Quinn asked.

That was a good question. Tamara bit her lip and looked down, a sure sign she was uncomfortable.

Ellen and Trevor reached the patio. "Yes, and you could have explained what was going on and why you wanted our help at the same time." Ellen's tone was frosty as she spoke, Jamieson disapproval dripping from each word.

Tamara straightened, threw her head back. Her actions reminded Christy that the woman had been through some pretty desperate times in the last few years. Jamieson disapproval was just the sort of thing that would trigger defiance and spark determination. "I thought it best to talk to all of you, together."

"Ah," said Quinn. He smiled in an encouraging way. A sweeping gesture indicated the others. "Well, you have us. What's up?"

"My father is about to be accused of murder." She turned wide, pleading eyes on Quinn, before she looked at the others.

Christy glanced at her mother, then her father, only to see them both staring fascinated at Tamara. They knew Christy and the others had investigated several mysteries back home in Vancouver, but the Yeagers had never been involved in their cases. Somewhat reassured that her parents were interested rather than horrified, Christy looked over at Quinn. He was frowning.

He shifted uneasily. "Look, Tamara, I understand, but I don't think—"

Tamara tensed, her hands curling into fists at her side as she rounded on him. "No, you don't understand. A man is dead. A man my father had an argument with the day he was killed. That horrible cop, Inspector Fortier, the one who investigated Frederick Jarvis' murder in Vancouver, is involved in this case. In Vancouver, he decided I was the killer and wouldn't consider anyone else. Now he believes my dad murdered this poor man in Ottawa. He's going to arrest my father, just like he arrested me. And Dad's done nothing wrong! His only crime is caring about people and helping them live better lives." As she spoke, her voice rose almost to a shout that ended on a choked back sob.

Sledge, standing uneasily beside Tamara, shoved his hands into his pockets. He looked around at each of them. "What's the harm in taking a couple of days and checking into it?"

Quinn sent him a smoldering look, but Tamara looked over at Sledge hopefully.

Sledge grinned at Quinn, not at all intimidated by his glare. "Come on," he said, his tone coaxing, his expression full of mischief. Christy could imagine him using both to dare Quinn into action when they were rambunctious teenagers excelling at getting into trouble. "You've got to admit it would be fun to take on Inspector do-it-by-the-book Fortier again. We showed him up before. We can do it again."

"We're not in Vancouver this time," Trevor said, sending his son a repressive look. "We don't know the territory and we don't have any contacts."

Sledge shook his head. His phone rang. He pulled it out of his pocket, then denied the call without even identifying who was trying to contact him. "We've got Quinn's investigative skills, Christy's charm—"

Christy made a small sound of suppressed amusement. Her mother beamed, while her father eyed Sledge thoughtfully.

With a wicked grin, Sledge continued, "Roy already has a pal in Fortier's sidekick, Sargent Doucet. If Fortier is working with him on this case, I bet he'd spill all the details. My dad can defend Mr. Ahern if he needs it, and Ellen will keep us all organized with her magic fountain pens and perfect paper."

"I'm not licensed in Ontario," Trevor said, his brows furrowed in a disapproving frown.

Sledge waved this away as a minor glitch.

"I left my pens and letterhead at home," Ellen said. Her tone was dismissive, her expression still Jamieson frosty.

"You could buy new ones," Rachael Yeager said helpfully. "There's a lovely pen shop in Ottawa."

"Is there?" Ellen said, sounding interested. Her expression softened and turned thoughtful.

Sledge's phone rang again and once more he denied the call without checking. "Great. Ellen can add to her collection and my dad can give excellent advice, even if he can't represent."

"Why don't you answer the phone?" Roy asked, rather impatiently, clearly annoyed by the distraction.

Tension etched Sledge's features for a moment then was smoothed away. "Because it's Justina Strong and she wants me to do some media gigs while I'm here in Ontario."

Trevor raised his brows. "And you don't want to?"

Sledge shrugged.

Roy's eyes gleamed. "Why not do some joint interviews?" A multi-published author, Roy had a new mystery series to promote. He lifted his hands with enthusiasm. "Hey, we could include Quinn. His new book is coming out in the fall. He could use the air time too."

"Dad," Quinn said, sounding disapproving.

Noticing the human action on the patio, Stormy the Cat had abandoned the chipmunk hunt. He galloped onto the patio, coming to an abrupt halt in front of Sledge. *Enough about interviews and book promotion. We've got a new case. What about me? What's my assignment?*

Sledge's eyes gleamed and he grinned with unrepentant devilry. "Your job is to cause mayhem."

The cat twisted around Sledge's ankles, until he faced the others, then he sat in his neat and tidy way, back straight, tail wrapped around his front paws. *Awesome. I'm in. When do we start?*

CHAPTER 3

Christy rolled her eyes. Of course Frank would say that. He was having a lot of fun with their detecting adventures. And Sledge was right, he did cause chaos.

She cleared her throat. Sledge shot her an amused look, his expression daring her to nix the whole project. She felt her jaw hardening, because that was exactly what she had planned to do. This was Noelle's vacation and she deserved to have her family's attention focused on her, not on Tamara's father.

Miles Yeager, who couldn't hear the cat and who didn't know Tamara, focused on the issue of book promotion. "When's your novel out, Roy? I know a couple of people at the Kingston Whig Standard. If you like, I'll give them a call. They'd probably love to talk to you, and to Quinn, about your books." He nodded at Sledge and grinned. "As for you, they'd be over the moon."

"Alice will want to arrange it," Sledge muttered, frowning, and looking harried.

Trevor waved his finger at him. "If you don't want the woman organizing your time, you need to set your priorities. Tell her an opportunity has come up and to contact Miles. No reason Miles shouldn't get the goodwill with the press that landing you would bring."

While this discussion was going on, Christy watched Tamara. As the conversation drifted away from her father's plight her eyes narrowed and Christy saw her jaw flex as her shoulders tensed.

Christy's assessing gaze wandered to the others. She saw that her mother was also keeping an eye on Tamara. Rachael's expression was the one she used when she had a disruptive student she feared would sidetrack her carefully crafted lecture into an interesting dead end.

Quinn was also watching Tamara. There was compassion in his gaze, and concern as well. Christy was willing to bet that if he'd been in Ontario on his own, he would have accepted her request without a second thought. That he had been about to turn Tamara down was because of her, and she loved him for that. She also felt guilty. She didn't want to become involved in a murder. That wasn't why they were here. Tamara could hire a private detective. She had plenty of money behind her if she chose to use it. The Jamieson-Armstrongs weren't her only option.

At that thought, she felt small and selfish. She drank some of her martini to push the idea away and told herself she needed to stick to her priorities.

Sledge's phone rang. He checked it, his jaw hardening. Holding it up, he said, "I've got to take this." He walked back to the house, saying, "Hello?" before he stepped into the kitchen.

Tamara watched him go. Her jaw moved and she pursed her lips. She must know he was her strongest ally, even stronger than Quinn, and his departure would make it easier for the rest of them to refuse their help.

Rachael shot a quick look at her husband. Christy almost laughed as she deciphered her parents' silent code. Rachael thought the situation needed to be defused and Miles needed to back her up to make that happen.

Miles said heartily, "Looks like Sledge is getting started on arrangements for that promo idea. We should decide on some dates."

Tamara's eyes narrowed further and her fists came up toward her chest. She lifted her chin and threw her head back. "Those dates should be a couple of weeks away. My dad needs help now. It can't wait for the two authors to chat about their books, or a pampered rock star to prattle on about his career."

"Hey there," Trevor said indignantly. "Sledge has worked hard for his success. There's nothing pampered about him."

"That was uncalled for," Ellen said, shaking her head with disapproval.

Noelle, who had paused at the bottom of the garden to collect the book she'd been reading before Stormy started hunting chipmunks, approached the patio. She hesitated as she neared. She too was watching Tamara, and she clearly sensed the tension in the air. Christy reached out to her. "Hey, kiddo. Come sit with me."

Noelle nodded. She moved one of the deck chairs. Christy followed her and they sat down together.

Roy rubbed his chin. "Tamara's got a point. We're here for the summer. There's plenty of time to do interviews."

Noelle leaned over to Christy. "What's going on, Mom?"

Frank was the one who answered. *Tamara's dad is involved in a murder in Ottawa and she's afraid he'll be arrested. She wants our help.*

Christy nodded.

Noelle frowned looking from the cat to her mother. "She wants you and Daddy and Quinn to solve it?" she asked, keeping her voice carefully low.

Christy nodded again.

Noelle tilted her head. "Why don't you?"

Good question, kiddo.

Christy shot the cat an annoyed look. Stormy stared back, green eyes unblinking. She said quietly to Noelle, "We'd have to go to Ottawa."

Noelle's eyes brightened. She raised her voice so her question wasn't just for her mom anymore. "Grandma, didn't you say we should go to Ottawa for a few days to see the museums and the parliament buildings?"

Rachael looked at Miles, who shrugged, then at Christy, who sent her a rueful look back. She smiled at Noelle. "I did say that, sweetie. You've got a good memory."

Noelle nodded, her eyes bright. "And didn't you say La Machine would be there soon?"

Rachael glanced at her husband and Christy again, then said, "Yes." She drew the word out as if she wasn't quite sure she should be admitting it.

"La Machine sounds so cool. I'm looking forward to it."

La Machine was one of the special events in Ottawa to celebrate Canada's Sesquicentennial. Two gigantic mechanical monsters were scheduled to roam the streets of Ottawa looking for each other so they could do battle. One was a dragon-horse and the other a giant spider. Apparently, it all had something to do with the enormous statue of a spider outside of the Art Gallery of Canada. It sounded weirdly fascinating to Christy, but she too wanted to see it.

Rachael drew a deep breath. "La Machine won't be in Ottawa for at least ten days, honey."

"But there are other things to see in Ottawa, aren't there, Grandma?" Nodding, looking very much a Jamieson in that moment, Noelle added, "If we leave now, we could go to the museums and see La Machine."

The adults all looked at each other.

Tamara said, "Does this mean you'll help my dad?"

"It does not," Quinn said, firmly. "Tamara, a visit to Ottawa for family vacation fun is different from visiting so we can dig into the underbelly of someone's murder."

The hopeful expression on Tamara's face hardened into anger.

At that moment, Sledge strode back onto the patio. He had the look of a man who had taken charge of his life and was happy about it. "Okay, it's all settled. Alice is booking us accommodations in Ottawa. I told her we'd need at least one suite, so we'd have a place to gather. She says we can do a hotel, but a short-term rental of a house is better. She'll fix it. She's also arranging interviews for me and she'll see if she can fit Quinn and Roy in. If we leave tomorrow afternoon, we can be at our place and settled by dinner."

"Really?" Tamara said. A smile lit up her face. "Oh, Sledge, thank you!"

Quinn stepped away from the barbecue, toward Sledge. "Call her off."

Sledge blinked then straightened, his posture tensing.

Oh, good heavens, Christy thought. The two of them were about to do battle with each other. She looked at Noelle, who was watching wide-eyed. She didn't want her daughter to see two men she looked up to going at each other. This needed to stop before it went any further.

She glanced rather desperately at her mother. Rachael nodded, then said, "It sounds like your Alice is better at taking orders than you thought, Sledge."

Sledge was staring fixedly at Quinn, but when Rachael said his name, his concentration broke and he looked over at her, frowning.

Rachael smiled at him. "Perhaps too good? I'm surprised she is so comfortable with the idea of you assisting in a murder investigation."

He shrugged. "It's not her business."

Trevor looked at his son shrewdly. "She doesn't know, does she?"

Sledge glanced his way, then shrugged again. "She thinks I'm on board with a publicity junket." He paused and cleared his throat. "She thinks you guys are coming because you're my entourage."

Trevor said with a sigh, "Oh, my boy." Miles looked bemused. Quinn was still clearly annoyed.

Ellen said tartly, "I have never been part of anyone's retinue and I do not intend to begin."

By this time, Sledge was looking uncomfortable and not a little shamefaced. "Well..."

Noelle whispered to Christy, "I like Tamara, Mom. She's uptight sometimes, but nice. I bet she loves her daddy, like I love mine."

There was a sigh in Christy's mind. *I love you too, kiddo.*

"Can we help her?" Noelle's gaze was fixed on her mother's face.

Her hopeful expression tugged at Christy's heart. "If we do this, we may not always be together as a family."

Noelle nodded.

"You may have to stay with Grandma and Grandpa, or with Aunt Ellen, while I go off with the others to investigate."

Nodding again, Noelle said in a normal voice, "That's okay, Mom. I love Grandma and Grandpa and Aunt Ellen."

Her words riveted the attention of the rest on them. Christy drew a deep breath. Her gaze fixed on her daughter, she said, "Noelle would like to go to Ottawa to help Tamara."

Noelle nodded.

Tamara gasped. Her eyes brightened and a smile split her face. "Oh..."

Moving so she was able to look directly at Tamara, Christy held up her hand. "I'll agree to this on the condition that our Ottawa trip is as much Noelle's vacation as it is helping Tamara. We'll try to clear your father, Tamara, but Noelle gets to see the sights, with her family around her, too."

Sobering, Tamara swallowed. It was clear that this wasn't exactly what she had in mind, but she nodded. "I understand."

Christy nodded back. "Then we're agreed. We're going to Ottawa."

Stormy hopped up onto Noelle's lap, then put his paws up on her shoulder and licked her cheek. Noelle giggled.

I always knew I had an extra special daughter.

They drove to Ottawa the next afternoon. Christy, her parents, Noelle, and Stormy used the Yeagers' SUV, while Roy, Quinn, Trevor, and Ellen were traveling in the van Christy and Quinn had rented. Alice had arranged for Sledge to have a sexy Fiat Spider convertible for his use while he was in Ontario, so he drove solo in the streamlined two-seater.

Frank wanted to travel with Sledge in the sports car, but Christy nixed that. She was certain that while Frank would love the adventure, Stormy would hate it. Though Frank had argued with her for most of the morning, she'd been firm. So, while Stormy stood on her lap and peered out the side window of the SUV, Frank sulked, remaining silent through the drive.

Before they'd left, Alice sent Sledge an email informing him she'd found accommodation for them for the next two weeks. She included the location address and the code to open the door to the parking garage, as well as the time of arrival. Though this seemed a bit odd when they were setting off from Kingston, it made sense once they reached Ottawa and their destination. Alice had rented them an entire multi-unit condo building.

Located in an area called New Edinburgh, the building was modern infill construction, only recently completed. The apartments weren't on the market yet, making them available for a short-term rental. That meant they were unfurnished, of course, but Christy realized Alice had seen to that too when they passed a moving van marked with the logo of a furniture rental company. It was pulling away from the building just as Miles turned into the driveway.

"I wonder what's going on," her mother said, sounding even more curious than she usually was.

The garage door slid upwards and Miles drove the SUV inside. "I assume we'll soon find out," he said. He pulled the SUV into a slot beside Sledge's red Fiat. Sledge was leaning against the trunk of the car, his suitcase on the ground beside him, looking at something on his phone. He'd blown past them somewhere along Highway 416, as he put the sports car through its paces on the long, straight roadway.

Christy heard a sigh in her mind. *Great car.*

Noelle giggled. Stormy meowed. Christy shook her head. "That it is."

Slipping his phone into the pocket of his jeans, Sledge straightened as Christy and her family exited the SUV. Christy and Miles collected their luggage from the rear hatch, while Noelle held Stormy. Rachael headed toward the elevator.

Sledge glanced at his watch. "We should wait here until the others arrive."

Miles raised his brows. "Why not go up to the lobby and find out what your assistant has in store for us?"

Sledge shrugged and tried to look nonchalant. "Alice asked we be here at precisely five o'clock. We're five minutes early."

So? Five minutes doesn't mean anything. Besides, the cat is hungry and he wants to use his litter box.

Noelle's eyes widened. "I'll get Stormy's box, Mom." She thrust the cat toward Christy, who gathered him up into her arms.

"Can you unlock the car for Noelle, Dad?"

Miles frowned. "I thought we were waiting until we'd figured out the accommodations before we brought up the cat's box?"

"Well..."

"Stormy needs to use it, Grandpa." Noelle added a nod for emphasis.

"How do you know that?" Miles asked.

As Noelle bit her lip in a guilty way, he looked from his granddaughter to his daughter. Christy laughed. "Stormy has a way of wiggling when he needs to go." On cue, Stormy moved restlessly in her arms, then meowed.

Miles nodded and said, "Ahh," before he clicked the car lock so Noelle could retrieve the litter box.

"Thanks, Grandpa," Noelle said, sounding relieved. She lugged the box to the front of the car and positioned it so it was between the wall and the SUV's front wheel, genteelly hidden beneath the bumper. Christy set the cat down onto the floor. Stormy minced toward it, pausing for a moment to rub against Noelle.

While the cat was busy using his box, the van with Quinn and the others entered the garage. Sledge waited until they were parked and had retrieved their luggage before he gestured to the elevator. "Okay, we can go up now."

"Nice of you to wait for us," Quinn said. "Any special reason you did?"

Sledge shrugged. "Alice wanted us to all arrive together."

Christy shot him a teasing look. "At precisely five o'clock."

Quinn glanced at his watch. "We'd better get a move on then. It's five-oh-two."

Sledge shot him a look through narrowed eyes and Quinn grinned.

Okay. The cat's done. We can go up now.

Rachael, closest to the elevator, had pressed the call button when Quinn and the others exited their car. Now the door opened smoothly. Noelle picked up the cat while the others grabbed their luggage and entered the car.

The building's lobby was decorated with marble walls and granite floors. Double glass doors looked out onto a small, but nicely landscaped front garden. Alice stood in the middle of the opulent foyer, waiting for them. "Welcome," she said as they piled out of the elevator.

Sledge nodded. "Thanks." He looked around the large open space. "What have you got for us, Alice?"

Alice pursed her lips, then said, "As you told me you needed at least seven bedrooms, one of which should be a suite so you could all gather together, I initially looked for a house to rent. However, houses with seven bedrooms are limited, so I considered a hotel. Then I found this building. There are six apartments on three floors and one here, off the lobby." She gestured to a doorway to her left. "I'll be staying here so I can monitor the building's door and be available to provide any assistance you need. I've allocated your apartment, Sledge. The rest of your entourage are free to choose their own accommodations." She gestured to the elevator. "If you will come this way?"

"You picked my place," Sledge said, as she pressed the call button.

The elevator door opened as Alice nodded. "Of course."

As they all piled back in, Sledge didn't have a chance to protest, but from his dark frown, Christy thought he was annoyed at Alice's high-handedness.

They rode up to the fourth floor, where Alice guided them to a suite on the north side of the building. She unlocked the door, handed Sledge the key, and entered.

The apartment consisted of two bedrooms, a living room, and a kitchen. The living room featured sliding doors that opened onto a balcony. Alice slid them apart, then turned and smiled at Sledge. "The green space to the north is the grounds of Rideau Hall. You have a lovely view of it from here, which is why I wanted you to have this suite."

Rideau Hall was the home of the Queen's representative in Canada, the Governor General. Evidently, Alice was impressed by rank and privilege.

Sledge raised his brows, not particularly affected by the information, but interested in his assistant's excitement. "Thanks."

She smiled with real pleasure. "You're so welcome. Now, let's look at the rest of this apartment and then we can explore the other suites."

As they toured the building, Christy decided Alice was firstly a miracle worker, secondly, that she must have a creative and flexible imagination, and thirdly, that she had to have a well of endless energy. In one day, she'd worked out the leasing arrangement for the building, then sourced rental furniture, and had the whole building stocked with everything they needed, from beds to sofas, to linens and kitchen necessities. She beamed the whole time they wandered through the building, making notes on which suites each person chose, and assuring them over and over again that they only had to ask and she'd find them whatever they needed.

By the time they returned to the ground floor, having left their suitcases in their respective apartments, Sledge was eying Alice with a bemused frown. In the lobby, she gestured to a doorway on the opposite side from the apartment where she would be staying. "When the condo is completed, the community room will be there. It's a large space I thought would be perfect for your gathering place. I've furnished it with a boardroom table, as well as sofas and chairs. I also included a large screen TV. Like the TVs in each of the suites, it's loaded with several streaming services." During the tour of the apartments, they'd already learned that the developer had installed Wi-Fi in the building. She glanced at her watch. "Now, it's almost six. Would you like me to make restaurant reservations or would you prefer takeout?"

Sledge rubbed his chin as he looked at Alice from under his brows. "We invited Tamara Ahern to meet us here tonight after seven."

Alice nodded briskly. "Takeout it is, then. Do you have a particular preference?"

"Pizza," Noelle said promptly.

Alice raised her brows and looked at Christy, who laughed and said, "I have no objection."

Alice nodded. "Very good. I know of an excellent pizzeria not far from here. If you'll give me your preferences, I'll call now."

In the end, Alice suggested they order a traditional pepperoni, plus the more innovative combinations developed by the restaurant, then she went off to put in the order.

As her apartment door closed behind her, Stormy wiggled in Noelle's arms. When she set him on the ground, he trotted over to the community room door. *Somebody open this door! The cat wants to explore and we need to get to work.*

CHAPTER 4

Along with the pizza, which was delicious, Alice also produced bottles of red and white wine and a dozen bottles of beer, presumably from a stash in her apartment. Once the remnants of dinner were cleared away, she set out coffee service and an assortment of patisseries for their evening meeting.

Not long after she came to the door, leading Tamara dressed in slacks and a button front shirt, and a tall, but rather stooped man whose sports jacket hung loosely from his shoulders. As they entered, he pushed gold-rimmed glasses further up the bridge of his nose and observed the scene through thick lenses.

"Your guests," she said briskly. "I'll be in my apartment if you need me."

"Thanks, Alice, for everything today," Sledge said.

She nodded without smiling and turned away. Tamara and her father entered the room.

The first few minutes were taken up by introductions, then Rachael said, "Come on, Noelle. You and I are heading upstairs for the evening."

Miles stood up. "I'll come up with you ladies. A pleasure meeting you, Todd."

Noelle pouted, but she'd been warned in advance that the discussion was adults only, so she said politely, "Nice to meet you, Reverend Ahern. See you soon, Tamara."

Tamara nodded and smiled. Christy kissed her daughter, promised she'd be up to say good night, then the Yeagers and Noelle went out, taking a selection of desserts with them. The rest settled around the boardroom table with cups of coffee. Christy set the plates of pastries in the center of the table before settling at one end. Stormy took up a position on her lap. She stroked him idly as Tamara opened the conversation.

"Thank you for agreeing to help my dad—"

"Even though it is quite unnecessary," Todd Ahern finished.

She turned on him, her eyes flashing, more animated than Christy had ever seen her. "It is necessary, Daddy!"

"It isn't," he said. His voice was soothing, rather than dismissive and there was a tender affection in his eyes. He might be Tamara's adoptive father, but it was clear he loved her unreservedly.

Tamara tapped the table with the kind of authoritative determination Christy associated with her. "Daddy, the cops see you as their prime suspect. Trust me when I say that means they'll look no further."

"Tamara, I've done nothing wrong. This will all sort itself out, you'll see."

Yeah, right. Stormy sat up a bit straighter so he could see over the top of the table.

Todd frowned and blinked a couple of times. Christy looked down at the cat then over at Ellen to see if she'd noticed the man's telltale expression. Ellen caught her look and returned it with a little nod.

"Dad," said Tamara, who couldn't hear Frank and so was oblivious to the revelation that her father probably could, "I know you believe everyone is as good and decent as you are—"

He laughed easily at her description of him. "Hardly, honey."

Tamara tapped the table again. "But they aren't. You need to be proactive. You must accept you need help and let my friends do what they do."

He heaved a deep sigh. "Tamara..."

"Let them help, Dad." She opened her eyes wide and softened her tone. "If for no other reason, do it for me."

His dubious gaze met her steady one, then after a minute he sighed again and said, "All right."

Finally.

He didn't move his head, but his gaze traveled from face to face around the table.

Christy tapped the cat on the nose, leaned close, and whispered. "Be good."

Spoilsport.

Todd's brows twitched. Christy looked at Ellen and shook her head. Sledge laughed. Trevor cleared his throat. Quinn shot an incredulous look at each of them, guessing what was going on.

Roy said, "Why don't you tell us about the murder and why the cops think you did it."

Todd clasped his hands in front of him. He paused, apparently to collect his thoughts before he began. "The poor man who was killed was Ralph Sharpe. He's a local businessman, very successful." Here Todd stopped and wrinkled his brow. "His company manufactures items for the home, kitchen gadgets and the like." He waved his hand. "I don't know the details. I do know he was wealthy because of the success of his company."

"Why would the cops think you'd kill a well-to-do business man?" Quinn asked, watching him steadily.

Todd shrugged and lifted his hands in a dismissive gesture. "I don't know! That's why I know nothing will come of this absurd idea that I'm a suspect."

"Dad," Tamara said. She sounded impatient. "Tell them about the argument."

Todd pursed his lips. "Tamara, it was nothing."

She tapped the table again. "Daddy!"

He sighed. "Oh, all right." He glanced at each of them. "This will be a long story, I'm afraid. Before I tell you about the argument, I have to provide a bit of background."

"Go for it," Roy said.

Yes, please do. This is putting me to sleep. The cat yawned.

Todd caught the movement. His eyes widened, an arrested look on his face. He dragged his gaze away from Christy and the cat, shook his head, and said, "Fifteen years ago, I was instrumental in the creation of a non-profit organization dedicated to helping young people from disadvantaged backgrounds develop their potential. Our goal was to teach them leadership skills, along with a social conscience, and an activist approach."

"Right on," Roy said.

Todd nodded. "Over the years, since our initial formation, we widened our scope to include young people from all socio-economic groups. Five years ago, Ralph's daughter enrolled in our summer program. While she was a student with us, Ralph expressed a desire to join our board. His request came with a large donation."

"You accommodated him, I assume," Ellen said, sounding very much a Jamieson.

Todd nodded. "We had an opening and his donation.... Well, it was substantial. We saw no reason to turn him down." He sighed. "I wish now we had."

"Why?" Trevor's question was a sharp demand.

Todd's steady gaze met Trevor's. "Initially, I thought he believed in the work we were doing. It was only later we realized his purpose was to completely remake the direction and mission of the organization."

Didn't see that one coming.

Christy smiled as innocently as she could as Todd's narrowed eyes focused on her and the cat.

Tamara reached out and squeezed her father's hand, which Christy saw had clenched into a fist. She raised her brows and Todd looked away.

"Was that what you were arguing about? His plans for the future of your organization?" Quinn asked.

Todd nodded. "I told him I wanted him off the board. That I couldn't let him destroy what was an important learning opportunity for young minds. He laughed at me and said he wasn't destroying anything. He was making it better. Better!" Color rose in Todd's cheeks. "He was subverting everything the organization stood for and I told him so."

"I take it someone heard your argument and reported it to the police after Ralph died?" Ellen said.

Todd nodded.

Christy could imagine how that argument might have looked to an outsider. Even now, Todd had lost what she thought was probably his usual calm demeanor. When he was face-to-face with a man he clearly despised? There had probably been shouting, angry words, perhaps even some shoving. No wonder the cops thought he was a viable suspect.

"How long before Ralph's death did you two argue?" Christy asked.

Todd swallowed, his expression guilty. "We argued in the afternoon. Ralph was killed that evening."

Again, Tamara squeezed her father's hand in a comforting way. Trevor shook his head. "The timing isn't good."

Todd roused himself from his gloom. He slapped the table and said fiercely, "I didn't kill him!"

Lounging in his chair, holding a pastry between two fingers, and completely unimpressed by Todd's show of defiance, Sledge pointed the pastry at him. "Then who did?"

"I don't know. That's the police's job."

Roy rubbed his chin. "Should be, but Fortier is a rigid kind of guy. If he's decided you're the main suspect, he won't look too hard at anyone else."

Todd glanced at his daughter. "That's what Tamara says, but how can that be? I'm innocent."

"Do you have an alibi for the evening of the murder?" Trevor asked.

Todd shook his head. "Though we originally set up YES!..." He broke off, then lifted his hand expressively. "The official name is Youth Empowerment Secretariat, but we use the acronym with an exclamation point for emphasis because our work is so impactful. Anyway, we set it up in Toronto, then ten years ago we moved our headquarters to Ottawa. I think you may know I live in Toronto, so I'm a visitor here. On the night of Sharpe's death, I was in my hotel room. Alone, I might add, as my wife didn't come with me."

Trevor leaned forward. "Did you eat in the hotel restaurant? Order room service?"

Todd shook his head. "When I left YES! headquarters, I stopped by a burger outlet and bought a takeout meal, which I brought back to the hotel. I ate my dinner in my room, worked on a speech I am to make next week, read a book, and went to bed."

"Would the clerk who served you at the restaurant remember you? Did anyone at the hotel see you return?" Quinn said.

Todd shrugged. "I doubt it. There was a line up at the burger joint and I don't think I even made eye contact with the kid who took my order. As for the hotel? It's a busy establishment and I don't make a lot of fuss. It's unlikely any of the staff would remember me in particular."

"Too bad," Trevor said.

"All is not lost," Sledge said cheerfully. He'd consumed his pastry, so now he used his coffee cup to point. "This Sharpe guy sounds like he probably pissed off a lot of people. All we have to do is shove a few more likely suspects in the good Inspector Fortier's face and he'll have to investigate them."

Tamara frowned at him. "Where would we find them?"

"Other members of the YES! board. People who worked for the organization," Quinn said.

"People who worked for Sharpe or his company," Christy chimed in.

"There," said Sledge, nodding, looking like he expected a pat on the back. "What did I tell you? It's easy."

His smile died as Todd pushed back his chair. Glowering, he stood. "I will not betray my colleagues and friends." Looking down at his daughter, he said, "Tamara, this has gone far enough. Finding Ralph Sharpe's killer is a job for the police, not a few amateur detectives."

"Sit down, Daddy," Tamara said gently, but firmly. Christy suspected that was the tone she used in emotionally charged situations with her medical patients.

Ahern frowned at her. She raised her brows and looked downward. Slowly, he complied.

When he'd resumed his seat, she said, "You're in a lot of trouble and my friends are here to help you. If they have to ask you difficult questions, you need to try to answer them to the best of your ability. Now, are there any members of the board who disagreed with Ralph, or who felt, as you did, that he should be removed from the board?"

Ahern didn't immediately reply. He stared at his daughter, brows knit, as if he was reassessing whether she was friend or foe. Finally, he sighed. "Ralph was something of a windbag. He liked to dominate the meetings. At some point or other, he annoyed most of the board members, but I can't see pontificating in a meeting as a reason to murder someone." He sighed again. "The only person who might care enough is Cooper Singleton. He is one of our longest serving members and he had to step down as chair when Sharpe bought his way onto the board."

"He resigned his position? So, Ralph wasn't just a board member, he was the chair of the board?" Christy asked.

"Yes, of course," Todd snapped. "How do you think he made so many changes to the organization?"

The cat jumped off Christy's lap onto the table and stalked over to Ahern. *Maybe because you're a bunch of naive idiots who didn't do your due diligence when you took his cash and gave him his reward?*

At the same time as the cat was getting his point across silently, Quinn said in a hard voice, "You're not a good storyteller, Todd, which is why Christy needed clarification. I'm also getting the impression you're not being particularly forthcoming."

Christy shot Quinn a thank you smile, then she winked and nodded toward Todd, who was staring at the cat wide-eyed. Quinn mouthed, "Really?"

Christy's smile broadened into a grin as she nodded.

He sighed and shook his head.

Suppressing a giggle, Christy turned to see Tamara watching them intently. She smiled as innocently as she could. Tamara was one of those who couldn't hear Frank and Christy wasn't about to let her in on the secret.

Todd dragged his gaze away from the cat, to focus on Quinn. "I am not withholding anything. I can't see any of my colleagues being violent enough to hit a man on the head, then throw him into the Rideau Canal."

"Is that how he died?" Sledge asked, risking a reprimand similar to Christy's. "Nasty."

"Passionate," Quinn said briskly.

"Angry," said Roy.

"Or made to look that way," Trevor suggested. "Where exactly did the death occur?"

"Along the canal path that leads from Wellington Street to the Bytown Museum. It's between the Parliament Buildings and the Ottawa Locks, which are part of the Rideau Canal system," Tamara said. "At night, it would be a place of shadows, and quiet as well."

"In other words, a good place for a clandestine meeting or to ambush someone," Trevor said. He was busy making notes on his phone, as Ellen had not yet acquired the pens and papers she'd need to resume her role as their secretary.

Todd thrust out his hands. "There, you see? It couldn't be Cooper Singleton. Or any other member of the board. Or the organization itself! It was probably a random attack by someone from the criminal element."

He looked so pleased with this statement, Christy thought they were unlikely to get much more out of him.

Quinn was shaking his head. "Why would a thief bash him over the head and kill him? He'd be much more likely to pick his pocket or point a gun at him and demand his valuables before he drifted into the night."

Todd shrugged.

"A quiet place with lots of shadows sounds more like a rendezvous point than somewhere a thief would be at work," Sledge said, sounding dubious.

"A rendezvous point." Roy's eyes were dreamy, his expression alight as his imagination took flight. "Are there any women who might be potential suspects?"

Todd hesitated.

The cat reached out a paw and tapped the back of his hand. *Answer the man.*

Todd snatched his hand away and rubbed the place where the cat had touched it. "Mia Goodwin, our Director of Curriculum Development may be a possibility. She was expected to become the CEO when Gordon Widdowson, our former CEO, resigned. However, she was passed over in favor of an outside candidate. She now believes her job is in jeopardy as the new CEO is a firm supporter of Ralph Sharpe's redirection." He looked resentfully at the cat, then at the others at the table. "But this was a violent crime. How can you think a woman might have killed Ralph?"

"I'll admit it's more likely that a man bashed him over the head than a female, but don't discount a woman just because she might not have the strength to do the deed." Roy waved his finger for emphasis. "There are ways around that, especially if the woman has money and motivation."

"What has money to do with anything?" Todd asked, confusion evident in his frown and tilted head.

She could have hired a hitman, doofus. Get with the program.

"I think a hitman is an unlikely circumstance," Ellen said.

Quinn's brows shot up.

Tamara frowned. "Who said anything about a hitman?"

"It was the obvious conclusion," Ellen said coldly. "As your father would have realized, if he had paused to consider the implications in Roy's suggestion."

Right on, Aunt Ellen. You tell him.

Todd looked from the cat to Ellen, his expression so desperate, almost frightened, that Christy felt sorry for him.

She shot a glance around the table, a be-good mom type look. Each of her champions assumed innocent expressions, while Sledge looked amused, Tamara confused, and Trevor thoughtful. "Getting back to our suspect list, is there anyone else we should be investigating?"

Todd shook his head. "I don't know anything about Sharpe's company or how he did business. He was well known in the community and served on a number of charitable boards, but I don't have any details."

The cat gave him one last, long look from wide green eyes, then picked his way across the tabletop to resume his position on Christy's lap. *Pathetic. What did I say about due diligence?*

Christy was inclined to agree, but from Todd's heightened color she thought he'd had enough for one evening. She glanced at her watch. "Mr. Ahern, it's been nice to meet you and I hope we'll be able to help, but right now I need to go up and say good night to my daughter." She pushed back her chair, the cat held securely in her arms as she stood. "If you'll excuse me."

CHAPTER 5

Later that evening, after Todd and Tamara had left and they were all settled in the living room of the apartment Christy shared with Noelle, the discussion turned to next steps.

"From what Todd told us, Sharpe was making sweeping changes to the organization," Quinn said from his place beside Christy on the comfortable loveseat. "He admitted that at least one of the board members was burned by Sharpe's actions. There were probably others."

"Not just board members," Trevor said. "Management was also affected." A matching sofa was set at right angles to the loveseat. Trevor and Ellen had taken positions on it, with enough space between them for it not to appear that they were cuddling. Roy was at the far end, one ankle crossed over the other knee.

"What about the alumni?" Miles asked. "From the way you described this organization, the experience was intended to be a formative one for a young person."

Rachael nodded. She'd grabbed the final easy chair, leaving her husband and Sledge to import straight-backed chairs from the dining room. "Particularly a disadvantaged youth whose life would have changed immeasurably as a result of the training."

"Not to mention the friendships formed with other students in your year and access to a graduate network that could lead to a successful career," Christy said.

Trevor nodded. "Interesting thought. Todd didn't mention any individual students, but you're right. A person who is passionate about a group might well kill in order to keep it intact." He shook his head, his expression dubious. "YES! has been operating for fifteen years. That's a lot of students to investigate."

"Easy enough to narrow it down," Sledge said. He'd turned his chair around and was sitting on it astride, his arms resting across the back. "Focus on the ones still involved." He grinned. "The groupies, as it were. The ones who stick around, maybe volunteer in some capacity."

His father nodded, a glimmer of a smile in his eyes. "Good idea."

Sledge winked.

"So, who does what tomorrow?" Roy asked.

"I'm taking Noelle to Dows Lake—it's part of the Rideau Canal system, but still within the city. You can rent kayaks there, which I think will be a fun way to start our Ottawa vacation," Christy said without hesitation. "If you need my help investigating, I'll pitch in, but my focus is on Noelle and her holiday."

Rachael looked at her husband, who nodded. "We'll come with you."

"I enjoyed kayaking when I was younger," Ellen said in an almost musing way. "But I would also like to purchase pens and paper at that shop Rachael mentioned. I feel quite lost without them. Perhaps..." She paused before resuming almost hesitantly. "Perhaps we could combine the outings?"

Rachael turned to her daughter. "What do you think, Christy? Shall we do both?"

Christy laughed. "Sure. We should probably include lunch in there as well."

"Absolutely," Rachael said.

"I'll take on Cooper Singleton, the board member Todd mentioned," Quinn said. "I can go in as a journalist, as well as a friend of Todd's. It might make Singleton open up to me more easily."

Roy tapped his ankle thoughtfully. "Good thinking. I'll do some research on Ralph Sharpe. Christy was right when she told Todd the murder might have had nothing to do with YES!."

Sledge sighed and dropped his chin onto crossed fists. "Alice texted me a while ago. She's set up an interview at one of the local radio stations tomorrow."

Trevor tapped his lips. "I'll see what I can find out from Fortier. I don't expect him to be forthcoming, but you never know. He might let something useful slip."

The meeting broke up soon after without any further revelations. The next morning, Quinn breakfasted with his father in the apartment they were sharing. Along with her other amazing organizational activities, Alice had stocked all the kitchens with breakfast foods, which got the day off to a quick start. He'd secured a meeting with Cooper Singleton for mid-morning. That allowed him enough time to organize his thoughts and decide what direction he wanted to take his interview.

Cooper Singleton was the CEO of a polling company that boasted a client list that included well-known lobbying firms, several think tanks, two political parties, and non-profits like the one Todd Ahern had created. His company was housed in a spacious old red brick building in the downtown, not far from the Parliament Buildings. Singleton's office was located in what had probably once been the master bedroom when the building was somebody's home. Now it was a roomy office with a large oak desk by the window, a small table with four chairs for meetings, and file cabinets that were tucked away in what had once been a narrow closet.

When Quinn was shown up to the office, Singleton rose and came round the sturdy desk with his hand outstretched. He was a tall, thin man with boney features and shrewd, observant eyes. His still thick hair was gray at the temples and combed from a side part. He wore a bespoke blue suit, a silver tie, and a pale mauve shirt.

"Mr. Armstrong, how do you do? I'm Cooper Singleton. Won't you sit down?" He gestured to the table tucked in the corner.

A coffee urn, along with two bowls bearing packets of sugar and powdered cream, and two cups emblazoned with the company's name and logo was positioned on one end of the table. Singleton poured coffee and offered one of the cups to Quinn before he sat down. "Todd Ahern told me you, or one of the other members of your group, would be contacting me with questions." He raised his hands, spreading them wide. "Go ahead. Ask whatever you want. I've worked with Todd for years and I respect the man. He would never harm someone, let alone kill him."

Quinn nodded. He set his phone on the table and said, "As Todd said, I'm looking into this for him, but I'm also a journalist and I know my editors will be interested in a story about the incident. Do you mind if I record this conversation?"

Singleton looked surprised and he hesitated, then he shook his head. "No. That's fine."

Quinn nodded, set the phone to record and asked an easy question to open. "How long have you been on the board of YES!?"

"Ten years. I joined when they moved their headquarters from Toronto to Ottawa."

"Do you know why that was done?"

Singleton picked up his mug and held it close to his mouth, but he didn't drink. "Many of the companies where the students intern are located here in Ottawa. Plus, there is direct access to federal politicians who support the program. It was easier for management staff to be here, rather than commuting from Toronto for meetings."

Quinn nodded. "How did the victim, Ralph Sharpe, become involved with the organization?"

"His daughter is one of the alumni. The program is designed for students in their last year of high school or their first or second year of university. It's spread over two summers and the students participate in workshops and group events where they learn leadership and other skills. They also are assigned to an employer in what is essentially an internship. By the end of the program, they have both business experience and a network of supportive co-workers and friends to help them move forward in their careers. Ralph became involved while his daughter was in her first internship. Karla Sharpe was an exceptional student and is now a mentor for incoming students." He lowered his cup and shrugged. "We assumed Ralph would be an excellent addition to the board."

"There was also a financial incentive, was there not?"

Singleton's mouth tightened for a moment, then he nodded as he put his untouched mug back onto the table. "A large endowment that came with strings attached. Namely, that he be instated as the chair."

"And if he wasn't made chair?"

"No donation." Singleton played with his mug, running his fingers up and down the handle in an unconsciously restless movement. "I must admit, I did wonder about that, but his daughter is a lovely young woman. I assumed, we all assumed, he believed in the organization."

That was interesting. Though Todd had admitted Ralph had been chair of the board, he hadn't admitted access to the position was tied into Sharpe's generous donation. "Who was the chair at the time?"

"I was. And I didn't think twice about stepping down. The endowment allowed us to enlarge the program by another ten students per year. That was huge. Too big to walk away from."

"When did the changes begin?"

Singleton's jaw hardened. He wrapped both hands around his mug as if to gather strength or comfort from the warmth. "Almost immediately. Sharpe announced he'd convinced several new businesses to become internship providers. Each of them was a for-profit organization, something we didn't endorse at the time. Our CEO, Gordon Widdowson, was reluctant to take them on. We on the board were also reluctant."

"Despite your reluctance, did you add them to your lists?"

"Oh, yes." There was bitterness in Singleton's voice. "Two board members who were the most vocal against the change suddenly resigned. Sharpe found two replacements who turned out to be supportive of his program ideas. A few months later, Gordon Widdowson abruptly resigned as well. He told me he'd been offered a job he couldn't turn down. I suspect that was Sharpe's doing, but I can't prove it. We'd long assumed that when Gordon departed, Mia Goodwin, our director of curriculum and events, would replace him. Mia would have been an excellent leader. She's a woman of enormous talent and vision. Instead, Sharpe insisted on an open competition and the person who won the position was the former president of the Dogwood political party."

Quinn knew the Dogwood Party. Fredrick Jarvis, whose murder Tamara had once been accused of, had been competing for the leadership of the Dogwoods when he was killed. Was this case somehow linked to that one, with an Ahern accused and at the center of each?

He put that thought aside for the moment. "What kind of changes did Sharpe and his new CEO make to the organization?"

Cooper paused for a moment to sip his coffee and perhaps to formulate his answer. "Casey Rees was hired early in 2014. He began by reworking our mission statement. That was followed by a new five-year management plan that enumerated significant changes to the goals we set for our students. Social justice is no longer part of the curriculum. Political activism is also on its way out, at least activism as allied to social justice. Mia told me last week that she's been made redundant at the end of this summer's program. She's now looking for a new position."

"Was she bucking Rees?"

Singleton nodded. "You must understand, she designed the courses. She'd been told to make sweeping changes to this year's program and she was appalled. She tweaked the content, hoping that would be sufficient, but..."

"It wasn't."

Shaking his head, Singleton said, "There was an almighty row when Todd found out. That's what he and Sharpe were arguing about the afternoon Sharpe was killed."

"Todd Ahern is passionate about this organization."

"Absolutely! He's worked tirelessly for YES! ever since it began. He believes...no, he knows it changes lives. Not just those of our students, but the people around them and the people they serve."

"Then it's possible that as Todd Ahern watched YES! being dismantled by an outlier, he became so angry he tried to force the man out. When Sharpe refused to step down, Ahern killed him in a fit of rage."

Before Quinn had even finished speaking, Singleton was shaking his head. "No, no, no! As I told you when you first arrived, Todd Ahern is incapable of harming anyone. Yes, he's passionate about the organization, but he's a man of intellect. He would never resort to violence to solve a problem."

Quinn nodded. "Point taken." He paused, studying Singleton. "What about other people in the organization?"

"Like me, you mean?" he said ruefully.

Quinn smiled faintly as he nodded. "Or Mia Goodwin."

Singleton leaned forward. "Like Todd, I believe in YES!. My company provides internships for the students. Several of our permanent employees are alumni. These young people ask questions, challenge authority, refuse to accept the status quo. They're exceptional individuals. I'm devastated by the changes Sharpe and his associates are making, but I'm a businessman, not a killer. I know there are ways to deal with this kind of situation. Legal, non-violent ways. So, to answer your question, no I did not kill Ralph Sharpe."

"Can you prove that?"

Singleton raised his eyebrows. "What do you mean?"

"Were you with someone on the evening Sharpe died? Someone who will confirm your presence at the time of his death?"

A faint smile touched Singleton's rather thin lips, then was gone, replaced by a serious expression. "I was with my wife, my daughter, who is an actress, and her husband. They were visiting for the weekend and we were celebrating because my daughter had just won the lead in a television series to be produced in Toronto."

Quinn smiled. "Congratulations to her."

Singleton nodded.

"And Mia Goodwin? Could she have been angry enough to have murdered him?" Quinn asked.

Shaking his head, Singleton sat back. "She's a woman! Ralph Sharpe was a big, hefty man. He was pushing sixty, but still a robust person. She couldn't have killed him. She isn't strong enough."

Quinn smiled faintly, thinking about Ellen's observation that a woman didn't necessarily have to do the deed herself. "Perhaps not, but that doesn't mean she wasn't involved in his death. She could have lured him to the murder site where someone else killed him."

"Good heavens." Singleton paled. "I never thought…No, that's impossible." He peered at Quinn from under furrowed brows. "What a horrible world you live in, Mr. Armstrong, if you think that is an option a normal person would use."

Quinn resisted the urge to say that his world was just fine, thank you very much. Instead, he smiled thinly and asked, "What will happen now that Ralph Sharpe is dead?"

Singleton blew out a deep breath. "To the endowment you mean?"

"And his position as chair. Will you or Todd resume control?"

"The endowment is secure, but the chair... Both Todd and I are capped. Board positions are indefinite, but you can only serve as chair for three terms. Unfortunately, of the board members who remain, one has medical issues and can't take on the kind of commitment the chairmanship entails. Another is retiring this year and a third has also been chair for three terms. That leaves one individual who is a great benefactor, but who is easily swayed by strong voices, or the two new members Sharpe planted on the board."

"By strong voices, you mean Sharpe's new appointments."

Singleton nodded. "I may not agree with their viewpoints, but both men are persuasive."

"So Sharpe's death changes nothing. The alterations to the organization will continue."

Slowly, reluctantly, Singleton nodded. There was sadness in his voice as he said, "Correct."

"What will you do?" Quinn asked. He watched as the man shrugged off the melancholy and straightened.

"I will fight, as will Todd. We will be strong voices to return the organization to its original mandate. We will not let it go without doing our utmost to keep it alive."

Quinn observed him for a moment, then nodded. "Thank you for speaking to me today. You've been very helpful."

Singleton stood when Quinn did. He thrust out his hand, which Quinn took to shake. "If you have any more questions, anything at all I can help you with, please contact me. I'll do whatever's needed to help Todd."

Quinn nodded. "Of course."

As he left the building, he reflected that Cooper Singleton was deeply and emotionally involved in YES! and he couldn't help wondering if the man was quite as non-violent as he claimed to be.

~

Mia Goodwin was angry. Hers was the kind of anger that simmered hot under the surface and boiled over at the least provocation. It was spilling out now as she sat on her side of her desk, hands clasped before her, and stared directly at Quinn. Short and plump, she was a tidy woman, middle-aged, and wearing the uniform of a mid-level professional woman—well-cut skirt suit in a dark blue, simple white silk blouse, minimal jewelry.

Her dyed blond hair was styled in a neat bob that reached her chin, and not a hair was out of place. Dark pockets below her eyes hinted at sleepless nights and lines around her mouth indicated recent pressures taking control. Right now, that mouth was a thin hard line turning down into a frown. Fury blazed from large brown eyes.

"I have been nurturing YES! for years. Years! My curriculum has been fine-tuned to provide the maximum benefit for the young people we educate. Then this... this—" She wrestled with herself, then shook her head and snapped, "This *pig* comes along with his money and his smug self-importance and decides it's his mission to destroy this organization!" She sat straighter and snapped her fingers. "In an instant, everything I worked for is gone. Gone! As if it never existed."

Quinn nodded. He didn't have to ask Mia any questions. Her views were pouring out of her and he figured that if he interrupted, he'd just stop the flow. So he said nothing, tried to look sympathetic, and let her vent.

"Five years ago, Ralph's daughter Karla participated in our program. She's a bright, intelligent girl, a pleasure to work with. She came to us a rich, rather spoiled, and certainly privileged child. She left us as a woman who had a vision for her future and a desire to serve the society around her. When her father spoke to Cooper Singleton about joining the board, we were all pleased. He offered us a donation that would take us into the future in a positive way. We thought his addition to our family was a wonderful step. Then..." Her voice lowered, became infused with venom. "As soon as he became chair, he started to dismantle our organization."

She stopped. Her mouth worked as she fought to contain her outrage.

Quinn waited a moment. When she didn't continue, he said mildly, "How?"

That brought her up short. Her mouth stopped moving, her brows furrowed, and she said, "How what?"

"How did he dismantle the organization?"

"As soon as there were openings on the board, he brought in his friends. Two men with the same mindset as his to support him and force through the changes he wanted to make."

Quinn nodded. "Okay, more board members to support him. What exactly were the changes they made?"

She glared at him as if he should know all this. And in a way she was right. He'd already known about the new board members. What he wanted were details on how Sharpe and his friends were changing YES!.

She drew a deep breath, apparently to help calm her. "Our students are with us for two summers. Each summer, they do enrichment and networking courses, but they're required to do an internship as well. We send them to carefully chosen organizations, from government departments, through worthy charities, to NGOs. The placements are individualized to enhance the strengths of the student and to help them overcome their weaknesses. All they have learned in our courses is reinforced during the work-study period, so the kind of organization they're sent to is important."

Quinn nodded. Mia was working up a head of steam again. His job was to listen and look interested.

"Ralph Sharpe and his cronies brought a whole new slate of companies into the internship pool. Private companies whose only purpose is to make a profit." Passionate anger blazed from her eyes. "The kind of companies we strive to teach our students not to waste their talents on. It's obscene."

She paused to draw breath. Quinn didn't even have to nod before she was off again. "I protested. By that time, though, our long-time CEO had resigned and Casey Rees, the man who replaced him, was one of Sharpe's plants. I was told the new placements would benefit a certain type of student and that broadening our internship pool was a good thing. Can you imagine?"

Quinn could. He had a talent for seeing multiple sides of a question and for understanding the reasons behind different viewpoints. Mia Goodwin clearly could not. Or, if she could, she didn't want to. She believed in the program she'd built with the intensity of the truly devoted. She'd pegged Ralph Sharpe as the enemy and any changes he, or his proxy Casey Rees, made that modified her organization were unacceptable.

Had Ralph Sharpe deliberately targeted YES! as Todd, Cooper, and Mia believed? Mia definitely saw his actions as part of a strategic campaign, during which he wormed his way into the organization, using the assumptions of board members and executives to gain a foothold, then making his changes in a series of quick, unexpected strikes.

The question was, why had he done it? Clearly, it must have had something to do with his daughter's time at YES!. Mia thought the girl had matured and grown, but had she actually been unhappy or frustrated? Had she observed weaknesses in the program that the one-track Mia couldn't see? Had she completed the program feeling coerced and bullied?

As he was deciding that Sharpe's daughter would be well worth talking to, Mia waved her hand, indicating the office around her. "All of this will be gone by the end of the summer. That's what Ralph Sharpe did to me with his odious changes and his vile crusade against us."

Quinn blinked. "YES! is folding? Cooper Singleton gave me to understand your funding was secure."

Anger blazed in Mia's eyes. "It might as well close its doors. As of September, it will exist only as a distorted shadow of what it once was."

A distorted shadow? Mia had clamped her lips shut, probably to add impact to that last melodramatic statement. Quinn raised his brows. "In what way?"

Her eyes blazed. "August thirty-first is my last day because I wouldn't make wholesale revisions to the curriculum and because I dared protest the new internship placements. I was told I needed to seek new employment and was given until the end of the summer before I was terminated. My replacement starts at the beginning of September." She leaned forward, her face contorted. "Do you know where he was last employed?"

Quinn didn't reply. He was pretty sure Mia was going to inform him.

He was right. Her jaw moved back and forth, her eyes narrowed, and her upper lip wrinkled in contempt. "He was the events planner at a conservative think tank! And now he will be managing my program, making changes that will violate the whole purpose of our work."

Moisture sparkled in her eyes and Quinn experienced a quick sympathy. Mia Goodwin had invested herself in YES! and its programs. The organization had become part of her and she felt the changes intensely.

She stared over his shoulder, dealing with tears of loss and anger, refusing to let them fall. Finally, she returned her gaze to Quinn's. It was melancholy now, the passionate anger burned out by a reality she couldn't change. "I worked closely with Gordon Widdowson, our former CEO, since he joined us ten years ago. Very early on he started mentoring me. I was to be his replacement, you see. The CEO position would be mine when he left the organization. He didn't define the exact date, of course, but he knew that when the time came, he would be leaving YES! in safe hands, as I'd be able to grow the organization and implement our mission." She shook her head, sighed. "Well, that didn't happen. And now I'm leaving completely."

Her unhappiness, mixed with the fury she'd exhibited earlier, all pointed to a strong motive to eliminate Ralph Sharpe. He'd come along, tearing up the programs she was so proud of, but, worse, he had cheated her out of a position she wanted and had every reason to believe would be hers. Quinn thought her passionate fury made her more than capable of violence.

In the heat of anger, he could imagine her whacking Ralph Sharpe over the head with an implement like a baseball bat. Or pushing him so he fell and hit his head against something solid. He even thought her personality was forceful enough that she'd try to cover up the attack by pushing his body into the canal.

He studied her for a moment. "Everything you've told me, Ms. Goodwin, indicates you have an excellent motive for murdering Ralph Sharpe. Where were you on the evening he was killed?"

Her melancholy expression morphed into incredulity. "You think I'd risk my freedom to do away with a dirty old thug like Ralph Sharpe?" Her lip curled. "Think again, Mr. Armstrong. I couldn't be bothered. The man was hated. I knew someone would get him eventually, but it wasn't going to be me. And now, I think that's quite enough." She stood up, extending her hand. "It has been interesting talking with you."

A clear dismissal. Quinn slowly stood. "Does that mean you don't have an alibi for that evening?" he asked as he shook her hand.

She snatched it away, the fire blazing in her eyes. "Good-bye, Mr. Armstrong!"

Quinn smiled ruefully. "Thank you for your input." He was relieved to be free of her emotional fury as he made his way out of the building that housed YES!. He also realized he'd found his first likely suspect.

CHAPTER 6

Alice Griffiths, wearing a sensible pantsuit and low-rise heels, pushed auto-dial for her boss, Justina Strong. She put the phone up to her ear as she hurried along the corridor of the local CTV affiliate. "Justina? Hi, it's Alice."

Dressed rock star cool in a torso hugging T-shirt, ripped jeans, and really expensive, roughed up black leather boots, Sledge sauntered down the hallway. He was pretending he wasn't paying attention to Alice, who was tripping along at his side. Every now and then, a staffer would pass by and greet him. Then he'd shake hands and smile. Occasionally, he'd sign his autograph—it was usually women who asked—but most of the time it was just the usual *Aren't-you?-Yes-I-am.-Wow-this-is-so-cool* kind of conversation.

But with Alice reporting to Justina, he wanted to know what she was saying, so he tuned in.

"Yes, the interview went well," she was saying. "Uh-huh. They're airing a teaser on the five o'clock news. Yes, the full interview will be on the eleven o'clock national news mid-week. Yes, the focus was on Sledge-Hammer's return to the music scene."

Return to the music scene, Sledge thought with disgust. Sledge-

Hammer never left the scene. Sure, they'd taken a hiatus from touring when their former manager Vince, had been murdered. His bandmate, Hammer, had then taken off with his girlfriend, Jahlina, to seek out her roots in China, but that was a holiday. A nearly yearlong holiday, but still. He'd been writing songs and keeping the band's name in the minds of fans and music lovers alike with his stint on the reality TV show that was a glorified singing contest.

Bringing the band back to life. Huh.

"Yes, I've scheduled interviews with the other networks." There was a pause, then her tone changed. "Well, I…"

Alerted, Sledge glanced at her. She was biting her bottom lip and stealing a look his way. He raised his brows, letting her know he'd heard. She bit her lip again, put her hand over the phone, and said, "Justina thinks a concert here in Ottawa would be an excellent venue for your return. She has a plan."

He frowned.

Alice hurried on, no doubt to counter his reluctance. "You'd be part of the concert that wraps up the La Machine weekend."

He knew about La Machine because Noelle was so excited about it. He didn't know there was to be a concert as the finale. "Hammer is in Vancouver."

"Causton Entertainment manages one of the bands that's already been scheduled. They could back you up."

Causton Entertainment was the company Justina and Alice worked for. It figured Justina would want to use him to promote one of her other acts. He shook his head.

"Sledge! It's important. It would be a great opportunity—"

"For who?" He shook his head again.

"But, Sledge—"

"I'm not going to argue with you in the hallway of a TV station." He kept his lazy smile in place, greeted another staffer in a friendly way, and kept walking.

Alice said into the phone. "I'll have to get back to you on that, Justina. Yes, difficult, yes."

Great, he was now being labeled a cranky creative type, instead of the consummate professional he really was.

They reached the main door and emerged on the sidewalk, which was crowded with people. The local CTV affiliate was located in the ByWard Market. In the early afternoon tourists, gawking at everything, jostled with civil servants heading back to their offices after their lunch break. The streets were crowded with stalls where farmers from the region sold their produce. As the afternoon gave way to evening, bars and restaurants would come to life as young people flocked into the area.

Sledge shoved his baseball cap over his shaggy locks and dipped the bill so it shaded his face. He added sunglasses and hoped that his emergence from the TV studio wouldn't alert the mob of people on the sidewalk they had a celebrity in their midst. He marched determinedly away from the station, not bothering to see if Alice was following or not. When he reached a restaurant that advertised it served the best pizza in Ottawa, he pulled open the door and sauntered inside. He heard Alice's footsteps hurrying along behind him.

The restaurant was a long, dark room with a bar running from the lobby area the length of the space. The bartender nodded acknowledgement and told him to sit anywhere. Sledge headed for a secluded table along the back wall.

A waitress appeared almost immediately, carrying menus and cutlery wrapped in paper napkins. She set these down, asked what they wanted to drink, and said she'd be back. He removed his sunglasses, but not his cap, opened his menu, and focused on the options. In his peripheral vision, he saw Alice pick up hers after a long moment staring at him.

He knew he was being a jerk, but he also knew Alice was like a terrier when it came to convincing him to make a career move he wasn't comfortable with. She was good at coming up with excellent reasons why whatever it was should be done, and she'd guilt him out until he finally caved.

He didn't want to do a concert without Hammer. Hammer was his partner, but, even more, he created the rhythm and the beat that dominated their sound. Sledge was the music, the voice, and the instruments.

Together, they were a complete package. That's why the band's name wasn't two separate words, but two names joined together into one whole.

The waitress reappeared with the beer he'd selected and the glass of water Alice had requested. She took their orders—a loaded special with every protein option on the menu and not one of the vegetables, for him, and a vegan special for Alice—then disappeared along with the menus. Alice put her hands on the table and leaned forward. Sledge pulled out his phone.

As he scrolled through emails, he could feel Alice vibrating with tension on the other side of the scarred oak table. She was going to burst soon and he'd have to deal with the whole concert idea. He hadn't decided how to handle it yet and he needed a distraction.

An email from Todd Ahern sent to all of them caught his eye. He opened it and suddenly his attention was caught. In their meeting last night, Ahern had promised to forward a list of the graduates of YES! and this, apparently, was it. He scrolled down, impressed by the number of names he was seeing. There had to be several hundred and at least a hundred of them were still involved with the organization, acting as mentors or now being internship hosts themselves.

The total was daunting. How were they going to sift through such a vast number before Fortier decided he'd done enough and arrested Todd Ahern? He thought about meeting Todd last night and about the tension he sensed in Tamara as they listened to her father's story. Tamara's fear wasn't surprising, really. She was living proof that when Fortier made his mind up, he didn't like to change it. She probably figured her father was doomed.

He liked Tamara. She was uptight, but fair. He liked to tease her because she always reacted with impatience, but she usually had to apologize once she calmed down. As well, he knew she must be worried, because she didn't approve of the Jamieson and Armstrong crew solving murders. To ask for their help must have been hard.

Thinking about the meeting the previous night had him visualizing the amazing digs Alice had arranged for them on such short notice. He stared at the long list in the email. Alice was good at sorting out details and arranging the impossible.

He put his phone on the table and shoved it toward her. "I have a ridiculously long list of names I have to cull through. I need to locate a person or persons so invested in an organization they'd kill someone. Can you find them?"

Alice blinked. Sledge was rather pleased to see that he'd pulled her up short and shaken her out of her obsession with the concert.

"You're talking about the murder that occurred a few days ago?"

Sledge nodded.

"That's why you and your entourage are here?" Alice's voice rose. The expression on her small, heart-shaped face was incredulous.

"Yup. The cops are looking at my friend Tamara's dad for it. He didn't do it, so we're here to help."

Alice's eyes narrowed and she leaned forward. "You're not going to unmask the killer at your concert like you did at the party in Vancouver, are you?"

Sledge grinned. A couple of months ago, the Jamiesons and Armstrongs had been involved in the hunt for the killer of a construction mogul in Vancouver. The suspects had all been invited to a grand party to celebrate SledgeHammer's new management. No one had intended that the killer should confess at the event, but that's what had happened. An enterprising individual had filmed the whole thing, then uploaded the video to social media. Sledge had been called the rock and roll detective ever since. "I might."

Alice shook her head. "Justina wouldn't like that."

"Why not? Any press is good press, right?"

"Sledge," Alice said patiently, "solving crimes isn't part of SledgeHammer's brand."

Well, fair enough. But… "It's part of me. My father's a lawyer. I'm all about defending the falsely accused. I grew up with it."

"But SledgeHammer is a rock band! Rebels fighting against the man…"

"Innocent until proven guilty."

She pursed her lips, acknowledging that innocence isn't always respected.

He tapped his phone. "The victim was busy dismembering an organization that lots of people loved. Somewhere on this list may be the name of the person who cares so passionately about the organization that they'd be willing to kill to stop him."

She raised her brows. "So?"

"I want you to find him. Or her."

She opened her mouth in an involuntary 'Oh' of surprise, and, he thought, disapproval. Then she thrust out her jaw and her expression changed to a little smirk of pleasure. "If I help you, you'll help me, right?"

Sledge had a sense he was standing on a fault line before a major earthquake began. He knew he should run away as fast as he could, but he couldn't seem to make his feet move. "Help you?"

She nodded.

The tremors began. The earth shifted and a gaping hole appeared. He felt his balance change as he teetered on the edge and he was helpless to control it. "How?"

"You do my concert and I'll help you find your killer."

She was looking quite smug now, which was annoying. "Only if Hammer agrees."

She thought about that, saw the sense of including the other member of the group in the deliberations, and nodded.

Pleased with himself, feeling more confident, he increased his requirements. "If Hammer is okay with it, I'll front for the band Justina wants to use. I'll sing with them and lend my name to the event."

Alice shook her head. "No deal. Justina wants to highlight you. She hopes she can get some promo for the other band, but you're the draw."

The yawning black void created by the earthquake shook him back into a panic. "All right. How's this? Justina's band can back me, but I'll only sing covers or other artists' work."

Alice shook her head again. "SledgeHammer hits."

Sledge shrugged. "Deal's off then. I don't sing SledgeHammer songs without Hammer. That's non-negotiable."

She sat back, apparently considering this. She was studying him, he realized, gauging his determination. He straightened, thrust out his chin, and eyed her back.

Finally, she nodded. "Okay, what about this? We'll get Hammer to come out and do the concert."

He rubbed his chin. That could work. And, honestly, he wouldn't mind doing an impromptu show. "Done. But if Hammer won't participate, I'll only do covers. Agreed?"

It was her turn to deliberate. After a moment she nodded decisively. "I'll talk to Justina and set it up." She looked down at his phone. "So," she said, as she started to scroll through the long list of names, "tell me more about this murder."

Sledge outlined what they'd learned so far. Alice nodded, forwarded Todd's email, then pulled out her iPad and began to work. The waitress arrived with their pizzas. Sledge thanked her with one of his trademark grins, making her blink. Alice muttered an absentminded thanks, her gaze on the web page she was scrolling through. She picked up a slice with one hand, still scrolling with the other and began to eat. Sledge sat back and enjoyed his beer and loaded pizza.

Two slices later, Alice looked up as she wiped her fingers with the paper napkin. "The way I see it, you have five possibilities and one very strong option."

Sledge raised his brows. "Only five? Out of all of those names?"

Alice nodded. "Most of the graduates move on to management positions in government or other organizations." Her brow wrinkled. "It's a testament to the quality of the YES! program. I'm impressed." She waved her hand. "But that's neither here nor there. What seems to happen is that in the first three to five years, the graduates stay in close contact. Many of them become mentors. Then, as their careers take off, they remain in contact, perhaps providing an internship placement for the new students, but their participation in group events dwindles."

Sledge nodded. That made sense. It happened with any group or organization. Experience and all of the bits and pieces of daily life changed a person's interests. Without regular contact, old friendships became stale, then nostalgic. The urge to participate in group activities withered away unless something special motivated a person to join back in.

"So, the people you've identified are all recent grads?"

"Yes and no. All six are mentors this year. Two graduated four years ago and both actually work for the same organization, an international health charity. One works for the government and graduated two years ago. Two others are last year's grads. They're both employed by nonprofits. The final one..." Here she paused for emphasis.

She was going to make him ask, he thought incredulously. He waited a heartbeat, another, then another. Her eyes gleamed. She was going to wait him out. Well, all right. If that was how she was going to do it, he'd play the game.

He beat a quick drumroll on the table, lifted his hand, palm up, pointing toward her, and said, "Spill."

"Grad number six, and our best option, is Cassandra Weldon. She completed the program ten years ago. Since then, she's participated in YES! activities every year, mentoring students and providing placements. She's been employed by two non-profits and is currently the managing director of an organization that works with the children of immigrants who are non-English or French speaking. The organization helps the kids learn one of the two official languages and ensures they're up to speed with the Canadian education system so they don't fall behind or miss a grade level."

"Sounds like a worthy cause," Sledge said. After Alice nodded, he added, "What makes you think we should look at this Cassandra Weldon for the murder?"

Alice tapped her iPad. "Cassandra Weldon is active on social media. Ever since she graduated, she's been posting about YES!, its program, the benefits of participation, and why people should apply. There's a fervor about her writing that's almost..." She paused searching for a word.

Sledge provided it. "Messianic?"

Slowly, she nodded. "She's a true believer, all right." She tapped the iPad again. "The thing is, in the past couple of years, the tone of her writing has changed. It's angry, bitter, resentful. Instead of lauding the organization, she urges caution. She still encourages people to apply and participate, but she warns them to remember that the goal is to give back, not your own advantage. At the same time, she rails against the new voices, presumably this guy, Sharpe, destroying the purity of a selfless institution."

"I suppose this started when Sharpe organized private companies to sponsor internships?"

Alice shook her head. "No. It started immediately after he was elected to the board. She wrote a post full of outrage asking why he'd been welcomed to the position and warning that his involvement would only lead to trouble. She's been following up on that ever since."

Sledge sat back in his seat. He rubbed his chin, the fashionable stubble of three days' growth of beard rough on his fingertips. "She sounds like a nut."

Alice's brow wrinkled as she considered this. Then she shook her head. "I don't think so. She's got a high-powered job and seems to have a good reputation in the community. She interacts with city, provincial, and federal officials and has elevated her non-profit from a small organization to twice its size in five years. I think YES! is her private, personal crusade and she's a fanatic about it."

Sledge grinned. "She sounds exactly what we need. I think we should talk to this woman."

Alice nodded. "I have her number. I'll call her and make an appointment."

Only it wasn't that simple. Cassandra Weldon wouldn't talk to Sledge of SledgeHammer. She informed Alice she was a busy woman who wasn't interested in overgrown boys who indulged in the trivial trappings of a material world. And that was that. She hung up without another word.

"A nut," Sledge said, nodding, when Alice glumly explained.

Alice sighed.

Sledge wasn't a guy who was easily put off. He rubbed his bristly chin and considered their options. After a moment, he grinned. "Try this. You can't call Weldon directly. She'll recognize your voice. Instead, phone her secretary. Tell her you're from McCullagh, McCullagh, and Walker, barristers and solicitors, and that Rob McCullagh would like to meet with Ms. Weldon."

Alice narrowed her eyes. "Why?"

"Why?"

"The secretary is going to ask the reason for the meeting."

"Good point." Sledge stared toward the ceiling as he considered. Bringing his gaze back to Alice's, he said, "Let's be upfront. Tell her it's about Todd Ahern."

She wrinkled her nose. "You think that will work?"

He leaned forward. "If YES! is her cult, then Todd Ahern is her spiritual leader." He nodded. "She'll bite."

Alice made the call.

Cassandra Weldon bit.

CHAPTER 7

Some two hours later, they presented themselves at an office located in a very old and rather down-at-heels building in Centretown, an area that had once been residential, but was now a jumble of businesses, government offices, and housing.

Parking was at a premium, so after rounding the block several times and finding nothing, Sledge pulled the Spider into the driveway of a house near their destination. He marched up to the front door and knocked. When a harried-looking woman holding a crying baby answered it, he politely explained he wanted to park in her driveway for a couple of hours. She stared at him for a moment, opened her mouth, then narrowed her eyes as he pulled a wad of cash out of his wallet.

She stepped out onto her porch to look past him to the flashy car in her driveway. The baby stopped crying, reached out, closed a chubby fist around his hair, which curled over his collar. The baby yanked. Sledge winced and the child gurgled, a sound something akin to laughter.

The woman held out her hand. "Two hours and not a minute more. The mother of this cranky handful gets home then and she won't be happy if she can't get into her driveway."

"I doubt we'll be here that long," Sledge said, wincing again as the baby tugged. He gently untangled the little fingers from his hair and the kid started to wail.

The woman glared at him. "See you're not." Clutching her cash and the baby, she retreated into the house. As the door closed behind her, Sledge could still hear the baby's wail.

"I'm never having kids," Alice said gloomily as they walked over to Cassandra Weldon's building.

Sledge laughed. "I don't think the babysitter is either."

"How much did you pay her?"

He shrugged. "Fifty bucks."

Alice made a tsking sound, but they'd reached their destination, so he didn't get a lecture on extravagance. Good thing too. He figured he had more than enough money for a small indulgence like this.

The building was an old house made over into an office. Five people were crammed into what had once been the living room and there were another three in the dining room. Everyone looked busy, working telephones, or typing energetically into computers. Someone, who didn't identify herself, told them Cassandra's office was upstairs, then went back to the phone system, answering calls. Sledge looked at Alice, who shrugged.

The stairs led to a compact second floor with a bathroom and two good-sized bedrooms. One had been converted into a conference room. The other was Cassandra Weldon's office. Sledge knocked on the partially open door to the office, then pushed it wider. "Rob McCullagh and Alice Griffiths," he said as he advanced into the room holding out his hand.

Cassandra Weldon stood and came round her desk. She was a heavy-set woman with broad shoulders, not much of a waist, and large hips. She was wearing a flowing skirt in a gorgeous shade of green that seemed to shimmer as she moved. It was topped by a tunic with bloused sleeves that fluttered when she shook Sledge's hand.

Gesturing to two chairs in front of her desk that appeared to be relics of the mid-century modern school of design, she returned back behind her desk and sat down. Clasping her hands in front of her, she said, "How can I help you, Mr. McCullagh?"

"You know Ralph Sharpe was murdered last Friday?"

She nodded. She had plump cheeks, but a thin compressed mouth and watchful dark eyes. Sledge couldn't read her reaction. She was guarding herself well.

"My secretary said you wanted to speak to me about Todd Ahern. What has he to do with Ralph's death?"

Sledge deliberately allowed surprise to play across his features. "You haven't heard then? Todd is the prime suspect for the murder. Alice and I are part of a team investigating on his behalf."

At his mention of Todd's situation, Cassandra gave a little gasp. By the time he finished, one hand covered her mouth and her eyes were wide with dismay. "Why would the police suspect Todd? He would never harm another human being."

She was the second woman Sledge had met who believed Todd Ahern incapable of murder. "And yet witnesses claim he and Sharpe had a violent argument that ended up in a physical altercation the same day Sharpe was killed."

Taking a deep breath, Cassandra released it slowly. She shook her head. "It wasn't like that."

Alice, taking notes on her tablet, looked up as Cassandra paused. Sledge said, "Then tell me what actually happened."

Having regained her composure, Cassandra wasn't about to give up more than she was ready to. "Have you talked to Todd about that afternoon?"

"Yes," Sledge said, "but I want to hear your version of events."

Her expression carefully uninformative, she said, "The anger, the violence, was all on Ralph's side. Todd was trying to reason with him, but Ralph wasn't having any of it."

"The police have a different interpretation of what happened. Why should I believe you?" Sledge allowed skepticism to seep into his voice and was pleased when she colored.

"Because I was there. I started the argument!"

Interesting. Sledge raised his eyebrows in an expression of disbelief. "Really? Todd never said anything."

"Of course not." The scorn in her voice was unmistakable. "He's not the sort of man to whine and lay blame. If someone accused him of starting the argument, he wouldn't deny it to save himself. He'd take the blame to protect those in his care."

Out of the corner of his eye, Sledge saw Alice throw him a startled glance. He'd been dead right about the way Cassandra Weldon felt about YES! and Todd Ahern. "Then it's time you gave me your side of the story. What happened that afternoon and why?"

The green silk of her top, a few shades lighter than her skirt, shimmered as she moved uneasily. She reached up to run her fingers through her dark hair, cut in a short practical style that lifted, then fell back into place once her agitated fingers moved away. She clasped her hands together on the desk, a visible attempt to calm herself as she began to talk.

"Classes for the first-year students finish at the end of July, then they go to a month-long internship before they return to their regular educational institutions in September. With the internships beginning in only a couple of weeks, I'd dropped into the office to make sure that the students I'm mentoring all had placements. I learned that two of my brightest students, both young men, had been assigned to Ralph Sharpe's company. I was furious!"

"Why?" Sledge asked.

Stiffening, she flattened both hands onto the desktop. Her eyes flashed. "Are you serious? Ralph Sharpe specializes in producing merchandise that is cheaply made and poor quality. He then promotes the product endlessly until the public discovers it doesn't don't work. At that point, he dumps it and moves on to the next big idea. He's the worst of the worst examples of evil corporate greed. And two of my students— my protégés!—are being delivered to his vile organization to learn what? That everything we've taught them is wrong? That service and respect for your clients is valueless, not the hallmark of a life well lived? That you can dispose of anything and everything carelessly, on a whim, in order to indulge your own lust for money?"

Sledge blinked, opened his mouth, then decided Cassandra Weldon was quite capable of switching from words into action at the slightest provocation. He really didn't want to get into an altercation with her.

She stared at him defiantly, almost tauntingly. When he merely raised his eyebrows, she said a little more calmly, "Someone told me Todd was in the office, so I decided to speak to him to see if he could do anything about the internships. When I got to the conference room, I found that Ralph was with him."

She drew a deep breath, looked out the window at the poor excuse for a garden behind the old house, and shook her head. "He and Todd were already talking about those internships. Ralph was blustering. Todd was calm. Todd said the second-year students could choose a private sector placement if they wanted, but he completely drew the line at first years being assigned one. Ralph got quite angry. His face went red and he told Todd that in another year or two all the placements would be in the private sector. Todd dismissed that and Ralph laughed. He pointed at Todd and said 'Little you know. Most of the internships are already privates.' Todd looked absolutely horrified. That's when I got involved."

When she didn't continue, Alice said urgently, "And? What happened?"

Cassandra drew a shaking breath. "When I said I agreed with Todd, Ralph laughed and said, 'Who cares? You'll be gone after this session.'" She shook her head. "He told us YES! was indoctrinating young people, not educating them, and he was going to stop that from happening. I think I gasped. I know I rushed up to him. And I slapped him." She stopped, opened and closed her mouth, sighed. "I'm not proud of that, but he was an evil man. He looked so shocked. Then, after a moment, he slapped me back. Todd hurried over, because, well, he wouldn't stand for that sort of behavior. He pushed Ralph away. That's when other people in the office showed up at the door. It must have appeared as if Todd and Ralph were fighting."

Sledge visualized the scene. Two angry men about to latch on to each other and indulge in a wrestling match. Cassandra, shocked and horrified, staring at them or shrinking away from the developing violence. A cluster of staffers watching, appalled.

"What happened next?" he asked.

Cassandra drew a deep breath. Her mouth was pursed, her lips turned downward. "Someone, I forget who, said something. Ralph realized he had an audience and he stepped back. He shook his finger at Todd and said 'This isn't over.' I remember that particularly because the words were so ominous and his voice—" She shuddered. "He snarled the words like a vicious, out-of-control animal. Then he stormed out, pushing people aside if they didn't move out of the way quickly enough. Awful man." Contempt laced her tone.

Alice had listened to this, her head tilted to one side in a detached, impersonal manner. "And he died that evening."

Cassandra looked at her sharply. Was there a guilty expression in her eyes? Or had she just not added the nasty scene and the violent death together and figured out that one could very well lead to the other? Sledge leaned forward. "Where were you that evening between eight and midnight?"

"Are you asking if I have an alibi for the night of the murder?" She sounded incredulous.

Sledge nodded.

"I don't have to tell you that."

"I'm not the cops, so no, you don't. What you've told us today adds you to the suspect list, though, so it would be a good idea if you did."

"You're going to take what I told you to the cops, aren't you?"

Sledge nodded.

She glared at him, her mouth working, her eyes hard. After a moment she slapped her hand onto the desktop and said, "Fine. I was here, finishing off the work I didn't get done that day, because I'd spent the whole afternoon on the phone with former internship providers, trying to find out if they were interested in providing a placement this year, and if they weren't, why not?"

"Was there anyone else here with you?" Sledge asked.

She shook her head. "No. After six o'clock when my assistant went home, I was alone in the building."

Studying her, he asked, "Did you order food delivered? Go out to pick up a sandwich? Take an hour to have dinner in a sit-down restaurant? Go anywhere someone might remember you?"

Again, she shook her head. "No."

This was bad news for Cassandra, but good for Todd, because it would provide Fortier with a viable alternative suspect, Sledge thought. "Okay, I think I've heard enough for now." He looked over at Alice. "Do you have anything you'd like to ask Cassandra?"

She shook her head. "No. I think you've covered it."

"Okay, then." He stood, holding out his hand. "Thank you for your time."

She blinked and nodded. Looking grim, she stood as well and shook his hand. "I'll see you out."

"No need," Sledge said cheerfully. He could feel her eyes boring into him as he and Alice left her office. Back on the sidewalk, he glanced at his phone. "Less than an hour. Our parking attendant-babysitter will be pleased."

Alice rolled her eyes.

"What do you think of Cassandra Weldon?"

"No alibi, hates the victim, good motive," Alice said promptly. She bobbed her head in a thoughtful way. "A good suspect," she added as they reached the car.

"That's what I thought." The engine caught with a satisfying roar. "Time to convene a group discussion. Let's go buy some pastries. Are there any good bakeries around here?"

CHAPTER 8

Preparations for dinner were well on the way when Christy emerged from the elevator carrying a box holding an assortment of dishes. She saw Quinn shove open the glass front door as he entered the lobby and felt, rather than viewed, Stormy streak between her legs as he bolted toward the slowly closing doorway.

She shouted, "Careful!" She wasn't sure if she was chastising the cat for almost tripping her, or warning Quinn to make sure the door shut behind him before the cat got there.

The cat paid no attention, focused on reaching the door before it closed. Moments before he arrived, the door snapped closed. Stormy skidded to a stop, his tail slashing from side to side in irritation. Then he turned and bolted for the community room and disappeared inside through the open doorway.

Quinn raised his eyebrows as he came over to relieve Christy of her burden. "What's going on?"

"Cat crazies. Frank's annoyed he didn't have a part in the detecting today and even though we left all the doors to the suites and the stairwells open so Stormy could move around the building freely, the cat's been alone all day. He wants attention." She shrugged. "Together, they're worse than a bored toddler."

Quinn laughed, and after a moment she laughed too before rising up on her tiptoes to give him a kiss.

He kissed her back, enjoying the rare moment of intimacy.

After a minute, Christy drew back and smiled at him. "That was nice."

He grinned at her. "It was, wasn't it?"

They went into the community room where the cat was now crouching on the back of the sofa, his tail lashing as he tried to catch a bundle of feathers attached to a fishing pole cat toy that Noelle was wielding. Ellen and Trevor were setting the boardroom table with silverware, so Quinn took the box of dishes over to them.

"Hi, Quinn!" Noelle abandoned the cat and bounced over to them. "What did you do today? Mom and Grandpa and Grandma and I went to Downs Lake—"

"Dow's," Christy said. "It's Dow's Lake, kiddo."

"Yeah, Dow's. It's right in the middle of Ottawa and they have kayaks and everything!"

"It's part of the Rideau Canal system," Ellen said, her tone indicating this was clearly meant to be an educational moment.

Noelle nodded, before she said with a great deal of glee, "We rented a kayak and I almost fell in."

Quinn shook his head and said with a twinkle, "Sounds like fun."

Noelle giggled. "It was. Then we went shopping and bought vegetables right from the farmers and Mom and Grandma and Grandpa made dinner."

Quinn smiled at Christy. "Definitely a good day."

She nodded. "It was. Ellen bought three fountain pens and an assortment of inks, then we all had lunch at a trendy little restaurant in an old stone building in the ByWard Market."

Hearing her name, Ellen happily described the new pens and the colored inks she'd purchased. She'd also acquired two journals, which would replace the letterhead she usually used for their notes.

Not long after Sledge sauntered in, followed by Alice, both carrying boxes obviously filled with dessert pastries. Rachael and Miles arrived a few minutes later, bringing the dinner they and Christy had prepared in Christy's condo kitchen. Tamara had called Quinn with news, so he'd invited her to join them. She rang the bell as the meal was being set up on the table.

They ate before they started discussing the day's results. The dinner was family favorites of garden salad and chicken fajitas, complete with pico de gallo and guacamole. The dessert Sledge supplied was an assortment of BeaverTails, an iconic Ottawa pastry in the shape of... well, a beaver's tail. Traditionally topped with a hazelnut chocolate spread, there was now a huge variety of flavor options and true to form, Sledge had purchased most of them.

"I think I'm going to burst," Christy said, after she'd finished sampling her third flavor.

Ellen sighed. "These are ridiculously delicious."

"Yum," said Noelle, licking her fingers.

Having decided that was enough dessert discussion, Tamara got right to the point. "Did you have a chance to do any investigating today?"

"Just a moment." Ellen wiped her fingers with a paper napkin she wielded rather disdainfully. Cloth, or better yet, starched and ironed linen, was more her style. "I need to get my pens and journals before we begin."

Alice brandished her iPad. "That's all right. I can take notes on this."

"Really." The word was long and drawn out. Ellen's eyebrows were raised and she managed to look down her nose at Alice, but the glare she leveled on Sledge was accusatory.

His expression sheepish, he cleared his throat, then shot Alice a wary glance before he said to no one in particular, "This afternoon, Alice helped me interview Cassandra Weldon. She's a grad of the YES! program and one of the mentors. Alice took notes then."

Ellen made a disapproving sound in her throat as she pushed her chair back. She went over to the built-in cabinets that lined one wall.

Tamara looked from Alice to Sledge then to Ellen, who was busy collecting her pens and journals from the cupboard where she'd stashed them earlier. "It doesn't matter who takes notes! Fortier came to the hotel to interview Dad again today. He told Dad not to leave Ottawa. I think he plans to arrest him!"

Christy stood. "I have nothing to report, so I'll do clean up. Come on kiddo, let's clear the dishes and take them up to our suite. Then you and I can watch TV together."

Noelle helped Christy gather dishes. Quinn decided to help, along with Roy, so the table was quickly cleared. At the counter where they were assembling the dishes, Noelle said in a low voice, "Mom, don't worry about me. I can stream a show on the TV down here. Go to the meeting."

Christy bit her lip, uncertain.

Noelle put her hands on her hips and raised her brows, as imperious as her Aunt Ellen in one of her finest moments. "Mom, I'm not going to listen in. The TV's on the far side of the room. You don't have to worry!"

Christy waffled a bit longer, then she nodded. Quinn smiled and Roy shot her an approving nod. By the time they returned to the table, the battle of who would be the scribe appeared to be over. With her journal open and her pens carefully laid out, Ellen was the successful combatant. Tamara's lips were pursed in an impatient line at the delay, but Alice didn't appear to be dismayed by her defeat. Rather, she was observing the action with undisguised interest.

The cat, who had escorted Noelle to the sofa near the TV, then sat with her while she got settled, returned to the table area, settling into Christy's lap. *Time to call this meeting to order.*

Roy poured himself a glass of wine and toasted the others. "Who wants to begin?"

Trevor cleared his throat. "I got hold of Inspector Fortier. He wasn't much help though. He took refuge in 'no comment' style answers. He wouldn't even confirm cause of death, so all we have to go on is Todd's assumption that Sharpe was killed by a blow to the head. He did acknowledge Todd was a person of interest, but he wouldn't commit to his being the prime suspect."

"Does Frontier have any other suspects?" Quinn asked.

"Not that he'd admit to. All he would say was that the case was progressing."

"What does that mean?" Roy asked, disgust in his voice.

Trevor shrugged. "Could be anything." He looked around. "I hope someone else has something more positive to contribute."

"Alice and I found a new suspect," Sledge said.

Quinn looked from Sledge to Alice, brows raised. "You and Alice? I thought you went down to the local TV station for an interview?"

Sledge grinned. "I did. Todd's list of students came in while we were grabbing a pizza after the interview. I asked Alice to gather data on the names, then give me some good options. She did."

Everyone looked at Alice, who smiled, then looked down demurely.

"Alice found me six names. Five possibles, along with one really strong probable. That's Cassandra Weldon, a former participant. We went to see her after we finished our lunch."

Alice is a woman of hidden depths. But then we figured that out when she miraculously furnished an empty apartment building at a moment's notice. Stormy hopped up onto the table, trotted down to the far end, butted Alice's hand, then licked it. She smiled and tentatively stroked him. The cat arched his back and preened.

"So why is this woman a potential suspect?" Roy asked.

"Cassandra Weldon runs a non-profit that works with the children of immigrants to help them to succeed in school. She believes absolutely in YES!. She hates everything Ralph Sharpe stood for and the changes he was making to the organization," Sledge said.

Alice nodded. "She's also very, very angry."

"And she doesn't have an alibi," Sledge concluded with a wink at Alice, who nodded back.

"Interesting." Christy's comment was more about Sledge's newfound connection with Alice, than about the suspect information.

"My father said the police were focusing on YES!, because of the conflict caused by Sharpe's changes," Tamara said. "Wouldn't they have already considered this woman?"

Sledge's grin widened. "They should have. She was involved in the altercation between your father and Ralph Sharpe. In fact, she slapped Sharpe, who hit her back. That's when your dad got physical with him. He was forcing Sharpe to back off. Cassandra said she wasn't surprised

Todd didn't mention that. She said he's the kind of man who'd never allow a woman's good name to be sullied, if he could help it."

"Sully a woman's good name? Did she actually say that?" Roy asked incredulously.

"Pretty much," Alice said.

"That sounds like my father," Tamara said. "He'd never accuse someone else to save himself."

Ellen made a note in one of her journals. She was using the other to identify things to do. "Someone needs to talk to Todd to find out if what this Cassandra Weldon says is true."

"I'll do that," Tamara said.

Ellen changed journals, chose a pen, and wrote up the task, then added Tamara's name under it. "Very good. What else have we got?"

Quinn said, "I talked to Cooper Singleton. He was the chair of the board when Sharpe joined it. He confirmed that Sharpe approached the organization with the offer of a substantial donation. The donation came with strings, mainly that Sharpe be appointed to the board as chair. Cooper confirmed that the donation was substantial, so he agreed to step down. Sharpe started making changes almost immediately."

These people do not sound like they have a lot of street smarts.

"And Ralph Sharpe did," Roy said, sipping his wine.

Rachael and Miles frowned. Christy rolled her eyes and Quinn raised his brows.

Alice looked around, confusion writ large on her features. "Did what?"

Sledge didn't even blink. "He made changes, of course."

Still looking confused, Alice frowned, though she didn't comment. Christy had begun to realize she had a formidable intelligence behind her quiet demeanor. They'd better be on their toes or she'd be asking questions Christy for one didn't want to answer.

Quinn cleared his throat and resumed. "Sharpe began by appointing friends to the board, people who shared his point of view. Then, when the CEO resigned to take a new position in another organization, he ensured a man with his political views was hired as the new CEO."

Miles said, "Political views? What do Sharpe's political opinions have to do with anything?"

Quinn shrugged. "I don't know, but that was how Singleton phrased it. The new CEO of the institution is the former CEO of the Dogwood Party."

Tamara gasped. "That's why Fortier is involved with this case. Ralph Sharpe was involved with the Dogwood Party!"

"I begin to see why Todd was so concerned about the direction his organization was going in," Trevor said.

"It gets worse." Quinn glanced around the table. "There was an internal candidate for the CEO position. The woman is currently the director of curriculum and events. Like Cassandra Weldon, she's dedicated to YES!. She was devastated at being passed over, especially since the new CEO recently told her her services would no longer be needed come September."

Christy leaned forward. "So, we have two viable suspects, both related to the institution. But, surely, as Tamara said, the police have already investigated these two people."

"You'd think so." Roy shrugged. "But remember how single-minded Fortier was when he investigated Fred Jarvis's murder. Once he'd latched on to Tamara as a suspect, he wasn't much interested in anyone else. What if the same thing is happening here?"

"Might be. Might not," Trevor said, unhelpfully.

"Where do we look then?" Tamara asked. There was a quaver in her voice as if she was holding back tears.

Once again, Alice entered the fray, this time with a shrug and a down-to-earth expression that said she thought what she was saying was obvious. "This Sharpe guy sounds like someone people could easily dislike. He may have tried to dominate everything he did. He certainly manipulated people. There must be tons of folks in his life who'd want to bump him off."

"Well," said Sledge, sounding amazed and approving at the same time. "So we investigate Ralph Sharpe, the individual."

Alice shot him a mischievous smile and nodded.

Sledge looked around the table. "Okay. Let's divvy it up. Who wants to do what?"

"Before we can act, we need to do research," Quinn said. "Get the basics about the man, where he lives, what his company is all about, who his family are. Look for inconsistencies that might indicate dark secrets."

"I'll do some research," Alice said.

Sledge gave her a sideways look and a small nod. "Good idea." To the rest he said, rather unnecessarily, "She's a whiz."

Quinn nodded briskly. "You make up a profile on him, then, Alice. I'll look into the Dogwood connection and see if I can get to the bottom of it."

"I'll see what I can find out about his family," Roy said. "Can you get me his home address, Tamara?"

She wrinkled her nose. "Maybe. I suppose the institution has his address on file. Why do you want it?"

Roy shrugged. "I thought I'd check out his home life. Maybe talk to his wife."

The cops always focus on the wife first in a murder, old man. They've probably already cleared her.

Roy shot the cat a frustrated look. With Tamara and Alice in the room he couldn't reply directly. Instead, he had to say, "A good rule of thumb in a homicide is to look at the spouse first."

"Are you planning to walk up to his front door and say you want to question his wife?" Tamara's expression said she thought this wasn't a very good idea.

"I'm not sure what I'll do," Roy said stiffly. He leveled a firm glance at Tamara. "I simply think having the man's home address, and the family's home phone as well, is a good idea. You never know when we might need it."

Tamara considered this, then nodded. "Okay, I'll see what I can do."

Alice's phone had pinged while Roy and Tamara were talking. Now, she said to Sledge, "Justina wants to do a virtual meeting with you and Hammer tomorrow afternoon about the concert."

Sledge nodded.

"What's this about a concert?" Christy asked.

Shrugging, Sledge said, "Justina thinks it would be a good publicity stunt for SledgeHammer to be part of a concert featuring one of her local bands—"

"Several, in fact," Alice said.

She was looking demure again. Christy suspected that innocent expression was one of the tools Alice used to achieve her ends. She almost laughed. Sledge was staring at Alice with narrowed eyes and a hardened jaw. She wondered how much Alice had altered the concert description to convince him to agree to participate in the event.

"Several?" Sledge not only looked dangerous but he also sounded it.

Alice met his angry eyes without a shred of apology in hers. "I told you the concert is the big splashy finish to the La Machine celebration next week. Justina has always wanted SledgeHammer to be involved."

"Planning for this event must have been going on for years. Why didn't Hammer and I hear about this earlier?"

Alice shot him one of her demure looks, staring at him from under her lashes. "Perhaps because your manager died and the band went into semi-retirement for a year or so."

There was a fuming silence as Sledge drummed his fingers on the table. "Okay. Maybe. But that's past. Why did she spring it on me this afternoon?"

Another telling look from Alice, raised brows this time. "You've been avoiding Justina's calls. Besides, we were only hired on as SledgeHammer's new managers a couple of months ago."

She's got you there, man. The cat nudged his fingers, which continued to beat an angry tattoo. *Give it up.*

Roy nodded. "Gotta go with the flow, man. La Machine is part of the sesquicentennial celebrations. A hundred and fifty years as a country. That's a pretty impressive accomplishment. Don't you want to be part of it?"

Sledge stopped drumming on the table and sighed. "Of course I do."

"Good. I'll bring you up-to-date on the details tomorrow," Alice said. "After we've talked to Justina and Hammer, we can go check out the venue."

Sledge nodded. His expression was a mix of shock and grimness.

Christy had the distinct impression that at some point in their earlier negotiations, Alice had played him big time.

In her role as scribe, Ellen flourished one of her new pens, commanding attention. "I have Quinn investigating the political connection. Roy will see what he can find out about the family. Sledge is otherwise occupied. Alice," she pointed the pen, "you said you'd create a profile for Sharpe. Does that task need to be reassigned in view of your SledgeHammer duties?"

"Heavens no." Alice smiled and waved her hand in a dismissive way. "I'll do the research tonight and email it to..." She hesitated, looked around the table. "To you, Ellen? To Quinn? Or Trevor?"

"Send it to me," Quinn said.

"Excellent." Ellen nodded and made a note. "Now where was I? Ah, yes, Tamara is going to talk to her father and find out more about students. She'll also find out Sharpe's home address and phone number for Roy. Anything else?"

"I'll try to convince Dad to talk to Inspector Fortier about that story Cassandra Weldon told Sledge." Tamara's lips drooped. "I don't think he will, though. But I'll still try."

Ellen nodded, made a note. When she was finished, she looked around the table.

Rachael said, rather tentatively, "Miles and I made plans to have lunch with two of our colleagues from Ottawa U tomorrow. We could ask what they know about YES! and the students who graduate from it."

"An outside opinion. Good thinking. You might also want to ask your friends if they know anything about Ralph Sharpe," Quinn said.

Miles nodded. "Hadn't thought of that. We'll add it to our list of questions." The look he shot his wife was conspiratorial.

"I'll see if I can get anything more out of Fortier, but I don't think he'll be receptive. He doesn't have to talk to me, since I have no official jurisdiction," Trevor said heavily.

"How about you, Christy? What do you have planned?" Quinn asked.

Christy smiled. "Noelle and I are going to the Natural History Museum." She thought from the expression that flitted across his face that

Quinn would rather have been with them than searching for Ralph Sharpe's killer.

Finishing up her note taking, Ellen looked back over what she'd written. "An excellent program, everyone. We'll reconvene here tomorrow evening to discuss what we've learned."

The cat sauntered across the table. He nudged Ellen's notebook with his nose. *How about you, Aunt Ellen? What will you be doing?*

She smiled beatifically. "My plans? I'm going to the museum with my family."

CHAPTER 9

Their roles decided, Tamara stood. "I'll talk to my father tonight." She chewed her lip. "With Inspector Fortier focused on him, I'm not sure if I'll get a chance tomorrow."

"Probably a good idea. Fortier is like a cat chasing a mouse. He'll stalk your dad until he's ready to pounce," Roy said.

The worry in Tamara's expression deepened. Quinn stifled an impatient curse. There were moments when his father's mouth got the better of his brain.

Roy's expression turned indignant. "I wasn't referring to our cat, of course. Stormy is nothing like Fortier."

Tamara frowned, looking perplexed. Great. The cat must have said something rude about Roy's comment. Time to break this up before Tamara—or Alice!—started asking questions. He stood. "I'll walk you out to your car."

He was rewarded with an appreciative smile from Tamara and a simple, "Thanks!"

As Tamara gathered up her purse and pulled out her car keys, he glanced over at Christy. She was helping Noelle load leftovers into a bag to take back upstairs. Her expression was carefully blank, but as he stared at her she looked over, then smiled. He realized she didn't like that he was spending time with Tamara, but she understood why he was doing it.

He smiled back, trying to show her he was simply being a friend to someone who was frightened and hurting, and that his heart belonged to Christy. He must have succeeded because her smile deepened and warmth entered her eyes.

Relieved, he followed Tamara out. When they reached the small visitor parking lot in front of the building, she paused at her car, her hand on the frame of the partially open driver's side door. "Do you think you'll find the real killer?" She chewed her lip again. Her eyes were moist with unshed tears, her expression woebegone.

He wanted to tell her everything would be okay, that her father wouldn't be charged or tried for the murder, but he didn't. He wasn't sure they could pull this one off. They were outsiders here in Ottawa, with no contact in the police to listen to their theories and take them seriously enough to investigate further. "I honestly don't know. We'll try, but we're assuming there was a reason he was killed. It could just be a terrible example of criminal violence."

"Like a mugging gone wrong, you mean."

From the tone of her voice, that thought wasn't cheering her up any. He nodded.

She sighed, opened the door wider and tucked her purse onto the passenger's seat. "Much as I hate the idea that someone my father works with might be a murderer, it would be a relief to know there was a reason Ralph Sharpe was killed, that he wasn't just the victim of indiscriminate violence."

She reached out, touching Quinn's cheek in an intimate gesture he didn't expect. She must have understood his surprise, because she drew her hand away quickly, with a little smile that might have been rueful or perhaps an apology of sorts.

"Thank you, Quinn, and thank Christy, and your father and friends, for abandoning their holiday to help me. I do appreciate it." She turned away, releasing the door, preparing to get in the car.

"We'll do our best to find the killer," he said, feeling inadequate.

She smiled and nodded as she slipped into the car. "I know," she said, before she slammed the door and turned on the ignition.

He watched her drive away, that feeling of being lost in unfamiliar territory enveloping him. She turned the corner, disappearing from sight. He turned.

In front of him was the small apartment building Alice had turned into sleeping accommodations and an investigative hub in the space of a day. A small miracle, if you thought about it. Certainly, it was testimony to the power of an inventive mind and a determination to succeed. He squared his shoulders, pushing his gloom away. As a team they each had their strengths and weaknesses, but collectively they were a powerful combination of out-of-the-box thinking. They were only at the beginning of this investigation. Who knew what they'd turn up? And if Fortier wasn't willing to listen, well, they'd find a way around him.

He went back inside.

Christy, Ellen, Noelle, and most of the dishes, had disappeared. His father, Trevor, and the Yeagers were in the conversation area talking and sharing a drink. Alice was focused on her laptop, but Sledge wasn't around. Quinn picked up the last of the dishes and headed up to Christy's apartment.

She was in the kitchen, wiping counters while Ellen put the leftovers into the fridge and Noelle stacked the dishwasher. She smiled when she saw him. "Thanks, Quinn. You've saved me a trip downstairs."

Noelle looked up from her task. "Wow, Mom. Looks like we're going to run the dishwasher tonight." She reached for the plates Quinn carried.

Christy laughed. "Not surprising. There were a lot of us at dinner." She added approvingly, "You're doing a great job, kiddo."

Ellen closed the refrigerator door. "I'll join the others downstairs for a bit, I think." She bent and hugged Noelle, then straightened and with a little wave, said, "Good night, all."

With the kitchen straightened and the dishwasher on, Noelle went off to the living room to watch an hour of TV before her bedtime. Christy and Quinn settled at the table in the kitchen nook. Christy poured white wine into glasses she'd placed on the table. "How was Tamara?"

"Worried," he said, appreciating that she spotlighted the big issue between them. He moved his glass on the tabletop, watching the wine shift and swell in the bowl of the glass. When he looked up, he said, "I feel sorry for her. This case must be bringing back painful memories and I don't think she's handling them well."

Christy nodded. "That's not surprising. First, she's kidnapped and imprisoned by rebels in Africa, then, when she's freed and returns home she's accused of masterminding her birth father's murder. Having the same cop accusing her adopted father of murder must be a nightmare."

He nodded.

She took a sip of wine, then smiled at him and said, "I'm not going to be contributing much legwork, but I'm here if you want to bounce ideas off me."

He returned her smile, relieved they were no longer on the topic of Tamara. "Delighted," he said, pitching his voice low.

She laughed.

After taking a contemplative sip of wine, he said, "I'll leave the surface research to Alice. She'll be able to find out the details of Sharpe's life."

"Like when and where he was born, when he got married, you mean?"

"His kids' names. Yeah, that kind of stuff. I'll dig deeper, see if the press has anything on him, but..." He shook his head as he let the sentence hang.

"You need someone local to give you a sense of where he fits into the community," she finished, understanding instantly.

"Exactly." He smiled at her. "What you and Ellen do so very well back in Vancouver."

The compliment brought pleased color into her cheeks as she nodded thoughtfully. "Both Tamara and Todd are from Toronto, so they're no help. And we don't want to involve the people who work at YES!, because they're potential suspects."

He nodded as she paused to think.

"My parents might find out something from those friends they're having lunch with tomorrow." She wrinkled her brow and laughed. "Academics are often so focused on their own projects and lives, though. They don't worry much about the broader community."

Quinn chuckled and agreed. They sat in companionable silence, sipping their drinks for a minute. Christy's suggestion has started his brain working and he was wondering if Trevor might have a useful contact when she said, "You were an international correspondent for years, Quinn. There's a big press contingent here in Ottawa, isn't there? Surely, you must know someone who can give you the scoop on the city's movers and shakers?"

At her words, a face flashed in his mind, a lot younger than it probably looked now, but exactly the man he needed for this task. "Brilliant," he said softly.

Her smile was impish. "You've thought of someone."

He nodded. "Bryant Matthews. We were in the Middle East together years ago. We worked for competing networks, but we were friends." He pulled out his phone, scrolling through his contact list. A few minutes later he'd sent a message and received a reply. "I'm meeting him tomorrow morning."

Christy threw up her hands and said in a dramatic voice, "My work is done!"

He laughed. "Not so fast. Now we have to figure out exactly what we want to get out of him."

Christy pouted at him. "Party pooper," she said. Then they got down to business.

~

By the time Quinn left Christy's apartment and retired to his, Alice had sent him a comprehensive document itemizing Ralph Sharpe's life in point form. Sources were identified and website addresses included. Quinn scrolled through it, impressed by what she'd dug up in a very short time.

Using her work and the focus he and Christy had decided on as a jumping off point, he settled in to do his own research. By the time he quit for the night, he'd developed a list of questions for his meeting the next morning.

Bryant Matthews had suggested they meet on Parliament Hill.

Consisting of three stone structures in a square U shape around an open green space, Canada's parliament buildings were designed in the Victorian Gothic style. A paved path bisected the lawns and led directly to the main building, called the Centre Block. This was where the House of Commons and the Senate were located. It was the core of Canada's government and Ottawa's premier tourist attraction. At ten in the morning the lawns were already full of people waiting to enter the Centre Block for their tour of the impressive chambers inside.

Quinn found Bryant standing on the grass, not far from the imposing wrought iron fence that separated the parliamentary compound from Wellington Street. He was a compactly built man, with a chubby face and a receding hairline. A few years older than Quinn, he'd been the seasoned professional on the foreign correspondent beat when Quinn first began. They'd become friends and Bryant had helped him out of a number of tight situations.

Now Bryant watched the milling tourists moodily, his hands in the pockets of his slacks. Knowing him of old, Quinn had bought two coffees on his way to this meeting. Reaching his friend, he handed him a paper cup. "Black, no cream, no sugar."

The moody gleam vanished from Bryant's eyes. He grinned as he accepted the beverage. There'd been many nights when they chased the same story, sharing coffee to keep awake, bonding over stress and adrenaline. "It's good to see you, man. Have to say, though, I never expected it to be here in dull old Ottawa."

Quinn laughed. "You sound like a jaded long-time resident." In fact, he knew Bryant had quit the international news scene to lead the Ottawa bureau of his news organization only a few years before.

His smile a little rueful, Bryant shrugged. "It doesn't take long to realize that Ottawa is two solitudes. Government workers and the politicos on one side, private industry and the real world on the other."

When he paused, Quinn raised his eyebrows and said, "And never the twain shall meet?"

Though he laughed, Bryant paused before he replied. He sipped his coffee thoughtfully, then said, "Not really. The politicos live in a world all their own. The rest of us watch them shoot themselves in the foot half the time and wonder how the hell they ever got here. But enough about my life. What about you? Are you here chasing a story?"

"I'm on vacation," Quinn said with a faint, self-deprecating smile, because really, he wasn't.

Bryant studied him for a moment, his gaze skeptical. "Sure. And I bet you're going to tell me you've got a bridge you can sell me, right?"

Quinn laughed. "You know me too well."

Bryant took a gulp of coffee as he poked Quinn in the chest with his free hand. "You got it."

Quinn laughed again. "It's true, I am on vacation. I'm staying with my girlfriend's family in Kingston…"

"Girlfriend! Whoa there, my friend. When did that happen?"

"Almost two years—"

Bryant's eyes opened wide. "Christy Jamieson?"

"How did you—"

"Hey, Mr. Bestselling Author, like half the population of this country I too read your book on Frank Jamieson's disappearance and death." He paused, nodded, then added, "Excellent work."

Surprisingly pleased by the praise, Quinn said, "Thanks."

Bryant nodded again. "I hear there's another book in the works."

Quinn's mouth quirked up in a small smile. "On the murder of Fred Jarvis."

"Ah," said Bryant. "The fellow who was running for the Dogwood Party leadership last year." When Quinn nodded, he did his finger-poking thing again. "You *are* on a story."

It was Quinn's turn to pause and sip coffee while he thought of the best way to phrase what he wanted to say. "I am and I'm not." Bryant raised his brows. Quinn shrugged. "I'm chasing a murderer."

That had Bryant appraising him carefully. "A local killing?"

Quinn nodded.

"Recent?"

Quinn nodded again, then sipped from his paper cup as he watched with appreciation as Bryant worked out the puzzle.

It took a moment, but Bryant's eyes were bright with interest when he said, "Ralph Sharpe."

"You got it."

"Huh," Bryant said. "Officially, the cops refuse to say much, but I've heard they're inches away from making an arrest. A do-gooder named Ahern, isn't it? So, what's your deal? Don't you trust the cops?"

"Todd Ahern is Tamara Ahern's father." Quinn watched as understanding bloomed on Bryant's features.

"Tamara… Oh, hell. I was glad when she was rescued from the terrorists and arrived back in Canada." He paused, ruminated. "She's been through a lot."

"And she doesn't need to have her father arrested for a murder he didn't commit," Quinn said.

Bryant peered at him. "He says he didn't do it?"

Quinn nodded.

"Do you believe him?" Bryant's gaze bored into Quinn.

He was a predator on the hunt, in this case a reporter scenting a juicy story. Quinn knew the signs. "My mind advises caution. My gut says trust him."

Bryant nodded. "Good enough for me." He cocked a brow and gave Quinn a sideways look. "Are you willing to share?"

Quinn knew this request would be coming and he'd decided his answer in advance. "When we find the real killer, you can break the story."

Studying him, Bryant considered that. "But you'll write the in-depth profile. I saw the article you did on the murder of that developer a couple of months ago." He laughed. "Exposing the killer at a SledgeHammer event in front of a room full of movers and shakers… Pretty awesome."

Quinn smiled but didn't reply. Instead, he waited.

Bryant rubbed his chin as he thought. "Murder isn't my beat. The political scene is." Then he shrugged. "Ralph Sharpe was a Dogwood bagman. I don't think he had a lot of influence with the party, or with their new leader, Archie Fleming, but the association is close enough for me to put some time into the story." He held out his hand. "Okay, it's a deal. How can I help?"

They shook, then Quinn said, "I've got a raft of notes about Ralph Sharpe, but the information is stuff that's available to anyone who wants to look. What I need to know is what kind of man he was. Who his friends were. If he beat his wife—"

Bryant laughed. "I get it. Who would hate the guy enough that he'd kill him."

"Exactly," Quinn said, nodding. "You're on the ground here. From what I've learned, Sharpe was well known in Ottawa. I figure you've come across him, interacted with him. I need your impressions as much as anything else."

"He was a smug bastard who had no loyalty to anyone but himself," Bryant said promptly. "Though he could lay on the charm when he wanted to."

Quinn nodded. This was the sort of information he needed. "How many people saw through the charisma?"

"Hard to tell. This town is full of big personalities pretending to be something they're not." He sighed. "Sometimes, I think they're all so busy focusing on themselves, they can't see anyone else. But..." He finished his coffee, crumpled the cup. "I heard there were problems at home. A row with his daughter over something. Probably political." He wrinkled his brow. "His company is going gangbusters. He produces that trash compactor, the Compress-a-Brick, that's the darling of the suburban environmentally conscious crowd. I've heard it's raking in hundreds of millions in sales."

Quinn nodded. "I saw that. His company is more marketing than manufacturing, isn't it?"

"Yeah, he has the product made cheaply somewhere offshore, then sells it for a wad of cash. Most of the cost is in the wall-to-wall marketing he does." He shook his head. "That's where the charm comes in. He was the ultimate salesman. He knew how to make people want something they don't really need and be willing to pay a premium price for it."

"A handy skill," Quinn said lightly.

Bryant laughed. "Yeah." He ruminated a little, watching the never-ending bustle of tourists taking pictures and gawking at the temple of Canada's freedom. "I can't be sure of this, but I've heard rumblings that he wanted to be something bigger with the Dogwoods."

"A candidate?" Quinn asked, interested.

Bryant looked rather grim as he shook his head. "No, a worm in Archie Fleming's ear. The backroom buddy who influences policy with no one to monitor."

"That can be a powerful position."

Bryant nodded.

"It could annoy a lot of people."

Again, Bryant nodded.

"Enough to have one of them decide to bump him off?" Quinn asked.

"Could be." Bryant wagged his finger. "Or maybe be willing to hire a hitman to do it."

Quinn whistled softly. "Any names?"

Bryant narrowed his eyes. His expression was crafty. "I might. How about I look into them and get back to you?"

Quinn raised his eyebrows. "We agreed to share."

"And I will," Bryant said heartily. "But I'll do my digging first."

Quinn sent a long, level look meant to let Bryant know he wouldn't be okay with being undercut, but, in reality, he'd expected something like this. Bryant Matthews was a consummate journalist, as tenacious as a terrier when he was on the scent of a story. He was also a good friend and if he promised he'd share, he would, though it might be later, rather than sooner.

Bryant grinned. "While I look into the politicos, you should go after the people who worked for him. He hated unions, and though I haven't heard people complain—too much!—about pay and working conditions, you don't make a fortune without annoying people."

Quinn filed this away as a good lead, then held out his hand. "I'm staying at a condo in New Edinburgh. Come by when you have something and I'll introduce you to the rest of my, er, sleuthing, team."

Bryant cocked his head. "And Christy Jamieson herself?"

Quinn nodded.

Beaming, Bryant took his hand, shook it heartily, and announced, "Deal!"

CHAPTER 10

The address Alice supplied for Ralph Sharpe's home was located in Rockcliffe Park, an area not far from the condo building. So, after Quinn left for his meeting with his former associate, and while Christy was still organizing Noelle and Ellen for their museum visit, Roy asked Frank if he'd like to go for a walk and scope out the area. Frank agreed, albeit reluctantly.

The Cat doesn't like museums, so I suppose we may as well go with you.

Roy resisted the urge to ask if Stormy had ever been to a museum, because he knew the cat hadn't. It was Frank who wasn't fond of museums. Instead, he said, "And museums don't like cats. Get over it, Frank."

Frank retaliated to that acerbic remark by refusing to help when it came time for Roy to load Stormy into the tote used to transport the cat from one place to another. Stormy resisted the indignity of being tucked into a bag with his usual verve and had Roy cursing before he finally managed to insert him inside.

New Edinburgh, where the condo building was located, bordered on Rockcliffe Park, so Roy opted to walk to his destination. The day was sunny and warm, but it was early, so it wasn't yet as hot as the weatherman promised it would be by the afternoon. As Roy walked, the house size slowly grew, as did lots they were on, until all around him were large two-or-more story homes set well back from the road and sometimes fenced and gated. At that point, he decided he'd reached Rockcliffe Park and paused to check the GPS on his phone to see how close he was to Sharpe's house.

As he suspected, he was in his target area and his destination was further down the road he was on, then around a corner, and off a side street. He looked about him thoughtfully. There was no one in sight and he hadn't seen a car for the last five minutes.

In Rockcliffe Park, he thought, life went on behind the closed doors of the big fancy houses, not in front yards, or on front porch steps, or on the street itself. How was he going to get information about Ralph Sharpe and his family relationships in this quiet, reserved area?

"Okay, Frank. Looks like we're going to have to knock on doors and pretend to be an encyclopedia salesman."

What? Are you nuts, old man? A salesman!?

Frank made the profession sound like something between toxic waste and an exotic dancer who was performing illegal acts on the side.

"What? You've suddenly turned into a Victorian prude? You've got a better idea?"

Tell them you're a journalist looking for dirt on Sharpe's death.

Roy stared down at the tiger striped head poking out of the tote. "They'd slam the door in my face! Aside from the fact that I don't look like a journalist, people in big houses like these don't want to talk to reporters."

Frank ignored the reference to big houses and asked with what sounded like real curiosity, *What does a journalist look like?*

"Quinn," Roy replied promptly. "Whenever he interviews a source, he dresses smartly."

He never wears a suit.

"He does sometimes. Anyway, that isn't what I said," Roy retorted with considerable irritation. "I said he dresses well. His clothes are pressed and the colors are coordinated."

There was a long silence. *Jeans should never be ironed.*

"He doesn't wear jeans to interviews. That's my point!" Roy said, fuming now. The bickering obscured one salient point, which Frank had been quite right about. No one would open their door to an itinerant salesman, let alone one who sported long hair tied back in a tail and wearing jeans and a checked shirt. If they did, it would only be to say no thank you before they closed the door in his face. He thought he was right about Frank's reporter suggestion, though. The result would be the same—an unopened door or a quickly closed one. So, what to do?

He looked down at the wide green eyes staring up at him. "We'll have to go for a walk."

We are walking. You've been walking since we left the condo.

Even while the voice was still talking, its tone definitely caustic, Roy was shaking his head. "Not walking from one place to another. A walk."

That statement resulted in a rather long silence, then a cautious, *Are you talking about THE LEASH?*

Roy nodded. "It's the only way."

Noooooooo! The cat's head disappeared into the tote.

"I tell you, Frank, if a neighbor comes out to walk their dog and sees me walking Stormy, it's a sure talking point. You have to convince Stormy to let me put on the halter and leash."

There was silence, then a long sigh, followed by a one-sided conversation as Frank worked to convince Stormy to wear the halter. Finally, he said, *All right, he'll do it, but under protest.*

"Noted." Roy crouched down, releasing the tote after he'd extracted the halter and leash from an external pocket. He quickly buckled on the harness and let the cat step out of the tote, before he picked up the bag and straightened. Then they ambled down the pleasant street, ogling the houses, but finding no one to talk to.

This is a waste of time.

Roy transferred the leash from one hand to the other as Stormy circled him, nearly tripping him up for the third time. He was beginning to think Frank was right when a woman, solidly plump with curly hair and bright blue eyes, turned a corner. She was wearing shorts and a T-shirt, walking the tiniest dog Roy had ever seen. Stormy instantly froze.

Is that a dog?

The woman stopped too, surprise and intrigue in her expression. The tiny dog bounced up and down, then began to yap, a high-pitched, annoying sound that had Roy gritting his teeth.

Stormy arched his back, fluffed out his fur until he was an imposingly large version of himself, then hissed. That was followed by a low keening growl Roy found very impressive.

So did the dog. It stopped barking, uttered short, terrified yips, and retreated quickly behind its owner's legs.

"Wow," said the woman. Her eyes were wide with amazement. Before Roy could apologize for his cat terrorizing her dog, delight slowly wreathed her rather plain features. "That was amazing! The little rat loves to bully other animals. I've never seen him intimidated before." She shoved out her hand. "I'm Evie, by the way. Are you new around here?"

Roy shook her hand as he nodded and said, "I'm Roy."

"Nice to meet you, Roy." She laughed as the little dog peeked out from behind her ankles, saw that Stormy was still fully fluffed, and quickly ducked away again.

At least Stormy had stopped growling. Roy thought the poor little dog might have a heart attack if the cat had kept up that seriously intimidating sound. He cleared his throat and said in a gossipy way, "Terrible thing about Ralph Sharpe, isn't it?"

Evie nodded. "The folks I work for live right beside his house and I'd see him and his family outside in the back garden from time to time."

Roy nodded wisely. "Barbequing, I expect."

Evie snorted. "Bickering, berating, and badgering, more like."

Well, that was interesting, not to mention alliterative. It seemed Evie had hidden literary talents. He shook his head and clicked his tongue disapprovingly. "So sad."

Nodding, Evie untangled herself from the dog, who, for some reason, had slunk between and around her legs, taking the leash with him. Stormy, meanwhile, had unfluffed and sat down, his now normal sized tail wrapped politely around his paws. He didn't appear particularly threatening, but one look in his wide green eyes belied that.

Evie dropped the leash, untangling it from her legs. The little dog stayed put behind her. "Mr. Sharpe liked to keep control of things, you know?"

Roy nodded and waited for more. It came readily.

"He had two nice kids. A boy and a girl. The girl was younger. He used to tell the boy he needed to be tougher and the girl that she'd have to manage her expectations, because girls weren't made to run companies." Evie shook her head. "Awful stuff, really. They're adults now and the boy works for his father. Why, I don't know. Seems like a terrible idea to me!"

Roy was about to agree when the little dog, perhaps emboldened by Stormy's polite appearance, suddenly bounded forward, yapping madly.

Shut up you little twerp and don't move until I say you can.

The dog fell abruptly silent, whined, then flopped onto his belly on the sidewalk, head low. Stormy didn't move.

"Would you look at that?" Evie said, her eyes wide and her expression astounded. "What did your cat do? I didn't see him move."

Roy realized with some relief that Evie couldn't hear Frank. "It's his eyes. He glares really well."

She laughed. "You wouldn't like to sell me your cat, would you?"

No one owns the Cat!

Roy didn't bother trying to reassure the cat as he usually did when Frank made that statement. He figured it would only confuse Evie. "Sorry. He's a one-man cat."

She nodded wisely. "I've heard of that."

"I had no idea Ralph was so difficult to live with," Roy said, getting back on track and probing gently.

Evie shook her head. "The stories I could tell. His daughter went out and got an education. Now she doesn't talk to him. The son, as I said, he's thoroughly cowed, poor guy. Mrs. Sharpe? Well, she's as loud and nasty as he was. I'd hear her going after him, sometimes, for nothing more important than not picking his pants up off the floor." Evie nodded confirmation of this ridiculous behavior, then shook her head, as if to reinforce how stupid she considered it to be. "Give the woman her due, though. She stood up for those kids. The donnybrooks that pair would have over something the kids had done! My heavens, what a family."

"I had no idea," Roy said, quite honestly. "I'd see Ralph's name in the newspaper, doing something positive for the city or donating money for a needy charity. It made him seem like an upstanding citizen."

Evie laughed. "I know. But..." She paused. "Strange, though it is, he *was* good for the community. His company employs a lot of people and he was generous with his money. But..." she said again, this time shrugging. "I wouldn't want to be part of his family."

Roy nodded gravely. "People have many sides."

"They do, don't they!" Evie replied enthusiastically, as if she'd never heard any statement quite so wise or with such depth before in her life. She looked down at the still cowering dog and jerked his leash. "Come on, Rat. We should get going."

The little dog jumped up and immediately took cover behind her legs when Stormy rose lazily and stretched.

Evie shook her head and sighed. "I'd better carry him. If I don't, we'll be out here until tomorrow." She bent and scooped up the now shivering dog. "Nice to meet you, Roy."

"And you, Evie," Roy said as they set off in opposite directions.

That dog was a wimp.

Roy couldn't help but agree. They walked on, going past the Sharpe house, which was a large traditional brick building, set in beautifully landscaped grounds behind a tall fence. They found no other useful contacts, though. Roy decided to call it a day after another half hour. He loaded Stormy into the tote bag—with Frank's help this time—then called an Uber to get them back to the condo. They hadn't acquired a lot of new information, but at least he had something to bring back to their next meeting.

He wondered how the others were doing.

~

While Roy had headed northeast from the condo, Rachael and Miles Yeager went southwest.

At midday, Ottawa's temperature was already up in the high eighties and the weatherman promised it would go even higher before evening came and the day started to cool. Rachael was regretting their choice of restaurant for the lunch with two colleagues she and Miles had known for years. They were seated at the back of the high-end eatery located in an old building in the ByWard Market. The stone structure had thick walls, but few windows, and the air conditioning wasn't robust enough to counter the scorching midday temperature.

Rachael didn't do well in the heat, which might have been why she was feeling so grumpy. She'd dressed for the meeting in a professional style pantsuit that was better suited to early spring or late fall than the height of summer. Or maybe it was Sawyer Starr, one of their lunch companions, who was making her cross. Like her, he was wearing a suit, but he didn't seem to be affected by the temperature. His dark hair was combed back from his face and not a strand was out of place. Nor was there any sweat on his high forehead or anywhere else on his soft, pudgy features.

Right now, he was droning on about the current state of the political situation in Canada, something he seemed to know very little about, but had strong opinions on. Their other companion, Shari Wilson, had probably known about the restaurant's air conditioning problem, because she was dressed in a sleeveless cotton dress and her long dark hair was tied back at her nape. She looked cool and comfortable. She was, however, fingering her wine glass, tilting it, swirling it, watching the wine flow from side to side, a sure sign she was agitated.

Rachael allowed indignation to rise. Sawyer might think he was the doyen of academics here in the capital, but Shari outranked him on many levels, not the least being her recent rise to Vice President Academic at the local community college. Sawyer, of course, assumed anyone in the college system was inferior to everyone in the university community, from teaching professors on up. He thought Shari wasted her talent by working for a college.

Shari thought he was the perfect example of why universities needed colleges. To her, they turned out students who were ill prepared for the realities of life and who needed the practical courses provided by a college to get a job and find success.

Perhaps it hadn't been the best idea to invite these two people to the same lunch, but Rachael was taking her small opportunity to help move the investigation forward very seriously. Sawyer really did know everybody who taught in the local universities and Shari had an administrator's viewpoint on students and student conduct.

Time to shift the conversation from national politics back to the academic world. When Sawyer paused to take a breath, Rachael smiled at him and said, "Sawyer, you know everything about everybody here in Ottawa. Have you ever heard of YES!?"

"I have," Shari said.

Rachael turned to her, but Sawyer wrestled the focus back onto him. "They have the most amazing program! Students who participate are, of course, the brightest and best of their academic year—"

Miles, dear man, raised his brows and said, "You sound like a paid spokesperson, Sawyer."

Sawyer, who knew that Miles was a professional skeptic, took no offense. He shook his head. "I'm not, though. I'm merely stating what I've observed through interaction with graduates of the program."

Shari snorted. "They may be the best and brightest, but they're also the most gullible and easily influenced."

Rachael turned to her. "You're not impressed the way Sawyer is?"

Shari sighed. "No, Sawyer's right. They're intelligent young people, but they are also incredibly idealistic."

Miles turned his perceptive stare onto Shari. "You have problems with idealism?"

"When it gets in the way of practicality." She twirled her glass as she spoke, the nervous gesture that told Rachael she figured she was about to be challenged and was preparing herself to deal with it.

She wasn't wrong.

"My dear Shari." Sawyer was shaking his head. His tone was avuncular, with a misogynistic tint that said she should leave deep thinking to those designed by nature to be up to it. "My field is mathematics, a most practical discipline! The students I meet who have been involved with YES! are a pleasure to teach. They study their materials, do their assignments, contribute in class. What more can a dedicated instructor wish for?"

Shari sipped her wine in a challenging way. She'd caught Sawyer's sly undercurrent and didn't like it. "Open mindedness? A willingness to learn and through it, change?" She put down her wineglass and pointed at Sawyer. "Your discipline is a science. It has expectations and boundaries. It does not have an emotional belief system underpinning every element."

Rachael leaned forward. "Shari, are you saying YES! brainwashes their students?"

Shari took hold of her wine glass, then moved across the table in an absent-minded way. "Not the word I would have chosen, Rachael, but the things I hear from my faculty make me wonder." She paused for a moment, gathering her thoughts. "A college like mine performs a very different function than a university does. Sawyer teaches pure intellectual math. My math profs teach accounting and business statistics. A university's purpose is to encourage learning and to instill a belief in the beauty of intellectual exercise. A college program is designed to help a student find a job and move forward in a career."

Rachael was nodding. She saw her husband was watching Shari with an intent, thoughtful expression. Sawyer was frowning. He wasn't keen on not being the center of attention.

"College students are practical students," Shari was saying. "They're there to learn how to get ahead, so they're open to new ideas." She stopped, shook her head. "But not the kids from YES!. A lot enroll in our public administration diploma. The objective of the course is to teach them how to run a non-profit organization or a government department. These kids? They think budgeting is on Attila the Hun's favorites playlist. Motivating staff? That's a laugh. Who needs it? Anyone who works for them will be dedicated to enhancing the lives of others and will work ninety-hour weeks to see the job done. They won't expect any extra pay, either. And when it comes to employment law? Well, it doesn't apply to them." She stopped and drew a deep breath. "I could go on, but my point is that they don't bend. Even when they're in a program designed to help them succeed, they figure they know better."

"Do they?" Miles asked. His eyes were bright with interest and curiosity.

Rachael looked at him sharply. Shari raised her brows.

"Succeed, I mean," he said.

A faint smile twitched Shari's mouth up. "Many of them do. As Sawyer said, these are bright young people. But they're often eclipsed by less gifted students who are more grounded in everyday needs. I've had instructors tell me that the YES! students who don't do well can become quite difficult. Angry, even."

"Sounds like YES! is more of a cult than an educational institution," Rachael said.

Shari pursed her lips thoughtfully. "Cult is too strong, but certainly their instruction is one-sided. It's a pity, really. The Youth Empowerment Secretariat—that's their official name, and what they were called for the first few years. When they first began, their mandate was a valid one. They prepped underprivileged kids to succeed at institutes of higher learning. Now? I think their agenda is more political than educational."

"Nonsense!" said Sawyer. "There's nothing political about the program. The students are taught how to succeed in academia and that's all. And they do succeed. I still endorse the program. Completely!"

Shari shrugged.

Rachael decided it was time to switch the subject. "Do either of you know Ralph Sharpe? He was the man who was killed a few days ago. He was on the YES! board, I think."

"Not well," Sawyer said. "I met him a few times at social events. He seemed to be a pleasant fellow. I know he donated to many worthy charities in the city."

Shari swirled her wine glass again. "My business professors aren't impressed by how he runs his company. He definitely doesn't apply best practices when it comes to his management style."

"A personal opinion," Sawyer said.

Shari gulped some wine then toasted Sawyer. "A good point that I'm not sure I agree with. I'll admit he was a charmer. He could make you think that what he said was what you wanted to hear. Until a couple of hours later when you had time to think about it. Then, not so much."

Miles studied her. "You didn't like him."

Shari shrugged. "I didn't know him well enough to care."

There wasn't much more to be got from Shari or Sawyer, Rachael thought. She glanced at Miles. He gave her a small nod, telling her he agreed it was time to switch the subject. Rachael didn't mind, though. They'd learned a lot.

Their first foray into investigating had been a resounding success.

CHAPTER 11

⚜

While Christy and Ellen were both scheduled to go to the museum with Noelle, Trevor decided to tag along when he was unable to get in touch with Inspector Fortier. They drove to the museum, as there was ample parking, something they'd already discovered was usually at a premium in Ottawa.

The natural history museum was housed in a large stone building affectionately known as "the castle." Built during the early twentieth century in glowing golden stone, its imposing structure featured multiple towers and turrets. Renovations in the twenty-tens included a blue tinted glass and steel rectangle erected over the carved stone entrance, a jarring contrast to an otherwise cohesive structure.

The natural history museum was Noelle's choice, because she wanted to see the dinosaur exhibit. She'd been fascinated by dinosaurs since she was old enough to understand what one was. There were other exhibits too—a mammals gallery, one on geology and minerals, another on birds. Christy would be happy if they skipped the insects display, and she figured they could give the water exhibit a miss, since Vancouver had an excellent marine museum. She was looking forward to the Canada goose gallery, which featured arctic animals.

They went to the dino hall first, while everyone was still fresh and feet weren't sore and tired. As she expected, Noelle lingered at every display, reading the labels and scrutinizing the giant fossils intently. Christy amused herself imagining her daughter as an intrepid paleontologist, even though Noelle hadn't yet expressed a desire for any career choice. She was chuckling at her mom fantasy when a woman standing at the next skeleton over turned and spotted them.

Her face lit up. "Christy Jamieson!" She bustled from her dinosaur over to the one Noelle was viewing. "Darling, how good to see you. But what are you doing here, in Ottawa?"

"Marian, so nice to see you." They exchanged air kisses.

Marian Fleming, the wife of the new leader of the Dogwood Party, former lover of the late Fred Jarvis, and to Christy's mind as kooky as they come, beamed at her. She was dressed in a dark blue sheath dress that made the most of her voluptuous figure while sending out a businesslike vibe. Her security officer, who had moved closer when Christy and her group neared her in the gallery, eased away.

Thinking Marian's appearance was a stark contrast to her own jeans and a simple sleeveless blouse, Christy gestured to the others. "Marian, you know Ellen."

"Of course. Ellen, how are you?" Marian said happily. She exchanged air kisses with Ellen, whose attire was more formal than Christy's, but nowhere near as stylish as Marian's.

Ellen submitted to the air kiss ritual with good grace. "I'm doing very well. Marian, may I introduce Trevor McCullagh?"

Trevor stuck out his hand. "How do you do?"

Marian was having none of that. She took his hand, leaned in, and landed an actual kiss on either cheek. Trevor looked resigned as she drew away. He knew all about Marian Fleming.

"And this is my daughter, Noelle," Christy said when Marian was once again free.

"How do you do, Mrs. Fleming," Noelle said, assuming her best Jamieson manners. Like Trevor she stuck out her hand.

Marian clasped it with both of hers and patted it gently. She smiled at Noelle, then said to Christy, "What a lovely child. Are you all here on vacation?"

Christy glanced at the others, then said carefully, "We're visiting my parents in Kingston. They suggested we come up to Ottawa for a few days."

Marian released Noelle's hand so she could clap hers together. "That's perfect! You must come to my get-together."

Christy blinked. "Your get-together? But..." She was about to say she had nothing to wear and didn't want to intrude, but Marian kept on talking, rolling right on over her protest.

"It's in honor of Ralph Sharpe, a local philanthropist, and a great friend of the Party. He died recently, and Archie and I want to do something to celebrate his life."

Christy glanced at Ellen, eyebrows raised.

Marian misinterpreted the look. She waved one hand dismissively and said, "It won't be gloomy, I promise! Our goal is to have everyone remember the good Ralph did for this city and for the Dogwood Party. Oh, do say you'll come. All of you." She paused, looked around as if searching for something, then added, "Is Quinn traveling with you?"

"He is," Christy said, watching Marian.

"Perfect! He must come as well. Archie will be delighted to see him."

That startled her. "Are you sure, Marian? It was because of Quinn that Archie's campaign manager, Colin Jarvis, quit in the middle of the leadership campaign. As I remember, Archie was very angry." Christy imagined the scene that might ensue if Quinn showed up at the get-together and Archie bore a grudge.

Marian, however, had no such qualms. "Oh, pooh." Another dismissive hand wave. "Archie is long over that. He won the leadership without Colin's help and he made a new set of allies in the process. He likes Quinn. He'll be delighted to see him."

Christy wasn't so sure, but Marian knew her husband, and her event would be an excellent way to discover another aspect of Ralph Sharpe's life. "Well, okay, it sounds lovely."

Marian beamed. "Perfect! Let me have your email so I can send you an invitation—to satisfy security, you know." She moved her head to indicate the hovering bodyguard.

Christy supplied her address.

Marian worked her phone then said, "There. It's sent. Now, I must rush. I'm on the museum board. That's why I'm here today. I always come a bit early to schmooze with the dinos before we meet." She initiated air kisses with Christy and Ellen, patted Noelle on the head, and this time only waved to Trevor, who had retreated out of easy hug range.

As she was moving away, Marian turned and said over her shoulder, "I forgot to mention, darlings, it's formal. This town does love to dress up!"

"Looking forward to it," Christy replied weakly, her hand raised in a little half wave.

Marian waved back, then sailed out, a force of nature to be reckoned with.

Ellen shook her head, her expression skeptical as she watched Marian depart.

"Formal," Christy muttered as she checked her phone to see when the party was happening. The date almost made her heart stop. She sucked in her breath then gasped, "Ellen. It's tomorrow evening!"

Frowning, Ellen returned her attention to Christy. "Can't be."

Christy showed her the email. Ellen's frown deepened. "Good heavens."

"And it's formal. What was Marian thinking?" Christy asked.

Ellen shook her head, then uttered a short rueful laugh. "That Jamiesons are always prepared. She must assume we travel with dozens of suitcases filled with clothing for every social situation."

Christy dropped her phone back into her purse. "We need to shop."

Ellen nodded. "Absolutely.

Trevor said, "I don't have a suit."

"Neither does Quinn," Christy said, chewing her lip.

"Mom." Noelle tugged at her hand, drawing her attention away from the prospect of a formal evening in the middle of a murder investigation in a city she didn't know or understand.

She looked down. "Yes, kiddo?"

"We're here now. Can't we see the rest of the museum?"

Ellen smiled as she nodded. "We'll shop tomorrow. I'm sure we'll be able to find something to wear."

Christy drew a deep breath. "You're right. We're here, so let's enjoy it."

Noelle gave a small, pleased nod.

About to move on to the next display, Christy had an idea. She pulled out her phone. "Sledge? Trevor and Quinn need suits and Ellen and I require evening gowns for a party. Do you think Alice could help out? When? The party is tomorrow evening. I know it's short notice but tell her price doesn't matter. What? Alice says easy-peasy? That's great! Thank her for us. Yes, we'll talk tonight."

She disconnected and grinned at the others. "Problem solved. Now we don't have to worry. Alice will sort it."

"Great!" Noelle said. "Look at this dinosaur, Mom. It's a Daspletosaurus. A meat-eater. Isn't it cool?"

"Very cool, though I'm glad I wasn't born in his time."

"I concur," Ellen said with the hint of a smile.

"Still, it'd be awesome to see a live dino," Noelle said wistfully.

The adults laughed. They all enjoyed the rest of the visit.

◊

In another part of Ottawa, Quinn was contemplating his next step. After he and Bryant parted ways, he wandered off the grounds of the Parliament Buildings down to Sparks Street, a pedestrian thoroughfare that cut through the middle of downtown, where he was able to find a coffee shop. There he settled in to do a little research and a lot of thinking.

Bryant might be right. Sharpe's murder could be a political one, but, somehow, Quinn didn't buy it. From what Bryant said, Sharpe was a wannabe, a man on the hustle, networking where relationships mattered, using his newly made fortune where money talked most loudly. He wasn't influential in the Dogwood party, but he was laying the groundwork so he someday would be. Once he achieved the position of backroom advisor, there'd be knives out for him, but now? Probably not.

It was much more likely the murderer would be found in his family and personal connections, or in his business relationships. Roy was checking out the family, so Quinn decided he'd take a closer look at Sharpe's business associates.

The first thing to look at was who was stepping into Sharpe's shoes. A scroll through the company's website netted him three vice presidents—finance, marketing, and production. Unfortunately, there were no names attached. He'd have to dig a little deeper.

Eventually, he discovered that the vice president of production was Hunter Sharpe. Interesting. Hunter was obviously a family member, but was he the victim's son? Brother? Nephew?

A check of Alice's profile identified him as Ralph's son. While one of the other vice presidents might be Ralph's designated successor, most likely Hunter was being groomed for the top position. If he were now head of the company, would Hunter be at work, guiding the business through that rocky period when an unexpected change of management takes place? Or would he be at home, helping his mother cope with her loss and planning his father's funeral?

His choice could be telling. Quinn decided the best way to find out what Hunter Sharpe was up to was to call Sharpe Productions and see if he was there. He found the extension for Ralph's secretary-assistant and dialed.

"Jennie Symmonds. How can I help you?" Her voice was brusque, not quite impatient, but not particularly welcoming.

"Good afternoon, Ms. Symmonds. My name is Quinn Armstrong. I'm a journalist—"

"All media requests for information are handled by Gretchen Beal, our Director of Communications. I'll transfer your call." There was no inflection in the voice, just that quick, no-nonsense way of speaking.

Quinn didn't want to be turned over to a slick communications professional who would know how to deflect his questions. He thought quickly. "Thank you, Ms. Symmonds. Before you transfer me, please allow me to offer my condolences for your loss."

There was silence on the other end of the phone line. Then Jennie said a lot less gruffly, "Thank you."

"It must have been a shock."

She sighed. "It was. And now—" She broke off, but Quinn heard the quaver in her voice before she stopped speaking. Change was happening in her world, probably in her job, and she wasn't certain it would benefit her.

"Now you've got a new boss and you're not sure you'll like working for him," Quinn said, sympathetically.

Jennie sighed again. "Hunter's a good guy, but he's different from his father. Listen, I'd better put you though to Gretchen now. Thanks for offering your sympathies. Not everyone does."

The line clicked and went dead before Quinn could reply. A moment later, another feminine voice said, "Gretchen Beal here, Mr. Armstrong. How can I help you?"

"I hope you can provide me with some information on Sharpe Products and Ralph Sharpe himself, but before we begin, let me offer my condolences on your loss."

"Thank you," she said with no change in inflection. "Sharpe Products is a manufacturing and distribution company that creates merchandise designed to help the modern, environmentally oriented homemaker. We are proud to be the developers of the runaway bestselling kitchen compactor, the Compress-a-Brick, which can be found at fine retail establishments throughout Canada and the United States."

Quinn thought with amused appreciation that she didn't even stop to draw breath as she rattled off the promotional material. "Tell me about the Compress-a-Brick."

Enthusiasm crept into her voice. "It's a wonderful product for our ecologically challenged era. Civic recycling services reduce the amount of waste that goes into garbage dumps, but there is always a certain amount of material that can't be recycled. That's where the Compress-a-Brick comes in. You put your non-recyclable garbage into the machine. When the barrel is full, you activate the compression mechanism. The machine then produces a solid brick you can use in garden projects like pathways, or to build planter boxes or other ecologically helpful containers."

"Interesting," Quinn said quite truthfully. He wasn't sure if he'd want a planter box made of garbage in his backyard, but that was him.

"Yes," Gretchen said. "Exactly. We're doing our world a great service with the Compress-a-Brick. Mr. Sharpe has been asking our R & D staff to focus on similar products that will help lessen the burden our urban society puts on the environment."

"This is excellent information, Ms. Beal. Ralph Sharpe was the president and CEO of the company, is that correct?"

"Yes, he was."

Was that caution he was hearing in the woman's voice? "Can you tell me who will be replacing him?"

"Mr. Hunter Sharpe is now the president and CEO."

Definitely caution. Quinn wondered why. "Hunter Sharpe is Ralph's son, is he not?"

"Yes."

A minute ago, Gretchen Beal had been eagerly talking up her product without so much as a pause to draw breath. Now she was providing only the barest of information. Something was wrong here. "I have a source who tells me Hunter and his father didn't get along."

That produced an unexpected explosion. "Jennie Symmonds! She's been told not to talk to the press—"

"Nor did she," Quinn said quickly, feeling guilty that he might have added another layer of stress to Jennie's current problems. "My information comes from an individual affiliated with YES!. Ralph Sharpe wasn't particularly well liked there and I've heard there was conflict over family issues and the way YES! organizes their program."

There was silence on the other end of the phone, then Gretchen said, "I have no knowledge of Mr. Sharpe's family activities. I do know Mr. Sharpe's philosophy was to give back to the community and to encourage others to do so as well. That, I believe, was why he became involved with YES!, but as I say, I cannot comment on that aspect of his life."

This woman was good, Quinn thought. She'd successfully wrestled the conversation from the conflict between Hunter Sharpe and his father and denied all knowledge of any issues with YES! at the same time. Well, he wasn't about to let her direct this interview. "Hunter Sharpe was the vice president of production before his father's death, wasn't he?"

A slight hesitation, then, "He was."

She was wondering where he planned to take this line of questioning. Quinn grinned to himself. He was about to have a little fun. "Was the R &

D team dreaming up products that couldn't be manufactured economically, therefore pricing them out of the market? Was that why Hunter and his father were at odds?"

"Our production team is excellent, Mr. Armstrong."

"But your R & D team isn't?"

There was a hiss along the phone line.

Quinn wondered if he'd stumbled on an important clue. "Or is R & D not coming up with anything worthwhile?"

Another hiss, swiftly cut off. "Really, Mr. Armstrong. What has this to do with an obituary on Ralph Sharpe?"

"Did I say I was writing his obit?" Quinn asked, allowing amusement into his voice.

Another silence, then cautiously, "What exactly are you working on, Mr. Armstrong?"

"What the public wants to know, Ms. Beal. Who killed Ralph Sharpe."

She drew a quick, startled, breath. "That's why you're asking about Hunter Sharpe's relationship with his father?" Her voice hardened and cooled. "I can assure you, Mr. Armstrong, that Hunter Sharpe would not harm his father. Family members within a family firm like Sharpe Products have differences of opinion and argue from time to time, but that is all they do. Argue. They do not kill each other. Now, I think I've told you enough. Good afternoon."

The line went dead. Quinn sat back. He'd got all he could out of Gretchen Beal. She wouldn't speak to him again. There was definitely something there between Hunter and his father, though. He wondered what it was. If he wanted to know, he'd have to go to the source, Hunter himself. That might prove difficult. He'd have to think of ways to approach the man.

He glanced at his watch and decided to make his way back to the condo. He wondered what the others had discovered and if they had enough pieces yet to start constructing the picture that would help them expose Ralph Sharpe's murderer.

CHAPTER 12

Christy had just finished setting the table for dinner when she saw Quinn in the doorway of the community room. She went over to greet him. "Hi. How was your day?"

She had to resist the urge to go up on her tiptoes and kiss him as she had the previous day when they were out in the lobby. Today, though, Noelle was in the community room talking to her grandparents and Ellen, and she and Quinn would be in full view.

He smiled down at her and said in a low voice, "Better, now that I'm here." He followed the words up with a lazy smile.

Christy blushed, then she laughed. "Keep talking that way and I might suggest we skip dinner and head up to your suite."

His smile deepened. "Sounds like a plan."

She blushed again and sighed, fully aware a private rendezvous wasn't going to happen.

He smiled ruefully as he reached up to touch her cheek in a light caress. "I see everyone except Sledge and Alice. They aren't back yet?"

Christy shook her head. "They were here most of the day, working on the logistics for the concert. Apparently, Hammer is on board with the idea and will be coming out in a few days, so the next step is for Sledge to rehearse with the other bands that are involved. I'm not sure how much we'll see of him once that begins." She shrugged, then laughed. "Alice was busy with the details of the event when we got home from the museum. She can be quite...focused."

Quinn shot her an amused look. "Bossy, you mean?" When Christy laughed again and nodded, he said, "How was Sledge taking that?"

Christy paused and cocked her head in thought. "Moments of irritation, but when she offered to supply dinner for tonight, he went off with her to help pick it up."

Quinn thought about that, the amusement in his eyes deepening. "Interesting."

Christy laughed. "Yes, isn't it?"

The sound of the elevator door opening was followed by footsteps in the lobby. Sledge shouted, "We're back. Food's on!"

"Sledge and Alice must have taken the Spider and come up through the garage," Quinn said.

Christy nodded. "Let's get everyone organized so we can eat."

The food came from a Southern barbeque restaurant in the ByWard Market. Christy piled serving plates with generous portions of ribs, fried chicken, barbeque chicken wings, pulled pork, potato salad, and sweet potato fries. Then, with the help of Roy, Trevor, and her father took them to the table for people to serve themselves.

The first topic of conversation was the museum—and the party.

"You should have come, Grandma, Grandpa!" Noelle said, reaching for a chicken wing. "The museum was awesome. And we met a friend of Mom's and Aunt Ellen's, when we were looking at the dinos."

Glancing Christy's way, Quinn raised his brows.

She grimaced. "Marian Fleming."

His fork hovered over potato salad he'd just piled onto his plate. "Fred Jarvis's Marian Fleming?" Disbelief colored his voice.

Christy nodded.

"That must have been interesting." He dug into the potato salad and raised it to his mouth.

Christy watched him with amusement. "It was. We've been invited to a party she's giving tomorrow evening."

Ellen nodded. "Once a friend, always a dear friend."

Quinn put his fork down again. "Archie Fleming sicced the police on me because I questioned Colin Jarvis and he quit as Fleming's campaign manager. I don't think he'd want me at his party."

Trevor laughed. "You'd be wrong then. Marian assured us everything worked out as it should and Archie made lots of new supporters in the process. You and I have to buy suits tomorrow."

Quinn looked around the long table. "Why?"

"The party is formal, of course," Christy said. Her smile was impish.

"Formal," Quinn said. "But—"

Sledge grinned at him. "It's okay. Alice has your back."

Alice beamed.

Quinn shot Sledge a narrow-eyed look. "How?"

"I've made arrangements for you at a high-end store that has an excellent reputation for discretion and quality," Alice said, as if no other possibility would do. "You and Trevor will choose a suit in the morning. Any alterations will be ready by the afternoon."

"Mom and Aunt Ellen are going shopping too," Noelle said. She'd moved on from the wings to the sweet potato fries, which she was dipping in a spicy aioli sauce.

"I'll escort you, of course," Alice said, nodding. "But I've ensured that the retailer has a sufficient selection of evening gowns available for you to choose from and any adjustments will be done before four in the afternoon."

"Would you mind if I joined you?" Rachael asked. "A girls' shopping day sounds like fun."

"Of course, Mom. We'd love to have you," Christy said smiling.

Noelle shook her head. "Grandpa, want to do something with me? Clothes shopping sounds boring."

Miles's expression brightened. "You bet, kiddo." He thought for a minute. "I know the perfect place to spend the day. Want to get lost in a maze? Play on a pirate ship? Cool down in a splash park?"

"Sounds awesome, Grandpa!"

He nodded. "Okay, we're on."

What about me? Are you all leaving me alone? Again!

Noelle's face fell. Christy bit her lip.

"Mind if I tag along with you and Noelle?" Roy asked. "I'm not going to the party, so I don't need a suit and I'd rather not spend the day shopping." He assumed an expression of hangdog dismay that made Miles laugh.

"Okay, sure. What do you think, Noelle?"

"Yeah. Let's bring Stormy too."

Miles, who didn't know Stormy was a very special cat, blinked. "But—"

"Only if Stormy promises to listen to me and do what he's told." Roy waved his finger at the cat. "Hear that, Cat?"

Yeah, yeah. I get it.

Miles looked astounded.

Noelle turned wide, pleading eyes on her grandfather. "He's really good with Roy, Grandpa. We took him camping last year and he never got lost."

Christy almost laughed as she watched her daughter twist her grandfather around her finger. Miles was no match for Noelle.

He cleared his throat and said, "I wouldn't want anything to happen to your cat."

"He'll come when he's called." Roy turned a steely look on the cat, who was sitting on Christy's lap, his head peeking over the tabletop. "Won't you, Stormy?"

The cat meowed. *Okay, I get it. I'll convince him.*

Stormy hopped down from Christy's lap, crossed the floor, then jumped up into Roy's. He put his paws up on Roy's shoulders, meowed, then started to purr as he rubbed his cheek against Roy's.

"See, Grandpa? Stormy and Roy are pals."

"Well—" Miles said, softening.

"Off you go," Roy said. "Go sit on the couch while we finish our dinner."

What? You're banishing me?

Roy tickled Stormy under the chin, then lifted the cat and put him on the floor.

Okay, okay. I get it. This is a test so Miles will let me go tomorrow. I get it, but I don't like it. Stormy shot an annoyed look at Roy before he strutted over to the seating area, every inch an annoyed cat.

Miles laughed. "Okay, I'm impressed. We'll take the cat with us."

Yay!" Noelle beamed.

Stormy sat on the couch, gave himself a good clean, then curled into a ball, his back toward the room.

Now you've done it. The cat's mad. He says you're rude and he's going to have a nap.

Christy almost laughed. Instead, she focused on planning. "Tomorrow's Saturday. I hope we'll learn something useful at the party, but there isn't much we can do until Monday."

"My friend, Bryant Matthews, told me Sharpe might have had aspirations of becoming something in the Dogwood Party." Quinn had managed to eat some of his potato salad and was reaching for a piece of fried chicken. He put the drum down on his plate and wiped his fingers with a napkin. "Finding out more about that will be our focus tomorrow, but Bryant also suggested that Sharpe's company, Sharpe Products, was more marketing than manufacturing. The communications person I spoke to let it slip that their R&D department is coming up dry."

"Companies grow through partnerships, acquisition, or new product development," Trevor said. "If Sharpe's company was striking out at creating new products, what was pushing them forward?"

"Or was the company stagnant?" Ellen asked thoughtfully. "You were looking into Sharpe's personal life, Roy. Did you discover anything?"

Roy rubbed his chin. "Sharpe had family problems. He and his wife fought, and his daughter moved away after university. My source told me he bullied his son as a youth, and probably still did, because the kid works for him."

"And now that kid is the new CEO of Sharpe Products," Quinn said. "I spoke to the company's PR person, who wasn't much help, but Ralph's secretary might be useful to interview. She hinted that the son wasn't all that popular and that he and his father were often at odds. She was pretty uptight about talking to me, though. Apparently, the word is out that the director of communications is to handle all external queries."

"I'll get her to talk, like I did with Cassandra Weldon." Sledge winked. "Easy-peasy."

Alice didn't smile at his use of her favorite phrase. "I don't know, Sledge. You'll have to do this on Monday and Hammer will be coming to Ottawa that day. And you know Justina doesn't like the idea of you being involved in murder investigations—"

Sledge shook his head at her. "First of all, Justina won't be here until Tuesday, so what she doesn't know won't bother her. Hammer's flight doesn't come in until the afternoon, so it doesn't matter if we go in the morning. Secondly, I'm in on this investigation, no matter what Justina thinks. So, it's settled."

Alice lowered her eyebrows and pursed her lips. Sledge met her disapproval with a cool look. After a moment, she sighed. "Okay. I guess."

"We'll have to wait until Monday, but I think we need to look more deeply into YES!," Miles said.

Rachael nodded. "I agree. From what Miles and I heard today, I'm concerned about some of their teaching practices."

"I'll make a note of that once I've cleaned my fingers," Ellen said. She had observed the finger-food offerings Sledge and Alice brought with some disapproval, but after discovering the food was delicious, she dove in. Right now, she was working on a messy pulled pork sandwich and some of the sweet potato fries.

Frowning as she made her notes, Ellen paused to tap her pen on her chin. "Do you think the strained family relationship was why Ralph and his son disagreed? Or could it have been the problems with their R&D department?"

"Could be either," Quinn said.

"We should find out what kind leader Ralph Sharpe was," Christy said.

"Bryant said he had charisma, but not everyone bought into it," Quinn said, nodding.

"We'll pry it out of the secretary," Roy said.

"We?" Alice said. She looked surprised.

Roy beamed at her. "I'll go along with Sledge. We'll take the cat."

On the couch, Stormy sat up, his sulk forgotten. *Sounds like fun.*

"You take a cat along when you interview suspects?" Miles said, rather wonderingly.

Roy nodded. "You'd be surprised at how seeing a cat on a leash shakes—"

Not THE LEASH!

"—up people," Roy finished, without acknowledging the interruption.

Sledge snorted. Alice cocked her head and frowned, evidently not understanding why he was amused.

Christy sighed.

Once more joining the group, Stormy hopped up onto a chair and put his paws on the table. *Great. Now that we all have our assignments, the cat wants more of the pulled pork.*

CHAPTER 13

Christy woke to the sound of voices in the suite she shared with Noelle. She yawned and stretched, then remembered she had a busy day today shopping for an evening gown for Marian Fleming's party tonight. Time to get up, she decided, though it seemed to be awfully early.

After using the en suite, she padded through the apartment to the kitchen. There she found her mother presiding over the stove, her expression intent as she poked at frying bacon.

Noelle noticed Christy first. She grinned and said, "Morning, Mom. Grandma's making breakfast."

Christy nodded. "Morning, kiddo." To her mother, she said, "Is there coffee?"

Looking remarkably put together for so early, it was Sledge who answered. He nodded toward the coffeemaker. "In the beaker."

"I'll get you a cup, Mom," Noelle offered. She hopped off the tall chair tucked up to the center island and headed over to the counter that lodged the coffeemaker. Rachael pulled a mug from the cupboard and handed it to Noelle, who carefully poured. Walking slowly, she brought the brimming cup to Christy.

She drank deep, then said, "Ah, I needed that. Thank you, Noelle."

"My pleasure," Noelle said, smiling proudly.

As the first few sips of coffee gradually unlocked her brain, Christy realized that the kitchen was rather crowded. Roy had staked out a place at the island beside Noelle. As well as a mug of coffee, he had his laptop open, and as usual he appeared to be absorbed in his work. At the table, Sledge was seated with a coffee mug in front of him, engrossed in something on his phone. Beside him, Ellen was drinking coffee, too, but from a cup with a saucer.

Quinn was also seated at the table, and as her somewhat distracted gaze connected with his, she realized he'd been watching her. There was amusement and, yes, tenderness in his expression. Her heart swelled and she smiled. He smiled back, looked at the chair beside him, and raised his brows. She went to sit beside him.

"Where are Trevor and Dad?" she asked of no one in particular.

"Your father was still sleeping when I came down," Rachael said. She winked at Noelle. "I figured I'd let him get as much rest as he can. He's going to have a busy day today."

Noelle giggled. "This park with the mazes sounds awesome. Grandpa and Roy and I are going to have fun."

"Trevor is still asleep," Ellen said.

How did Ellen know that? Christy looked at Quinn, her eyebrows raised.

Quinn's answering glance held laughter. Clearly, he figured she knew the good old-fashioned way.

Sledge shifted in his seat, not quite as absorbed in what was on his phone as he appeared to be. It jingled in his hand and he jumped before he answered.

After a moment, he said, "You're on speaker. Say that again, Alice."

They all sat quietly as Alice's disembodied voice came through the phone. "There's a man at the front entrance who claims he's a cop. He says his name is Inspector Fortier. He wants to speak to Quinn."

"Fortier?" Quinn said. "I wonder what he wants."

He looked intrigued and Christy thought he'd be happy to go downstairs to meet with the cop.

Sledge had other ideas. "Tell him he's here too early and no one is up. He can come back later, say around noon. We'll all be out by then."

"Okay." Alice drew out the word. "Why?"

"I don't like him. He's annoying."

"Okay." She said, more cheerfully this time. "I'll be up when he's gone."

She hung up. Sledge put the phone onto the table and looked around at the assembled group in a challenging way.

Christy laughed. "I'm glad you sent him away, Sledge. I don't want to have to start my day dealing with pompous bullying."

"My sentiments exactly," Ellen said, though her eyes were bright. She looked like a woman ready to take on officialdom, even though it wasn't quite eight in the morning.

Sledge's phone rang again. He put it on speaker. It was Alice. "Sledge! He won't go away. He says he'll order up a SWAT team and break the door down if I don't let him in."

Rachael was stacking slices of French toast onto a plate before she added crisp bacon to another, necessary preparations so they could all enjoy breakfast together. She paused, spatula raised. "Good heavens! Can he do that legally?"

"We need Trevor," Ellen said.

Roy snapped the lid on his laptop. "I'll get him." He leapt to his feet and headed out of the room.

"Alice," Christy called. "Can you hear me?"

"Yes," Alice said, sounding doubtful.

Sledge handed Christy the phone. She smiled and nodded thanks. "Alice, tell Fortier we will see him, but not for another half hour at least. If he still insists on entering the building, show him to the common room and leave him there, on his own."

"Let him kick his heels in solitude," Ellen said, with some venom, earning her another startled look from Rachael.

"What then?" Alice asked.

"Then we have breakfast," Christy said.

And that was what they did. Forty-five minutes later, after they'd consumed Rachael's French toast, then showered and dressed, they gathered together at Christy's suite before they took the elevator down. Noelle stayed upstairs with Rachael and Miles, who had been roused from his sleep-in. The cat, who had rushed upstairs fifteen minutes earlier to tell them Fortier was pacing the length of the common room and was shouting at Alice, came with them. Sledge had wanted to barge downstairs to rescue Alice, until Frank told him Alice was in no way intimidated and was keeping Fortier in line.

They exited the elevator with Ellen in the lead. She was dressed in tailored slacks and a silk blouse. Her jewelry was moderate, but her expression was haughty. There was a steely look in her eyes that didn't bode well for the inspector.

Beside her was Trevor, also dressed in the most professional clothes he'd brought. Christy and Quinn followed them. Like Ellen, Christy was wearing tailored slacks and a pretty summer blouse. She regretted that she didn't appear more intimidating, but she was on vacation and her clothes were mostly casual.

Beside her, Quinn was also casually dressed, but ranging alongside them, Sledge was wearing one of his SledgeHammer world tour T-shirts and ripped jeans. The costume and his saunter were a study in cocky defiance. Roy brought up the rear, dressed in his usual jeans and checked shirt. The cat was in his arms.

Alice, hovering by the door to the common room, pulled out a key when she saw them. "I had to lock him in when he got boisterous," she said as she inserted the key and turned it in the lock. "I don't think he'll be pleased to see you."

Through the windowed door Christy could see Fortier pacing the length of the room. Alice was right. The man was fuming.

"Good," Ellen said. "You've done very well, Alice. Thank you."

Alice opened the door and Ellen sailed into the room. Fortier stopped at the sound of the key. His back to them, he said, "Finally, you've come to your senses. You will regret this insult." His tone was furious. Then he turned.

His mouth gaped open as he saw them crowded just inside the doorway. "*Mon Dieu*! It is the madwoman who called the local police when I was arresting Tamara Ahern."

Ellen waved a hand dismissively. Her voice was contemptuous. "You were creating a scene, Fortier, as you are now. What is so important that you can't call on people at a civilized hour?"

Fortier's eyes narrowed and his jaw hardened. "The only one making a scene was you, *Madam*. I was doing my job."

Another wave of Ellen's imperious hand. "Of course, you would think that, you silly man. Who was it who discovered Fred Jarvis' killer? Not you. It was Detective Patterson, was it not?"

Fortier's eyes narrowed even further and his whole body went rigid. Roy set Stormy on the ground. The cat prowled through their legs to sit in front of Ellen. He tucked his tail around his feet and sat motionless, watching the cop.

"I am not here to trade quips with you, *Madam*. I have come to give *Monsieur* Quinn Armstrong a friendly warning."

Quinn stepped forward. "Is that a threat, Fortier?"

He shot Quinn a hostile look. "Take it as you will, *Monsieur*."

On the other side of Ellen, Trevor spoke up. "What kind of warning? This sounds suspiciously like police harassment."

Fortier closed his eyes for a moment. When he opened them, he cast a fervent look heavenward. Christy heard him mutter, "These people," before he schooled his features into a stern expression. "It would be advisable for you to stop poking into the affairs of *Monsieur* Ralph Sharpe."

His hands in the pockets of his jeans, thumbs out, Quinn sauntered toward him. "I struck a nerve, did I, Fortier? Is there something about Ralph Sharpe or his company the cops figure should be kept under wraps?"

"The public only needs to know that *Monsieur* Sharpe has died. Nothing more. You will stop your inquiries."

Quinn raised his brows. "Trying to muzzle the press, Fortier?"

Fortier clenched his jaw again. "You and I both know you are not here as a reporter."

"I'm an accredited journalist, Fortier. If I want to dig into the murder of a prominent man, it's my call. I'll write the story, then I'll sell it to every news outlet in Canada. Hell, if the story's good enough, I'll write the book. You'll see it on bookstore shelves in the next couple of years."

Fortier's eyes had narrowed to slits. "If you continue, you may find yourself in a jail cell for interfering in a police inquiry, *Monsieur* Armstrong. Do not push me."

"When we met you during the investigation into Fred Jarvis' death, you were part of some kind of task force looking into political crimes," Trevor said. "Why are you on this case? It appears to be a simple homicide. It should be worked by the city police force."

"Appearances can be deceiving," Fortier ground out.

"Trite," Roy said from the back of their phalanx.

Fortier sent him a smoldering look, but he didn't rise to Roy's bait.

Quinn cocked his head to one side. "One of my contacts tells me that Ralph Sharpe had political ambitions. He wanted to be a big shot in the Dogwood Party. Is that why you're here? Are you afraid we'll step on some tender political toes?"

"I have given you my warning. Go back to Vancouver. Leave this case alone."

"Unfortunately, that is quite impossible," Ellen said. She bestowed a superior smile on Fortier when he turned his furious gaze on her.

"How so, *Madam*?"

Ellen tapped her chin. "Marian would be most upset."

"That's Marian Fleming," Christy said, kindly filling in the inspector when he looked baffled. "We've been invited to her party tonight."

He opened his mouth, closed it with a snap, then drew a deep breath and tried again. "Who invited you to this party?"

"Why, Marian, of course," Ellen said. She stepped to one side as she made a shooing motion with her hands, aimed at the cop. The others moved so a path opened to the door. "Now, inspector, you need to be on your way as we have much to do today to prepare for the party."

He looked at each of them in turn. His expression was mulish. "Listen to me, all of you. This is work for the police."

"Provided you do your work and don't target Todd Ahern because you're afraid you might get tangled up in a scandal you don't want anyone to know about," Quinn said.

"I will not discuss this case with you, reporter." He glared at them. "After the Flemings' party, go back to Vancouver. It is my last warning."

Lounging against the doorframe, Sledge, shook his head. "Sorry, man, no can do. We're here for La Machine next weekend. SledgeHammer is headlining the closing concert. Haven't you heard?"

Fuming, Fortier shook his head. "Fine. Just stay out of my way." He passed through their gauntlet, his head high.

They watched him march to the front door, which Alice, anticipating his departure, held open. It closed slowly behind him as he left.

He's trouble.

"Yes," Trevor said. "He is."

CHAPTER 14

The Rideau Centre, just south of the ByWard Market, occupied a city block and included three floors of shopping. A mix of high-end boutiques and national chain retailers, it also housed a Nordstrom department store. This was where Alice had arranged for them to work with the division heads for men's and women's clothing to find their perfect outfits.

At the main entry, they synchronized watches, separating into their respective sexes and agreeing to meet back at the entry in an hour and a half to compare notes and decide if they needed to find alternate vendors.

In the ladies' wear department, Christy quickly found a gown she liked. The skirt would have to be shortened and it needed a tuck or two in the bodice, but the effusive manager assured her the alterations would be ready by four o'clock that afternoon. Ellen was more difficult to please, finding four dresses, all of which had flaws she wasn't sure she was willing to live with. That necessitated deep discussions in the change room between all four women, the manager, two sales clerks, and the department seamstress. In the end, a compromise was reached, and a dress chosen. It too would have alterations, but would be ready by four.

Back at the entryway, they found Quinn and Trevor lounging on a bench in the mall. They found suits within the first half hour. Their trousers would be hemmed that day, and, like Ellen and Christy's gowns, would be available by four that afternoon.

With their critical needs taken care of, Alice departed to join Sledge, who was already at the rehearsal venue. Their afternoon would be dedicated to working with the other bands on the concert, but she assured them she'd be available should a glitch occur in the alterations schedule.

The rest had a few hours before they could pick up their new garments. They decided to enjoy a leisurely lunch, then do a bit of shopping in the massive mall while they waited.

Since the ByWard Market wasn't far away, they walked to a restaurant in the area that was highly recommended in the tourist literature. Located in an old stone building, the dining room featured exposed granite walls and polished hardwood floors. On the tables were starched white tablecloths and crystal bud vases with miniature roses in each. The cuisine was French, the prices over the moon, but the food was delicious.

"Do you think someone from the Dogwood Party, or involved in the party, even in a secondary way, could be Ralph Sharpe's killer?" Christy asked once their food orders had been taken and the waitress had left them alone.

"My friend Bryant Matthews thinks it's a possibility," Quinn said. He rubbed his chin. "I'm not so sure though. Sharpe was a wannabe. Eventually, he might have become a power in the party, but he wasn't there yet. If someone thought he was a problem, there are lots of ways to undermine him. You don't have to kill him."

"Unless you're an idealist," Trevor said, his expression grim.

"Which circles us back to YES! and Todd Ahern," Quinn said gloomily. "YES! is left-leaning. Ralph Sharpe, if his affiliation with the Dogwoods reflects his views, was right of center. He was using his money and influence to change the direction of the organization. Todd, as the originator of YES!, had a vested interest in keeping the association the way it was. It wasn't surprising the two men clashed."

"I wonder why," Ellen said, her expression puzzled.

They all looked at her. "Why what?" Trevor asked.

Ellen shrugged. "Quinn's right. YES! focuses on social advocacy and encourages their students to dedicate themselves to helping those at the bottom of society, but their focus is on building a network of like-minded people who will bring change by working from within. Ralph Sharpe was a capitalist entrepreneur. He wasn't interested in helping the lowest in society, but he appreciated the group's core mandate to build strong support networks. My question is, why get involved with YES!? There are other organizations that focus on bringing people together and creating networks. Why did he want to go to the considerable effort of pushing YES! in a new direction?"

"That is a good question," Trevor said.

"Because he could?" Rachael offered.

"You mean, he was just being contrary, Mom?" Christy asked.

Rachael shook her head, then made a face, scrunching up her nose and pursing her lips. "This may venture into the realm of conspiracy theory, but he wanted to be someone in the Dogwood Party, right? What if he thought turning YES! away from its left-wing orientation would prove to the movers and shakers in the party that he was someone who got things done, who would be useful to them."

"His ticket to ride, you mean," Quinn said slowly.

Rachael nodded. "Exactly."

Christy laughed. "That's twisted, Mom!"

Rachael laughed too. "I know. Who thinks like that, right? But, well, there are people who do."

"It's something to keep in mind for tonight," Trevor said. "I think we should try to get a sense of what people thought of Sharpe and how they're packaging his legacy. It will tell us a lot."

"Hopefully, by the end of the evening we'll know whether we need to pursue the political aspect, or whether we should be looking at other parts of his life," Quinn said.

Their meals arrived at that point. When they'd finished and were enjoying an after-lunch cup of coffee, Christy said, "We have another couple of hours before the clothes are ready. I think we should head back to the Rideau Centre. I'd like to check in with the store a bit early to see if they've got the alterations completed." She laughed. "And if they don't, well, fussing will keep them on their toes, so to speak."

Ellen nodded. "And make sure they know we expect them to honor their delivery time, if not be early."

"Would anyone mind if we found a store that sells those garbage compactors Sharpe Products produces?" Rachael laughed. "I'd never heard of them before we became involved in this case, but now I'm intrigued by them. It sounds like such a good idea. If it really works, I'd like to buy one."

Christy shot her mother a rueful look. "I've got to confess. I'm like Mom. I'm fascinated."

"Garbage does not interest me," Ellen said.

"Me either," said Rachael, shaking her head. "But those little bricks. What a great idea! You know, back in the day when I was a young woman, having a trash compactor in your kitchen was a cool way to save the environment. Then recycling started and no one talked about trash compactors anymore. Now we're hearing that a lot of the plastic we recycle just goes into a dump somewhere. Why not reduce it to a cute little brick that can be reused instead of being discarded?"

"You're an environmentalist," Ellen said, studying her.

Rachael blushed, but she shook her head. "Maybe a little, but nothing as passionate as Roy is. No, I just want to do my bit to divert as much as I can from landfills."

"It's a great idea, Mom. Let's see what Ralph Sharpe's signature product is all about."

They found an interesting shop selling all kinds of items for the kitchen without any problem. The front part of the space was dedicated to brand-name glassware and dishes, but at the back of the store, along with rice cookers, electric pressure cookers, and other appliances, they found what they were looking for. There were two in stock and each box had a different name.

"Compress-a-Brick and Compact-a-Brick," Rachael read. "I wonder why Sharpe Products created two different versions?"

A smiling sales clerk heard her question and said, "Because Compress-a-Brick and Compact-a-Brick are made by two different companies." He picked up the box for the Compact-a-Brick. It retailed for a hundred and fifty dollars more than the Compress-a-Brick. "This one has three different sizes for their bricks. It's made here in Canada and it will last you for twenty years or more. It's a quality item."

He put the box back on the shelf, then gestured to the Compress-a-Brick. The Sharpe Products logo was prominently displayed in the carton's graphics. "Now this one you can buy for less than two hundred dollars, but the bricks are only one size and the machine itself is made offshore. Very cheaply, in my opinion."

Rachael's eyes twinkled. "So, you'd recommend the Compact-a-Brick?"

"Absolutely."

Smiling rather mischievously, Rachael looked at the others. "I'm going to buy the Compact-a-Brick for myself. Should we get the Compress-a-Brick and do a comparison test on them?"

Christy laughed. "Let's just go with the Compact-a-Brick, Mom."

Ellen was staring at the two boxes, intrigued. "No, I think Rachael's right. We should buy both. Let's do it."

Christy looked at Quinn, her brows raised. He chuckled. "If nothing else, we can always write a consumer review comparing each product."

Rachael laughed and picked up the Compact-a-Brick. "Wow, this is heavier than I expected."

Quinn took it out of her hands. Trevor picked up the Compress-a-Brick. He frowned. "This one isn't bad. Maybe there's something to the clerk's assertion that the Compact-a-Brisk is better quality."

"Looks like we'll find out soon enough," Christy said. "Let's pay for these, then pick up our clothes. We have a party to get ready for!"

∼

Archie and Marian Fleming lived in Rockcliffe Park, not all that far from the New Edinburgh condo. The Uber driver who deposited Christy, Quinn, Ellen, and Trevor in front of the house was impressed by the address. And why wouldn't he be?

 Despite being close to the downtown of a major Canadian city, the house was set back from the road in green manicured grounds. A stately wrought-iron fence separated the property from the sidewalk. Both halves of the gate were open and men in dark suits stood in the opening, monitoring arrivals. They piled out of the Uber and produced ID, which was checked against a guest list. After being let through, they set off for the house.

The walk that led to the house cut through a carefully maintained lawn. Broad flowerbeds, all abloom, adorned the front of the house. There must have been cameras monitoring the entry because the front door opened as they climbed the porch stairs.

"Welcome," said a young woman, smiling. She was wearing black trousers and a starched white shirt, indicating she was a staff member. Christy wondered if she was part of a catering team or if the Flemings lived with a full complement of household servants.

The woman took Christy and Ellen's wraps. "The guests are congregating in the living room." She indicated a large formal room opening off the foyer. "But the bar is in the dining room across the hallway. There's also a buffet in the dining room. I'm not sure where Archie and Marian are at this moment, but I know they'll be pleased to greet you. Our guest of honor, Hunter Sharpe, hasn't arrived yet, but when he does, Archie will be saying a few words about his father. In the meantime, please enjoy your evening." With a nod and an even warmer smile, she went off to hang up their wraps, then returned to her station by the doorway.

"Well," said Christy. "Which way do we go? Dining or living room?"

"Why don't Quinn and I go to the bar, while you and Ellen get started in the living room?" Trevor suggested.

Christy looked at Ellen, who nodded. Christy took a deep breath, donned her Jamieson Princess persona, and said, "Okay, let's do this."

Like the front entry and the hallway, the living room was traditional. This didn't surprise Christy, as she remembered the Flemings' North Vancouver home was decorated in the same manner. Eggshell blue walls met wainscoting stained a dark walnut. The paintings adorning the walls were by the Group of Seven, well-known Canadian painters, while others were fine examples of eighteenth-century European artists. The sofas and chairs, which had been moved from the center of the room to accommodate standing groups, were padded and upholstered in silk. Side tables were dark, gleaming wood. Some held crystal vases filled with summer bouquets. On the far wall, French doors opened to a patio and a pleasant garden beyond.

"A lovely room," Ellen commented, surveying the space.

"Yes, it is." Christy smiled faintly. Marian and Archie Fleming might have traditional tastes in décor, but their personal life was far from traditional. She wondered how many of the people milling about in this room had any idea how spicy the Flemings' past was.

A compact man wearing a well-cut suit detached himself from a group of lavishly gowned women and came over to greet them. His broad smile revealed a crooked front tooth, but its warmth seemed genuine. He held out his hand. "Hi. Welcome. I'm Ezra Gaynor."

Ellen and Christy introduced themselves. Was it her imagination, Christy wondered, or did his smile dim just a little?

"Friends of Marian's," he said. The smile had definitely dimmed.

"That's right," Ellen said. Her gaze had cooled along with his smile and she was very much a Jamieson. She'd caught the hint of disparagement in his tone and she didn't like it. "Are you attached to the party somehow?"

Gaynor bristled. "I'm the party president."

"Ah," Ellen said. In that one sound she put a wealth of meaning, making it clear to Ezra Gaynor that he hadn't made the social cut, that he was not one of the elite, that he was merely a cog in the political party's wheel.

He flushed and the smile disappeared completely.

"The young woman who greeted us said Hunter Sharpe would be coming tonight," Christy said, drawing his attention back to her. "This must be a terribly difficult time for him and for his family."

Gaynor relaxed a little. "It is. Hunter and I went to university together and we've been good friends ever since. He's a strong supporter of the party. He was the one who got his father interested in us."

Christy said sympathetically, "Hunter and his father were close, then?"

Gaynor nodded. "Very. Ralph was a good man. He was generous both with his time and his money. He will be missed."

That sounded like a practiced, and rather pat, pleasantry, and from what Roy had discovered, untrue. Christy noticed Gaynor's gaze was shifting as he checked out the room.

"I'm sure he will be," Ellen said.

"The way Ralph died, well, it was horrible," Christy said. "How is the family taking it?"

Gaynor glanced at Ellen, then looked back at Christy as she spoke. "They're devastated, as you can imagine," he said rather curtly. "If you'll—" He stopped abruptly and his eyes narrowed as he noticed someone over Christy's shoulder.

Christy turned to look. She saw Quinn and Trevor carrying glasses of wine.

"Quinn Armstrong," Gaynor said. "Inspector Fortier told me you'd be here." He didn't sound pleased.

Quinn passed Christy one of the glasses he was carrying. He raised his brows. "By invitation."

Christy hastily introduced Ezra Gaynor to Trevor, who was handing a glass of wine to Ellen and mentioned that Marian had specifically invited Quinn.

Gaynor didn't bother with polite small talk. "Fortier told me you're trying to whitewash Ralph Sharpe's killer so you can get a good story. Let me tell you, that's not okay with me. Not here, not tonight, not ever."

"I don't invent facts, nor do I cover them up," Quinn retorted, staring coldly at Ezra Gaynor.

"Darlings!" Marian Fleming bustled over, her arms open wide. "You came! I'm so glad. Ezra, Archie is somewhere about. Can you find him and bring him over? I know he'll want to say hello."

Gaynor glared at Marian, but he departed to do as she asked after shooting one last hostile look at Quinn.

Marian sighed. "Such an officious little man. How Archie puts up with him, I don't know." She brightened. "But he seems to work quite well with him, so all's well."

Ellen said, "How are you, Marian? Having a memorial for another person associated with the party must bring back memories of Fred's death last year."

Tears welled in Marian's eyes. She'd been Fred Jarvis' mistress before he was murdered during the campaign for the leadership of the Dogwood Party, a campaign he was fighting against Marian's husband Archie. The private lives of the new leader of the Dogwood Party and his wife were complicated.

"Dear Fred," Marian said. "I still miss him, you know."

Ellen nodded. "You were together a long time."

"Yes." Marian sighed. "And as you say, this dreadful business with Ralph Sharpe. Well, it has brought it all back." She looked around carefully, then said in a low voice, "And to have Inspector Fortier involved.... Again! It's... well, it's just bizarre."

"How deeply was Ralph involved with the Dogwood Party? Did you know him well?" Christy asked.

Marian shook her head. "Not particularly. I would see him at events and he liked to schmooze with Archie—rubbing shoulders with power, you know."

Ellen nodded in a way that implied she knew the type.

"And he was a contributor. We all liked him. He was a charming man and so helpful when something needed to be done."

"But he wasn't part of your inner circle," Ellen said shrewdly.

"Oh, no. Nowhere close."

And that seemed to be perfectly fine with Marian. Ralph Sharpe had been one of the many clamoring for attention around her husband Archie. Christy had the sense that he was rather like the furniture—useful, but not something you worried about.

"Christy Jamieson, Quinn Armstrong. Good to see you." Archie Fleming came up behind his wife to join their group. He shoved out his hand. Quinn shook it. For Christy, there were the obligatory air kisses.

Ellen, who already knew Archie, introduced Trevor. Archie made friendly small talk. After a moment, Quinn said, "Have you had any contact with Colin Jarvis recently, Archie?"

Quinn's comment was a bold move. Archie had been furious at one time and Christy supposed that Quinn wanted to see whether Archie's friendliness was a false front or something else.

Archie directed a serious stare at Quinn, then he smiled faintly. "I've heard Colin is doing just fine. We don't speak."

"Such a shame," Marian said.

Archie nodded. "I was angry at the time, Armstrong, but I won the campaign without Colin's help." Colin Jarvis had been Archie's campaign manager before he learned that his father and Marian had been in a relationship for years. Quinn had been the one who informed Colin of the liaison and, as a result, Colin had resigned from Archie's campaign. "Marian likes your Christy." He shrugged. "I'm prepared to be friends."

"I'm working on a book on Fred Jarvis's murder. It's scheduled to come out in December next year," Quinn said, watching him.

"Will I be upset?" Archie asked, his voice cool.

That was code for, "is the book a tell-all about Fred's sexual peccadilloes," Christy thought. She waited to hear what Quinn had to say.

"I had to include some of his sexual promiscuity, but I didn't mention Marian's name. You're part of the story, of course, because you were direct competitors for the leadership of your party."

Archie nodded briskly. "Not a problem then. He smiled faintly. "Would you send me a copy of the book prior to publication? I'm sure the press will have questions and I'd like to be prepared."

Quinn nodded. "I'll ask my publisher to provide a review copy."

"Thank you." A new guest arrived. Archie smiled and said, "If you'll excuse us."

He moved away. Marian floated along beside him, cheerfully greeting everyone she passed.

"That went better than I'd expected," Christy said.

Quinn nodded rather grimly, then he laughed. "If I put everything about Fred Jarvis' relationships in my book, no one would believe me. Keeping Marian out of the story is a complete necessity."

CHAPTER 15

Christy thought the meeting with Archie Fleming had gone reasonably well, but Quinn wasn't so sure. Archie had been absolutely furious when Colin Jarvis had quit his team. Would he really be sanguine about it, even now a year later? He shrugged and told himself it didn't really matter. They were here tonight to see what they could discover about the life of Ralph Sharpe, not to rekindle a damaged friendship.

Still, he liked Archie Fleming, despite his involvement in Fred Jarvis' deeply flawed social and sexual network. He laughed to himself as he decided that dating a woman whose dead husband was living in her cat had certainly shifted his deeply rational journalist's mind.

"Time to work the room," Christy said, breaking into his thoughts. She looked up at him, her smile intimate. He felt a little part of him seize up. It never failed to amaze him that she'd chosen him.

Trevor said, "There were several groups in the dining room. Why don't Ellen and I begin there?"

"Good idea," Quinn said.

Christy smiled and linked her arm with his. "Where shall we start?" She wrinkled her nose. "Not with the people around the obnoxious Ezra Gaynor. What about that couple by the French doors?"

"His face is familiar." Quinn searched his memory but couldn't come up with a name.

Christy laughed. "Let's go find out why."

The man smiled as they approached. "Hello. I'm sorry, but I don't believe we've been introduced."

"I'm Christy Jamieson," she said, smiling warmly.

The man's eyes brightened and he said, "Of course."

Christy indicated Quinn. "And this is my friend, Quinn Armstrong."

The man sent a calculating look Quinn's way and suddenly something clicked together in Quinn's mind. He smiled and held out his hand. "You're Randy Dowell. Nice to meet you." Randy Dowell was the Dogwood Member of Parliament for one of the ridings in the British Columbia interior. He was said to be a good friend of Archie Fleming. If Quinn remembered correctly, the two men were about the same age and both had attended English Bay University. The years had treated Archie more kindly than Randy, though. The silver in Archie's dark hair gave him a distinguished look. Randy's thinning brown hair just appeared washed out.

After introducing his wife, Colleen, Randy said, "You're the reporter who cracked Fred Jarvis' murder. Good work."

"Thank you," Quinn said, surprised. He'd written several articles about Jarvis's murder, but he'd never mentioned his own involvement in solving the crime. Archie Fleming could have known, though. Did that mean he'd shared the information with Dowell?

"Did you know Ralph Sharpe well?" Christy asked.

Colleen Dowell, a heavy woman wearing a dark brown gown that gave her a funereal air, pursed her lips and looked downward. She seemed to be fighting tears. Christy put her hand to her mouth and said, "Oh, I'm so sorry. You must have been close friends. I didn't know."

Randy said heavily, "Not close friends, but fellow sufferers afflicted with the same mental anguish."

"Oh, my," Christy said faintly. "How terrible."

Colleen sniffed and nodded. "Like us, Ralph lost a daughter to that odious cult."

Quinn's attention was caught. Was Colleen referring to YES!?

"A cult!" Christy said. "My daughter is only ten, but I can imagine how awful it would be to not have her in my life. Can you tell me what happened?"

Colleen looked relieved as she nodded. "When she was in grade twelve, Carrie, that's our daughter, her school nominated her to a so-called networking organization called YES!." She nodded toward her husband. "Randy had just been elected to Parliament and he was here in Ottawa while I stayed in BC with the kids."

As Colleen choked back a sob, Dowell took over the tale. "YES! is located here in Ottawa, and Carrie had been accepted to a university in town, so we thought it would be a great way for her to acclimatize to the city, and to make friends in the area before classes started." He broke off, shaking his head.

"What happened?" Quinn asked, though from the looks of these two people he thought he already knew the answer.

"YES! is a combination of classes and practical experience," Randy said. His expression was grim. "After the first month, Carrie was telling me I was a social dinosaur and that I needed to reevaluate my priorities. We argued. As the summer went on, she became more and more belligerent. In September, when university classes started, we were both relieved she'd decided to live in residence for her first year, but once she'd moved in and school began I barely saw her."

"We all gathered at home in BC for Christmas," Colleen said sadly. "It was not a happy visit. She called us backward, privileged, and uncaring. She even called Randy a misogynist! Which he's not," she added with a fierce look.

"The next summer, Carrie stayed in Ottawa and went back to YES! for their second semester, but she didn't stay with me. She rented an apartment with a friend she'd met in the program." Dowell looked down into his glass, then up again. "We had another three years of bickering and fighting while she completed her degree. When she graduated, she moved to Toronto. We haven't seen her since."

"She won't even talk to us," Colleen said mournfully.

Impulsively, Christy reached out and touched Colleen's arm. "I'm so sorry. I don't know how you were able to deal with that. It must have been very hard."

Colleen shot a quick glance at her husband. "Ralph helped us through it. His experience was similar to ours. His daughter Karla participated in the YES! program too, and he lost her as well. It was harder for him, I think. She was a bright girl and he hoped she would join his company. After being involved with YES!, she absolutely refused to work with him. She told him his products were garbage and he cheated his customers. She said she wouldn't be party to that. Can you imagine?"

Christy shook her head, her expression sympathetic.

"Why, then, was Ralph involved with YES!?" Quinn asked. "I understand he was on the Board of Directors. In fact, he was the chair."

For the first time, Randy's features lit up in a smile. "Ralph was a smart man. He said shutting down YES! would be next to impossible. So, he'd do one better. He'd rebrand it." Dowell laughed shortly, though the sound wasn't amused. "He told us he'd slipped his own people onto the Board, arranged for the student internships to be with private companies, not nonprofits, and he'd engineered the hiring of a new CEO supportive of his ideas."

"His plan was working, too," Colleen said. "Otherwise, why would Todd Ahern murder him?"

"You think that's why he was killed?" Christy said, sounding shocked.

"Why else?" Randy Dowell said.

Archie Fleming came up to them, a young man beside him. Quinn saw that Trevor and Ellen had followed him into the room.

"Randy! Good to see you." Archie clapped Randy Dowell on the shoulder. "You and Colleen know Hunter Sharpe, of course. Hunter, this is Quinn Armstrong and Christy Jamieson." As the others joined them, he nodded and said, "And here are Ellen Jamieson and Trevor McCullagh. They're all friends from Vancouver on a visit to the capital."

Hunter Sharpe was a tall man with thick brown hair and pale blue eyes. His suit was black, his shirt a crisp white, his tie black silk. He said the appropriate things and shook hands, then accepted the condolences of the little group with quiet thanks. His expression was somber, as Quinn would expect for a man grieving his father.

Introductions over, Hunter zeroed in on Quinn. "You wrote *Finding Frank Jamieson*."

It was a statement, not a question. Quinn nodded.

"Inspector Fortier told me you're investigating my father's murder."

Quinn studied him. "Fortier is not pleased that I'm looking into the crime. I had the impression that someone was putting pressure on him to get the case closed quickly. Any idea who that might be?"

A faint smile curled Hunter's rather thin lips. "I imagine you think my father's life and death would make a good book."

Strangely, Hunter's voice was without inflection. Quinn couldn't tell what he was building up to. Would it be something like a rant about the evils of the press intruding on people in the middle of a painful and emotional time? Or would he ask Archie to kick them out for intruding? Then again, he might just be holding on to his emotions so tightly he couldn't let go for any reason.

Quinn said cautiously, "I plan to write an article once the police solve the case."

"They already have," Hunter shot back. "Todd Ahern killed Dad and he'll be charged for it."

"As I said." Randy Dowell nodded.

Hunter turned to him, a look almost of relief on his features. "Dad said they turned your daughter the same way they corrupted my sister. I was sorry to hear that."

As Randy nodded again, Trevor frowned. "Corrupted is a strong word, Hunter. Do you have proof?"

When Hunter raised his brows in a haughty way, Archie said, "Trevor's one of the best defense lawyers in Vancouver, Hunter."

Christy looked at Ellen, surprise in her expression. Ellen raised her brows. Trevor had been part of the investigation into Fred Jarvis' death when they met Marian and Archie Fleming, but he'd been on the periphery. Quinn concluded that Archie had done his own bit of investigation after Marian invited them all to this party.

"Yes, I have proof," Hunter said crisply. "Before she became involved with YES!, my sister was in line to become the general manager of one of our divisions, what would become the new Compress-a-Brick line, in fact.

It was still on the drawing board at that time, but the plan was that she'd shepherd the product from inspiration to the thriving division it is now." He stopped, his mouth set in a tight line.

"What happened?" Christy's compassionate tone drew Hunter's gaze to her. She smiled in an encouraging way and some of the tension eased in him.

"Karla, that's my sister, had finished her first year at university when she became involved with YES!. One of her professors told her that she'd benefit from the networking part of the program. So, she enrolled. By the end of the summer, she was arguing with my father over how he handled the company. The next summer, after her second year at university, she went back to YES! for more courses and another internship. The battles between her and my father worsened. He thought she'd come round and we made plans to integrate her into the company. But after graduation, she announced that she would never work for Sharpe Products, because my father's business practices were morally corrupt."

"Harsh words," Quinn said.

Hunter nodded.

"Your father was fortunate he had you to work with him," Christy said.

Hunter straightened a little. "We did work well together, a good team. I'll be carrying on his legacy."

Archie squeezed his shoulder and Colleen said, "Oh, how wonderful." Her voice was thick with emotion.

Quinn thought that statement was more bravado than fact. Hunter was playing the role of dutiful son and valued heir. He wondered if he'd be able to shake out some information that wasn't quite so gilded. "If your family's experience with YES! was so painful, why did your father get involved? He provided a large donation and was active on their board. In fact, he was the chair, wasn't he?"

Hunter curled his lip. "Can't you guess?"

There was arrogance in his tone, a disdain that grated on Quinn. "Why don't you tell me?"

"They duped my father and he didn't like it. When Karla first started talking about YES!, Dad thought it would be a great addition to her education. The kind of polish she needed to succeed in business. It was nothing of the sort, of course, but Dad had already become involved."

"How did that happen?" Christy asked.

Hunter said impatiently, "When Karla said she was going to apply, he gave the organization a large donation. They offered him a seat on their board and he was happy to oblige. As he learned about the YES! philosophy, he became concerned. By the time Karla started talking about corporate greed, he'd already decided change was needed."

Trevor was looking at Hunter rather skeptically. "If he didn't believe in the organization, why continue on their board? Surely, it would have made more sense for him to resign."

"And have other families like the Dowells and his own be torn apart by revisionist thinkers masquerading as legitimate educators?" Hunter snapped. He shook his head. "No, that wasn't my father's way. Throughout his career in business, he'd acquired many companies with a corporate structure and culture very different from that of Sharpe Products. He knew how to assimilate an organization, keeping the part of it that had value, but sectioning off what was ineffectual. That's what he was doing at YES!. And he would have succeeded, too, if Todd Ahern hadn't realized Dad was remaking his precious organization and killed him."

"The ultimate hostile takeover," Ellen said, eyebrows raised. She sounded interested, though not enthusiastic.

"Absolutely necessary," Randy Dowell said heavily. "Your father had my support, Hunter. Have you any idea what will happen now he's gone?"

"When Todd Ahern is tried, that will be the end of YES!. No one will ever entrust their children to the place again. I intend to make sure that happens." His voice was hard, his determination, driven by anger, clear in the words.

"What if Todd Ahern isn't guilty?" Quinn asked, watching him. To his mind, Hunter Sharpe was playing to an audience. He wondered how far the man would go in what was starting to seem like a vendetta.

Hunter shrugged. "The trial will destroy YES!, even if Ahern gets off somehow."

Trevor said, "The investigation isn't over yet. Todd Ahern may not be the killer and he may never be arrested."

Hunter glared at him. "That isn't possible. It won't happen."

"What if it does?" Quinn said.

"My father was murdered by Todd Ahern. Who else would want to kill him?" Hunter's jaw was set and his eyes were hard. He'd staked his ground and he wasn't moving from it.

"You're right that there was a lot at stake for Todd Ahern and YES!, but there could be other people who had a motive to kill your father. We may not know what that is yet, but once we do, it will be much easier to discover who did it."

Hunter's expression was grim, but he wasn't shaking his head, refusing to listen. "Look, Quinn, I get what you're saying. And you're right. My dad had a big personality and he lived a public life. He was active on many boards, and was relentless in business. He could have had enemies. I believe Todd Ahern killed him, because Ahern was invested in that damned organization of his and Dad was taking it away from him. He had a solid motive and, from what Fortier said, he doesn't have an alibi."

Pausing, Hunter shook his head. "But if my Dad wasn't killed by Todd Ahern, I want to know who the killer is, and I want to see that person punished for it."

His eyes locked with Quinn's and Quinn saw a bleakness there that covered deep, aching grief. Hunter Sharpe wanted an answer, one that was reasonable, one he could accept and believe in. Right now, Todd Ahern fit that criterion, but he was pretty sure that if they could provide solid proof that someone else was responsible, Hunter would accept the alternative.

Emotion hung heavy amongst their group as Marian Fleming flitted over. "Darlings!" she said with her usual buoyancy.

Quinn wasn't sure if she was deliberately trying to defuse the tense situation or not, but her warm smile was working. Colleen Dowell brightened, Randy no longer looked quite so weary, and there was a glimmer of warmth in Hunter's eyes. He caught Archie's gaze and saw there was amusement there. The leader of the Dogwood party knew he had a valuable social hostess in his personable wife.

"Hunter, so lovely to see you, though it's at such a sad time." Marian managed to execute a light hug and a couple of air kisses with the tense Hunter, then she linked her arm with his. "It's such a lovely evening, Ezra and I have set up the podium in the garden. Archie, would you help Ezra encourage our guests to come outside? Now, Hunter, come along with me and I'll get you seated." She smiled at the rest of the little group, as she began to lead Hunter away. "We'll see you outside."

Archie marched away to round up guests. Randy Dowell sighed heavily. "A sad story, but I admire Ralph's determination." He glanced at Quinn and Trevor. "You're wrong, you know. Ralph was murdered because of his work at YES! and Todd Ahern was the one who killed him." He nodded in a definitive way. "Come on, Colleen. Let's go out."

Trevor stared after the departing Randy. "I'm not convinced."

"Nor am I," Quinn said. "I think we need to talk to Karla Sharpe."

Trevor nodded rather grimly. "Sooner rather than later."

CHAPTER 16

Breakfast the next morning was being hosted in Rachael and Miles's suite. Christy, along with Noelle carrying the cat, rode up in the elevator. They were both dressed for their day, in shorts and T-shirts, though Christy's was V-necked and striped in pastel colors, while Noelle's featured a dinosaur and the logo of the natural history museum.

On arrival, they discovered Rachael standing at the kitchen island surrounded by all the men in their little group. She was explaining the similarities and differences of the Compress-a-Brick and the Compact-a-Brick in enthusiastic detail. The men, like Christy and Noelle, dressed for the day's activities, were listening with fascinated expressions. Alice was at the stove frying bacon and humming a SledgeHammer song. Christy noticed that Sledge was humming the same song, though his attention was clearly fixed on the intriguing new machines. Noelle put Stormy onto the floor. The cat immediately leapt up onto the counter, yet another male beguiled by the lure of new technology.

"Morning, Alice. Anything Noelle and I can do?"

Alice dragged her gaze away from the pan, looking as if she'd been inhabiting some other universe and was surprised to find she'd landed in this one. "I thought we could have pancakes. There's a box of mix in the cupboard if you want to get started."

"I'll do that," Noelle said firmly. "I'm an expert pancake batter mixer."

Christy laughed. "I'll get the box and a bowl, then it's all up to you, kiddo. I'll set the table, Alice," she added, as she found the pancake mix and a large bowl.

"Once the machine is full of the stuff you want to compact, you press the start button," her mother was saying. "The Compress-a-Brick works faster, but it's also louder." She reached inside and pulled out the material she'd obviously compacted earlier. "And here's the brick."

Christy, pulling cutlery from a drawer, paused to look. So did Noelle. Alice remained focused on the bacon.

The brick was rectangular and about the size of a normal concrete brick you might use on your garden path. It wasn't as dense as a normal brick, though. Christy could see spots where the compression hadn't quite bonded the different materials from which it had been made. It was also multi-colored, reflecting the many sources that composed it.

Her mother dropped the brick into Quinn's hand. He weighed it thoughtfully. "It's heavier than I expected." He passed it on to Trevor who was standing beside him.

Rachael nodded. "I think that's because I used the pizza boxes for this brick. If I'd used Styrofoam and other plastics, it would have weighed virtually nothing."

The brick made it round the little circle of men about the same time as Ellen entered the suite. Her brows rose. "What's this? Show and tell?"

"A comparison of the Compact- and Compress-a-Brick machines. My mom was busy last night."

"Morning, Ellen," Rachael said. "Christy's right. I just had to try them both out." She held out another brick. It was larger than the first and the materials were tightly melded together so it was impossible to know where one ended and the next began. "This is a Compact-a-Brick. Same materials but look how much tighter the bond is in this brick. And!" She reached into the machine and pulled out a second brick, smaller than the first. Another brick that was even smaller followed. "Look! Different sizes. Isn't the little one cute? I could see using a bunch of these to make a small planter box for the garden."

Ellen's eyes glazed over. "Good heavens."

"You need a coffee," Christy said. "So do I."

"How does this look, Mom?" Noelle had been industriously working on her pancake batter while the adults contemplated a new method of recycling.

Christy peered into the bowl. "Looks great. Alice, what do you think?"

Alice plated the bacon over paper towels to drain before she checked out the batter. "Excellent. Okay, time to get to work, kid. You pour."

Christy left Alice and Noelle to cook the pancakes. As Ellen sat down at the table to sip her coffee, Christy took hers to the little group by the compactors. "I'm getting the impression you think the Compact-a-Brick is the better product, Mom."

Rachael nodded. "The sales clerk at the store was absolutely right. Better options, better quality results."

"Interesting," Christy said.

"Yes, it is, isn't it?" Quinn was comparing bricks from the two compressors thoughtfully. "I wonder which came first?"

"You mean who stole whose idea?" Rachael asked, wide-eyed.

"Probably no one," Roy said. "People come up with ideas that appear to be the same all the time. It may seem like one is stolen from the other, but, really, it's just two people thinking about a problem and figuring out a way of dealing with it that's remarkably similar."

Quinn put the bricks down and Sledge picked them up. He put one on top of the other and peered at them. "It's a fun idea." He winked at Rachael. "If you lived in Vancouver, I'd let you build me a Compact-a-Brick flower pot." Rachael laughed. He shifted the bricks so they were horizontal to each other "How would you stick them together? Glue?"

"Some sort of cement, I suppose," Trevor said.

Sledge nodded. "Yeah, I guess."

This is garbage. Are you people nuts? Stormy knocked the smallest brick and sent it flying. When it landed on the floor, he followed it down and batted it again. It skittered across the ceramic tiles on the kitchen floor. He raced after it, pouncing on it before it stopped moving. Grabbing it in his paws, he flopped down on his side, raking it with his hind feet. Scratches appeared, but the structure of the Compact-a-Brick held firm.

"Here," Roy said. With a flick of his wrist, he threw the Compress-a-

Brick toward Stormy. It landed, bounced, then landed again to skate across the floor directly past the cat. Stormy abandoned the Compact-a-Brick to pounce on the Compress-a-Brick. Capturing it, he followed the same pattern as before. His back claws raked the product, digging great jagged holes in it. Bits started to flake away.

"Wow," Christy said. "Mom's right. The Compact-a-Brick is much better quality." She retrieved the Compress-a-Brick from the cat before Stormy reduced it to shreds. Unimpressed, Stormy pounced on the Compact-a-Brick and sent it flying.

"Breakfast!" Alice announced. "Come help yourselves."

The pancakes were a hit and Alice looked rather pleased when she joined them at the table, the last one to serve herself. Talk was lively as they ate. Miles and Noelle told them about their visit to the maze, with a few add-ons from Roy. According to Noelle, the day had been awesome, which both men nodded agreement to. The highlight was the maze—for all of them. Frank in Stormy had played hide and seek with Noelle until Stormy the Cat discovered the maze was the home of many families of field mice. He'd spent considerable time darting between the hedges chasing one or another of the creatures. He'd caught several and brought them as offerings to the adults and Noelle, much to Miles's bemusement.

Roy and Noelle were used to this behavior, and Noelle had been firm in her disapproval. Each time the cat had released his captive as she wagged her finger at him and told him to be good. The mice had all survived to be chased another day. Miles, unaware that his son-in-law resided in the cat, thought it was cute how well Stormy responded to his granddaughter.

With the meal consumed, they lingered over coffee to plan their day. It was Sunday, so it was impossible to do any work on the case. They tossed around ideas of how to spend the day, then finally decided they'd head out to the Mackenzie King Estate, across the Ottawa River in Gatineau. In the 1930s the estate had been the rural getaway of one of Canada's longest-serving prime ministers and was nestled in Gatineau Park. The property boasted walking trails as well as King's home and gardens, which meant they wouldn't have to leave Stormy alone in the condo.

The day proved a wonderful interlude. Ellen and Trevor wandered off to inspect Mackenzie King's house and were gone for most of the afternoon. Roy fell into conversation with one of the guides and learned about King's spiritualism and his belief he was in regular communication with his late mother. The guide confided that King had kept this quiet while he was prime minister. Roy could understand why.

Christy, Quinn, and Noelle, along with Miles and Rachael, took one of the walking trails and chatted lazily as they went. And Stormy found a red squirrel that seemed to enjoy being chased—and taunting the cat when he couldn't be caught.

At the end of their day, they stopped for dinner at a restaurant in Chelsea, a quaint little town that was a combination of rural retreat and commuter village. The venue was located in an old house on the main street and inside had the dark warmth of a British pub. The food was all Quebecois though—pea soup, poutine, Montreal smoked meat sandwiches, tourtiere pie—hearty, filling meals designed to feed hungry appetites.

By unspoken common consent, they didn't talk about the murder until the next morning when they were organizing their respective days. They converged in Christy's kitchen. Her mother cooked plates of bacon and eggs while they talked. Noelle helped her grandmother, buttering toast and carrying plates to the table.

"We have to get this cult thing sorted out," Christy said. "The Dowells and Hunter Sharpe make it sound as if their daughter and his sister were brainwashed by the people at YES!. I'm not at all surprised Inspector Fortier is focused on the organization and, of course, Todd Ahern as the key figure in it."

Quinn nodded. "Hunter even said his father was on a mission to save other families from the same fate, which sounds like a stretch. There was one thing I found interesting, though. Hunter described Ralph's involvement as a hostile takeover and said that was something his father was used to doing."

Christy nodded thoughtfully. "They're not the same motivations, are they? On one hand, Sharpe is trying to help others in a similar situation. On the other, he's pursuing purely personal goals."

Quinn accepted a plate of eggs and bacon from Noelle with a smile and thanks. As he added a piece of toast from the plate in the center of the table, he said, "But they both benefit him. If the Dowells see him as a fellow sufferer working to resolve their mutual problem, he creates a bond with them that will help him ingratiate himself into the Dogwood party. If he puts himself into a position where he can change the direction of the organization, he controls it and achieves the revenge he desires. It looks like a win-win to me."

Christy sipped some coffee. "Which do you think would be more important to him?"

Quinn grinned at her. "Let's find out, shall we?"

She smiled back. "What are you suggesting?"

"My friend Bryant Matthews may have something for us, and he told me he'd like to meet you. Why don't we have lunch with him today?"

"Grandma and Grandpa are taking me to see the Parliament buildings today, Mom."

Noelle looked totally innocent, but Christy thought she saw a little bit of mischief lurking in her eyes.

"We're going to start early to see if we can beat the tourist rush," her father said. There was definitely amusement in his eyes. "We thought we'd go to the aviation museum this afternoon."

"Well..." Christy said, torn.

"I need to talk to Tamara and her dad about YES!," Quinn said. "I thought I'd arrange to see them this afternoon after we'd talked to Bryant."

His comment gave Christy an opportunity to both be active with her daughter and be part of the investigation with Quinn. Her parents didn't need her trailing around with them while they visited Parliament Hill, but a visit to the aviation museum with Noelle would be fun. She could have her time and Noelle time all in one day.

So, she nodded to her daughter, her father, and Quinn. "I'd love to come to lunch with you Quinn, but the aviation museum sounds like fun, so I'll join Noelle there. How does that sound, kiddo?"

"Like a plan," Noelle said, adding a cheeky grin.

Christy laughed.

Alice took her plate over to the kitchen and slipped it into the dishwasher. As she returned to the table, she looked at her watch in a rather pointed way. "It's nine-fifteen."

Sledge yawned. "Yeah. It's early. So?"

"Are we still planning to interview Ralph Sharpe's secretary this morning?" Alice tapped the face of the watch and shot him a determined stare. "Hammer's plane gets in this afternoon. We need to be here by four to greet him."

Sledge blinked, but he sat up a little straighter. "We'll meet him at the airport."

Alice shook her head, her expression disapproving. "Not a good idea. If people recognize you both it will create a scene."

"So?" Sledge raised his eyebrows. "Then we do an impromptu press conference and promote the concert."

Alice cocked her head, a tiny frown between her brows as she considered the possibility from all sides. Then her expression cleared and she nodded. "A win-win, no matter what happens."

"Where is Hammer staying?" Ellen asked.

Sledge drank some coffee. "With me, in the extra room in my suite."

Ellen sent a pointed stare at Alice. "I suppose Hammer has an assistant too?"

Sledge nodded. "Jayden Torres. Hammer thinks he's great."

"He'll be staying in the second bedroom in my suite," Alice said absently, as she scrolled through something on her phone. "Okay, Hammer's flight gets in around three-thirty. We should get going."

"Why so early? I haven't had my breakfast," Sledge said, rather plaintively.

"Coming up," Rachael said from her spot by the stove.

Rachael plated Sledge's eggs and bacon. Noelle brought it over to the table. Sledge winked at her and gave her a high five before he tucked into his meal.

"We won't all fit in that tiny little car of yours," Roy said. "I'll order an Uber. For what time?" He looked at Alice. "Will ten o'clock work?"

She tapped her chin as she thought, then she nodded. "Should work."

"Doesn't give me much time to finish my food and have another coffee," Sledge grumbled.

Suck it up. There are some of us who want to get going.

Christy almost laughed at the shocked look on Sledge's face.

Roy worked his phone and ordered the cab. Alice said earnestly, "We don't know how long it will take to get to Kanata and talk to this Symmonds woman. Better to leave a little early than to get to the airport too late to catch Hammer."

With the cab ordered, Roy refocused and noticed the cat was up to something. Stormy was standing on a chair with his front paws on the tabletop. He was eyeballing the remaining sliver of bacon on Sledge's plate. He clearly had designs on it.

Roy cleared his throat. When Sledge looked over at him, he pointed to the plate. Stormy's paw was reaching out, moving closer....

Sledge snatched up the last of the bacon and popped it into his mouth. He shook his finger at the cat. "No, you don't. Mine."

Spoilsport.

"You betcha."

When Alice looked puzzled, Roy cleared his throat. "Right. The taxi's ordered. I'm going to go get ready. I'll meet you two in the lobby at ten."

Alice nodded. "We'll be there."

Hey, old man! What about me? I'm coming too.

Roy nodded—in response to Frank's statement, not Alice's, Christy thought—and stood up.

He looked at the cat. "Don't be late or we'll go without you."

Fat chance!

CHAPTER 17

Once he was ready to go, Sledge was all for swaggering into the Sharpe Products office and letting his celebrity do the heavy work to get them a meeting with Jennie Symmonds, the late Ralph Sharpe's secretary and personal assistant, but Alice wouldn't let him. She said it was beneath his dignity, which annoyed him.

Whatever attributes he had, dignity wasn't one of them. Drive, determination, good nature, compassion, kindness: he'd cop to all of them, but dignity wasn't on his list.

Alice, however, was adamant that she needed to call ahead and make an appointment. While they were arguing about what excuse she could possibly make to get them into a meeting with Symmonds, Roy took matters into his own hands.

"Stormy's in the tote bag and he's getting antsy. The cab's waiting at the door. We've got to go. Are you two coming?"

The old man's right. I can't keep the poor guy in here much longer.

Sledge fixed a look of bored acceptance onto his face before he looked over at Alice and shrugged. Though he was rather pleased the decision had been made, he was in dead center between two determined personalities, not that he himself wasn't stubborn, not at all. Alice liked to organize things her way and Roy simply went wherever he wanted to go. It would be interesting to see who managed the logistics of this expedition. He was betting on Alice, but Roy would give her a good workout.

Sharpe Products was located in a medium-rise office building in north Kanata, a suburb of Ottawa. The taxi ride took forty minutes along a highway congested with traffic and in many places, bottlenecks. Once he realized they were visitors, the driver, a cheery fellow, kept up a stream of tidbits about the areas they were passing through. Since they were on a major highway, there wasn't much to see, but the driver's chatter kept Alice from second-guessing their plan and calling ahead.

When they reached Kanata, the taxi turned off the expressway and onto a four-lane secondary road. Along with everyone else using the road, the driver gunned it as soon as he merged with traffic. Small strip malls, then a series of low-rise office buildings, bordered the boulevard. Eventually, the taxi turned into the parking lot of a gray concrete structure that looked rather like a cheese grater and the driver announced they'd arrived. He offered to wait for them, but after he heard the cost, Roy shook his head, a horrified expression on his face.

Alice commented that it would be unwise to send the cab away since they didn't know if Jennie would see them. Sledge, in solidarity with Roy, paid the fare. As the driver gunned it out of the parking lot, they headed for the entry.

Open the tote bag! It's stuffy in here.

Roy opened the bag and the cat's head popped out. *That's better. Are you going to let the cat down?*

"We should wait until we're in the building," Roy said.

Alice looked at him curiously. "Wait for what?"

Sledge grinned as Roy shot him an anguished look that begged for help. "Long car rides affect Roy. Well, you know."

To his surprise the usually imperturbable Roy went bright red. So did Alice. "Oh, I... ah, I didn't mean..."

Sledge patted her shoulder. "It's okay. It's just that we don't talk about it—"

"So, let's not," Roy said gruffly. "Look, we're here. What's our story?"

"The truth," Sledge said, and walked into the building.

The reception area took up a good portion of the lobby. A high ceiling, lots of windows, pale granite floor tiles, and white walls gave the space a light, airy feel. Sledge advanced to the desk. He smiled at the receptionist, a pretty blond who looked to be in her mid-twenties. "Rob McCullagh to see Jennie Symmonds."

She shot him an assessing look, taking in the casual shirt, jeans, and boots he was wearing, then shifting her gaze to the equally casual Roy carrying a tote bag with a cat's head sticking out of the top, and Alice, more uptight in slacks and a blouse. Her brow furrowed. "Do you have an appointment—" She stopped abruptly as she took another look at Sledge. Then she gasped. "You're him. You're Sledge!"

Sledge smiled but didn't reply.

"You want to see Jennie? Of course." She clapped her hands together. Excitement brightened her eyes. "Absolutely! She'll be delighted. Come with me." They set off before she even checked to find out if Jennie was actually in her office.

Along the way to the fourth-floor suite that had once belonged to Ralph Sharpe, she batted her eyelashes at Sledge, letting him know she was up for some light flirting. He cheerfully gave her what she wanted while Roy glowered and Alice ignored them.

The cat sighed. *Once upon a time...*

The CEO's suite consisted of a reception area and two offices. It was painted a muted gray and a matching carpet covered the floor. The suite was empty now, except for one office where a woman in early middle age who was wearing a dark skirt suit and medium heels appeared to be in the process of vacating it. Sledge found himself wondering if the dark clothes were out of respect for her employer's recent demise, or her ordinary choice of business attire.

"Jennie!" the receptionist said, pausing in front of the open doorway. "Rob McCullagh is here to see you."

Jennie Symmonds glanced up from the papers she appeared to be putting in order. She looked Sledge up and down, then said briskly, "I'm sorry, Mr. McCullagh. I don't believe I know you."

The receptionist moved deeper into the room, perhaps intending to remain for the interview, and ushered them in. "He's Sledge, Jennie! Sledge of SledgeHammer."

Jennie blinked, looked from the receptionist to Sledge, then back to the receptionist again. "Okay. What's SledgeHammer?"

The receptionist gasped. "The rock group? Jennie, you must have heard of them. Everyone has!"

Jennie shook her head. She turned to Sledge with a pleasant smile. "I'm sorry, Mr. McCullagh. I'm not being deliberately rude, but I'm not a fan of rock music. I prefer classical symphonies. What can I do for you?"

Well, that put paid to his idea of using the built-in goodwill that went with being the lead singer in Canada's premier rock band. Out of the corner of his eye, he saw Alice roll her eyes and shake her head. His jaw clenched.

Roy cleared his throat. He stepped around Sledge and shoved out his hand. "I'm Roy Armstrong," he said.

And I'm Frank in Stormy the Cat.

Frank's introduction of himself had no effect, but Roy's name did. Jennie frowned, her gaze searching his face. Then her eyes widened and she put her hand to her throat. "Oh," she said. "Oh! Roy Armstrong. Roy Armstrong, the writer?"

Roy nodded.

"Oh," she said again, the hand now waving in a distracted way. "Oh, do come in. Please sit down." She gestured to a couple of chairs positioned in front of her desk. Sledge let Roy and Alice have the seats while he propped up the doorframe and watched this turn of events with considerable amusement.

The receptionist sighed, as she shot Sledge a sad and disappointed look. It appeared she was taking Jennie's ignorance as a personal slight on Sledge's behalf. He smiled warmly at her and winked. She blushed. The disconsolate expression disappeared and a teasing smile took its place. As she slipped past him on her way out, she whispered, "Will you stop by before you leave?"

He nodded. She gifted him a big smile, then shut the door behind her as she left. He caught Alice rolling her eyes again and decided to ignore her.

"I've read all of your books," Jennie was saying to Roy. "But I love this new direction you've taken with the murder mystery. You're very good at it. I didn't guess who the killer was, but when he was revealed, I realized all the clues were there in the book. I love that." She blushed a little, probably hearing herself rattle on like a besotted fangirl, but that didn't stop her from blurting out, "Are you writing another mystery? Will this be a series? Do promise you are and it is!"

Roy smiled at her, as at ease with his own set of fan questions as Sledge would have been with his. "I am. The new book should be out for Christmas."

She clapped her hands. "Wonderful!"

"In fact, that's why I'm in Ottawa. I'm doing a bit of research..."

Jennie caught the nuance immediately. "Murder," she breathed, drawing out the word.

Roy nodded.

Her eyes gleamed. "You want to talk to me about Ralph's death."

Gotta admit, this woman is quick.

Roy ignored the cat's comment. He kept his gaze steady on Jennie's as he nodded again. "If you wouldn't mind."

She waved her hand. "No problem." She sounded excited, even joyous. "What do you want to know?"

"Why are you so eager to talk about your late boss?" Alice sounded disapproving. She certainly looked disapproving.

Jennie blinked. It appeared she'd forgotten Alice was there. Not surprising, since no one had bothered to introduce her.

"This is Alice Griffiths, my assistant," Sledge said. He wondered impatiently what it was she was so upset about. They'd come out here to dig some dirt on Ralph Sharpe. Back at the condo, Alice had been all for this excursion. Why was she getting so bent out of shape now they were here?

The frown between Jennie's brown eyes disappeared. She nodded, her expression now understanding. "And because you're protective of your boss, you wonder why I'm not. I get it." She shrugged. "To answer your question, I owe Ralph no loyalty. He's dead. My position has been made redundant because his son, who now owns the company and will be the new CEO, is replacing me with his own assistant. I've been given a month's notice and a reasonable severance package."

"That's too bad." As quickly as she'd flared up, Alice's expression was now full of sympathy at the way Sharpe Products was treating Jennie.

After a brisk nod that was acknowledgement of sympathy offered, but in no way an acceptance that any was needed, Jennie turned back to Roy. "What would you like to know?"

"What was Sharpe like to work for?"

"Demanding. Temperamental. At times, insensitive. When he met the public or was networking, he was all cheerful charm, but that was on the surface. Underneath, he was driven."

"Tough boss," Roy observed.

"He could be," Jennie agreed.

"How long have you worked for him?"

"Five years, two months, and twenty-two days," Jennie said promptly. She grinned at Roy's startled look. "I calculated my time with the company to be sure I was given the severance package I deserve."

"And were you?" he asked.

"I was." She added thoughtfully, "I will say this about Sharpe Products, they don't nickel and dime when they're getting rid of people."

"Do they get rid of a lot of people?" Sledge asked incredulously.

Jennie nodded. "A fair number. The company has grown largely through acquisition. As part of the assimilation of a new company into ours, the two staffs are integrated. That means a lot of jobs become duplicates and people have to be let go."

"You must have a lot of angry former employees," Roy said. "Got any names or examples?"

Jennie looked at him for a minute. "Your son is Quinn Armstrong, the investigative reporter, isn't he?"

Roy smiled proudly and nodded.

She glanced at each of them, then focused on Roy. "You're not just doing research for a new novel. Your son's trying to solve Ralph's murder, and you're helping, aren't you?"

Roy nodded. "He is and we are."

"Oh!" said Jennie, delight on her face. "This gets better and better!"

Sledge wanted to laugh, but he didn't. Jennie Symmonds had just lost her job. If she was having fun telling tales on her former employer, who cared?

"Okay," she said. "If you give me a minute, I'll contact some people and see if they're willing to talk to you. If they are, I'll give you emails and phone numbers so you can connect directly."

She set to work on her phone. Several whoosh sounds indicated text messages sent. Subsequent pings told of replies received. She read the responses, typed busily into a document on her computer, then printed it at a machine set up to one side of her desk.

Grabbing the printout, she handed it to Roy. "Two people have agreed to talk to you. One is a redundancy, like me. He worked for Sharpe's for twelve years, but when we acquired a competing company, it was his position that was eliminated, not the position of his counterpart in the other company." She pointed to a second name. "This man is very angry. He was a long-time supplier for one of the companies Sharpe's acquired. Ralph insisted that he rebid on all his contracts and he forced the man to undercut himself to keep the contract. Even worse, every year we issue new RFPs and he's required to rebid. He feels he's been badly treated indeed."

Roy looked at the two names. "This is great! Thank you, Jennie."

She smiled at him. No, Sledge thought, she beamed at him. "You are very welcome, Roy. Now, if there is anything else I can help you with, please let me know. My contact information is there along with the other names."

"You bet we will," Roy said, his eyes gleaming.

She nodded briskly. "Good."

He paused, his head tilted to one side as he studied her thoughtfully. "Jennie, can I ask you something?"

"Of course!" The expression in her eyes was as warm as her smile.

"Would you like to be a character in my next book?"

Delight bloomed on her features. "Oh, yes! Yes, of course! Do you really mean it?"

He nodded.

When they left, she was fanning herself and saying, "Oh, what a wonderful day. Oh, how exciting. Oh, my. I have to tell my husband!"

CHAPTER 18

Once they were back in the parking lot, Roy immediately realized they had a problem.

The cat, of course, vocalized it. *Should have kept the cab.*

Should have indeed. Around them was nothing but parking lots attached to low-rise office buildings with vast physical footprints. The road that bisected the area was two lanes in either direction. Traffic roared along it at eighty kilometers an hour. There were no sidewalks. Why would there be? There was nowhere to walk to.

Alice, of course, was making good use of her phone. "If we order a taxi, it will get here within a half an hour. An Uber will take twenty minutes."

She didn't say, "I told you so," which was nice of her because she'd been right. Sending their ride away had been a bad idea.

Sledge was working his phone too. He appeared to be energized by the predicament they found themselves in, which was heartening. He looked up and around, figuring out the location, then he pointed to the other side of the road. "If we cross the racetrack, er, street, and walk about two kilometers, there's a golf course and hotel complex."

"What good would that do us?" Roy was feeling grumpy, mainly because he was the one who had got them into this situation.

Not in the least disturbed by his gruff manner, Sledge grinned at him. "First off, it gets us out of this parking lot. I'd rather wait a half an hour for a taxi in a hotel where they have a bar and a restaurant than standing around here."

Alice nodded. "Not good for your reputation."

"There is that," Sledge said, nodding amicably. "Then there's the chance that the doorman at the hotel can get us a cab faster than the apps are projecting. They might even have a taxi stand with cars waiting."

Her eyes narrowed, her gaze intent, Alice nodded. "And if they don't, they'll make sure you get transportation. You're Sledge of SledgeHammer, after all."

Alice was nothing if not single-minded about her boss and his position in the world, Roy thought, still grouchy.

They set off, traipsing through parking lots and across the narrow grass borders that separated one from the other. They reached a traffic light, crossed the highway, then followed Sledge's GPS directions to the hotel.

At the beginning of the walk, Stormy had his head poking out of the tote, an interested observer of all that was going on around him, but when they crossed the roadway he disappeared back inside and couldn't be coaxed out again for almost five minutes.

They found the hotel fifteen minutes after they left the Sharpe Products building. There was no taxi stand outside. Roy thought rather uncharitably that if they'd stayed in the parking lot, the Uber would probably have arrived by now and they'd be on their way to wherever they were going next. Instead, they were footsore and winded at a way station where they'd have to wait for transportation to arrive.

Sledge pulled open one of the big double doors and sauntered inside the glossy hotel. Alice hurried after him. Roy sighed and followed them both.

The hotel was decorated in black and silver, with dark wood accents. The front desk was opposite the front door, easy to find. Sledge made his way to the desk.

An attractive young woman with long dark hair and a wide, welcoming smile said, "Good morning, sir. How can I help you?"

Sledge gifted her with one of those smiles of his that seemed to melt female hearts. She blinked, then frowned. She must be trying to figure out where she'd seen him before, Roy thought, as he joined the other two at the desk.

"I'm afraid I'm lost," Sledge said, contriving to look remarkably contrite as he said it.

"I'm sorry to hear that," she said.

Her frown deepened, but Roy saw the moment when she realized who she was talking to. Recognition flared in her eyes but was quickly quenched. Her professional smile widened, though. "I can help you with that, sir. Where are you trying to go?"

Alice pulled out the sheet with the two names Jennie had given them and said, "We're trying to get to Terry Fox Drive."

The Terry Fox address was news to Roy. He thought they were planning to go back to Ottawa.

The woman looked at the address. "Not a problem. You're only about a ten-minute walk away."

Roy propped the tote filled with cat onto the reception desk. It had gotten rather heavy during their fifteen-minute hike and the cat was pushing at the sides. Frank probably wanted in on the action, Roy thought as he opened the fastening. The tote fell away as Stormy pushed his body out. *At last, we can stretch! I'm so tired of being cooped up.*

The woman's eyes widened and she looked over Sledge's shoulder as if seeking a source for the voice she'd just heard.

At least, that was what Roy figured was happening, from the way she was reacting.

Frank did too. *Hey, beautiful. I'm over here.* Stormy stretched in that sinuous way cats did, then he sauntered across the desktop and butted her hand with his head.

"Oh," the woman said. "You have a cat. What a gorgeous guy. I love cats." She rubbed her cheek against Stormy's. Ever sociable, he started to purr.

Ignoring this interaction, Alice said, "According to Jennie Symmonds, Vernon Pratt, he's the fired employee she mentioned, now works at that address on Terry Fox. Why don't we call him and see if he'll talk to us? It would save us coming back to Kanata another day."

Sledge raised his brows and looked at Roy, who shrugged. "Works for me."

Alice retreated to make the call. The front desk clerk was now scratching Stormy below the chin. His eyes were slitted and his purr was a loud rumble. The voice sighed with pleasure.

Alice bustled back moments later. "He'll talk to us if we can be there in twenty minutes. That's when his lunch hour starts."

Roy coaxed a reluctant Stormy back into the tote with the help of the front desk clerk, who then gave them directions on how to reach their destination. With no transportation available, they set off, walking briskly.

～

Vernon Platt was a middle-aged man with only a little of his hair left and a round, good-natured face. He met them in the lobby of his company's building and suggested they adjourn to a nearby park to talk.

The park was nothing but a little plot of green at the end of the rambling, low-rise building. Furnished with three picnic tables, there wasn't a tree or flowering plant in sight. They all sat down at one table. Roy put the tote back on the grass and Stormy gratefully emerged. Vernon didn't seem to notice, which was all to the good, Roy thought. It remained to be seen whether or not he could hear Frank, though. If he did, they'd deal with it when the time came.

"You want to talk to me about Sharpe Products," Vernon said, clasping his hands in front of him on the tabletop.

Sledge nodded. "Jennie Symmonds thought you might be willing."

Vernon studied them. "She called me to let me know. Why do you want information on how Ralph Sharpe dealt with severed employees?"

"We're investigating his murder. We need to know everything we can about him," Roy said, shrugging.

Vernon studied them for a moment longer, then he nodded. "Jennie told me that too." He smiled. "Okay. Ask your questions and I'll answer as best I can."

Sledge led off. "Why were you fired?"

Vernon smiled faintly. "I was surplus to requirements."

"That's pretty cold," Alice said, her brows raised. She sounded scandalized.

Vernon shook his head. "Not really. You have to understand how Sharpe Products works. Ralph Sharpe never had a new idea and his R&D department sucked, but he was really shrewd at assessing the market value of any product and he knew how to create a marketing campaign that would turn even the biggest skeptic into a believer."

"So, he was a great marketer," Roy said. "What has that got to do with firing people?"

"Sharpe Products grows by acquisition," Vernon said patiently, echoing what Jennie Symmonds had told them. "Ralph would keep his eyes open for little companies that had great ideas, but not enough capitalization or the marketing skills to push the product into the big time. He'd make the owners an offer that seemed enormous to them, and buy them out. Then he'd mass produce the product, cutting a few corners in the process, and create an aggressive marketing campaign designed to sell an enormous number of items in a short period of time. If the product did really well, he'd keep pushing it. If it didn't, once he'd made a profit over and above what he paid for the company and the manufacturing, he'd dump it."

Alice leaned across the table. "Expansion by acquisition. I've heard of it. I suppose he made the former owners sign non-compete agreements when he purchased their companies?"

Vernon nodded. "Always."

"Okay," Sledge said. "He expanded by buying up other companies. What's that got to do with you being fired?"

"Everything." Vernon shrugged. "One of the things he did when he acquired a new company was to look for ways to cut costs. The first thing he did was absorb it into Sharpe Products so it became a division instead of a separate company. He scrutinized each position to see if there was someone in Sharpe Products who was doing the same or a similar job. If there was, he'd load the duties from the new company onto the Sharpe Products person and fire the person from the new acquisition."

Sledge was frowning at that. "Why? Why was it so necessary to get rid of the new acquisition's staff?"

Vernon's mouth twisted into a grimace. "Most of the companies purchased by Sharpe Products were a year or two past being start-ups. Whatever product they were selling, the people who worked there cared about it. They'd created it, they'd developed it, they'd finessed it. They perfected it. Like I said, when Ralph got hold of a new product, he liked to keep the price down and to do that he usually rejigged the manufacturing specs to include cheaper materials. People who create new products and build companies out of nothing care about quality. They'll protect the product they've developed and they'll protest if the company is disbanded. So, Ralph got them out of the way as quickly as he could."

"Cold," Alice said again.

Vernon shrugged. "I suppose it was."

"What happened to you?" Roy asked.

"I'm a marketing manager. I was part of a team that handled the household goods Sharpe sold. Ralph acquired a computer company that developed an app that turned your appliances on remotely. It also opened your garage door for you when you were halfway down the block or locked up your house if you'd forgotten to do so. He didn't think anyone on the household goods team had enough technical know-how to produce a top-notch ad campaign for the app, so he took a risk and kept the marketing exec from the new company. Then he redistributed the household products accounts within the Sharpe Products team and fired the most expensive team member. Me."

This time it was Sledge who said, "Harsh."

Vernon laughed. "No, it was great. Ralph was a crazy perfectionist. If he gave you a product to hype and it didn't sell the way he thought it should, he'd be on your case. He liked to yell and lay blame. When he fired me, he gave me a generous package and a great reference. I'm a capable guy. I managed to find my current job in less than a month. Now I have a nice little nest egg in the bank and I'm working with people I really like. All of it thanks to Ralph Sharpe. The guy did me a favor."

CHAPTER 19

With Noelle on her way to the Parliament buildings with her grandparents, Christy prepped for her lunch with Quinn and his friend Bryant Matthews. She didn't have a big selection of outfits. Saturday night's evening gown was obviously out of the question and she didn't want to wear ever so casual shorts and a T-shirt. Finally, she compromised on a pair of tailored slacks and a loose blouse with a boat neck and short sleeves.

As she applied her make-up and made sure her red-brown hair was neatly styled, she reflected that it was lunch with a friend and not meant to be formal. The problem was, she'd seen Bryant Matthews reporting on television news programs for years, which gave him a kind of celebrity, or at least a notoriety, and he was Quinn's friend, so she wanted to get meeting him right. She stepped back, checked herself out in the full-length mirror mounted on the back of the bathroom door, and nodded. The green of the blouse looked good on her, and together with the slacks, gave her a trim appearance.

Quinn smiled when he saw her and Christy saw appreciation in his eyes. They'd decided to Uber to the restaurant, as he and Christy would be going their separate ways after lunch—Christy to join her parents and Noelle, and Quinn to meet with Todd Ahern.

Bryant had chosen a diner on Elgin Street for their lunch get-together. The place was a large space packed with booths that were made up of hard-wearing Formica tables with brown tops flanked by yellow vinyl bench seats. The floor was a faded, worn linoleum in a dizzying pattern of black and white squares. The walls were a mustard yellow that might have once matched the vinyl seat covers. When Quinn and Christy walked in, Bryant was talking cheerfully with a youthful waiter who seemed to know him well.

The man she'd seen on the television screen was middle-aged with a compact build and a moon-shaped face. He delivered his stories in a straightforward, unemotional way that gave him the same kind of vibe as an accountant lecturing his client on the intricacies of the tax system. Emotion, it seemed, wasn't part of his makeup.

When she met him, he was still visually that same man, though a little slimmer in person, but she discovered his private persona was different.

As Christy and Quinn arrived, the waiter slapped down menus and promised he'd be back in a few minutes. Quinn waited until Christy had eased into the booth, then he slid in beside her. He smiled at his friend. "They know you well around here?"

Bryant nodded. He shoved his hand across the table and said to Christy, "Hi, I'm Bryant Matthews."

"Christy Jamieson." She smiled as she took his hand and shook.

"Pleased to meet you." Bryant's blue eyes twinkled as he glanced at Quinn.

Then he winked. And since he grinned at the same time, Christy figured she'd been part of a conversation between the two men when they met earlier. She stole a look at Quinn. His color was high, and he wasn't a man who reddened often. Yup, she'd been a discussion point.

Quinn cleared his throat. "Find out anything interesting about Ralph Sharpe's political aspirations?"

Christy moved on the bench seat, shifting so she could watch Quinn more easily and suppressed a smile. He was definitely a man changing the subject. Quickly. She found his embarrassment rather endearing.

Matthews' cheerful countenance turned thoughtful. "He donated up to the legal limit every year and was an active fundraiser, but he was still on the periphery when he was killed. His son, Hunter, now, there's a different story."

Quinn nodded. "Hunter Sharpe is a close friend of Ezra Gaynor, the current Dogwood Party president."

Bryant raised his brows. "That's quick work. How did you find out? It's not widely known."

Quinn grinned. "I have my sources."

As Bryant narrowed his eyes, preparing to dig deeper, Christy laughed. "Marian Fleming invited us to the celebration of life ceremony the Dogwoods held for Ralph a few days ago."

Bryant waved his hand up and down in a 'hot stuff' motion. "You snagged an invitation to that shindig?"

How hovered silently at the end of his sentence. Christy saw no reason to hold back information. "Marian is a friend of mine." She laughed again. "We bumped into each other in the dino gallery at the museum of nature. She immediately invited us to the event and insisted we come."

Bryant was staring at her with a fascinated expression on his face. "The dinosaur gallery."

Christy nodded. "She's on the museum's board and she likes to spend some time in the museum's galleries before every meeting. Dinosaurs are her favorites."

Bryant's brows shot up and laughter animated his features. "What an opening. I could make some really bad jokes about conservative politicians and extinct animals."

Quinn winced. "You have no idea how far out in left field you'd be."

Though Bryant looked intrigued by that statement, the waiter arrived at that moment and they had to scramble to select their lunch options. When their orders were given and he'd gone, Bryant had to admit he couldn't find any solid connection that might have been a motive for someone in the party to eliminate Ralph Sharpe.

"So Fortier must be involved in the case because of Randy Dowell's connection to YES!, nothing else," Christy said as their meals were served. Quinn had already filled Bryant in about the Dowells' estrangement from their daughter due to her participation in YES!.

Though they threw ideas back and forth while they ate, by the end of the meal Quinn was shaking his head. "The more we brainstorm, the more I'm convinced that the killer is someone from Sharpe's personal or business life. Both intertwine with YES! unfortunately, which complicates matters, but the motive is somewhere within that group of people. I'm sure of it."

Bryant rubbed his nose. "My sources don't reach into that part of the city, so I can't help you there. Any idea how you can get the data you need?"

"I'm meeting with Todd Ahern this afternoon. I expect him to dismiss the accusation that YES! is a cult, but I'm hoping he'll have the proof to convince me the accusation is coming from people who are hurt and angry and looking for someone or something to blame."

"But you're not sure," Bryant said softly, reading his expression.

Quinn shook his head. "Todd Ahern is an idealist with no head for business. He expects everyone to be as decent as he is."

"Which we all know isn't always true." Bryant grinned. "This gets more interesting by the day. You have to keep me in the loop."

Christy laughed, but she reached over to Quinn and put her hand over his. "If nothing else, your conversation with Todd will give you clarity one way or another and it will provide us with a different direction to concentrate on."

At least she hoped so.

~

Todd Ahern, dressed in slacks, a white shirt, and a sports jacket, looked suspiciously at Quinn. "You didn't bring that cat, did you?"

"Daddy! Why would he bring his cat? And where would he put it, for heaven's sake?" She gestured to Quinn, who was wearing a shirt, chinos, shoes, and socks.

"It's Christy's cat," Quinn felt impelled to point out. This was not how he expected the meeting to begin.

Tamara rolled her eyes.

Todd continued to look nervous. "Cats are crafty creatures. It might have slunk through the door while we weren't looking."

Tamara's lips pressed together into a firm, disapproving line. She was dressed in sensible slacks and a cotton blouse that did nothing to enhance her figure. She was still dealing with the traumas left over from her years of captivity, Quinn thought.

Remembering that Todd could hear the cat, and was spooked by the possibility, Quinn took sympathy on him. "And, no, the cat isn't with me." He resisted the urge to add that the cat was on another assignment. Instead, he said, "Look, I asked you to meet with me this afternoon because there's a charge that YES! is a cult. I need to get to the bottom of that before we go any further."

At the word cult, Todd's expression went from worried to bewildered. Already annoyed, Tamara's eyes flashed with temper. "Daddy's organization is not a cult. What a stupid accusation!"

Quinn nodded. He, Tamara, and Todd were sitting in the breakfast room of the chain hotel where Todd was staying. The hotel guests who would congregate there in the morning to partake of the free continental breakfast provided by the hotel were long gone, but the hotel staff kept the area open and a pot of coffee going all day, so in the afternoon it was a quiet space to have a private conversation.

"The two men we talked to on Saturday evening were adamant that young people were being drawn into a cult that deliberately separated them from their parents and families." He looked from Tamara to Todd. "The word cult was used specifically."

Todd was shaking his head. "No, no, no! A cult is an organization with an extreme religious orientation. YES! is not like that at all. Our goal is to help young people, particularly disadvantaged young people, be successful in our complicated and often dysfunctional world."

"You are a religious person and you founded YES!." Quinn kept his gaze locked with Todd's and his voice quiet.

"I'm a United Church minister," Todd said, aghast. "There is nothing extreme about my beliefs!"

"This is crazy." Tamara slapped her hand onto the tabletop. Not perfectly level, the table rocked. She pulled her hand back guiltily, perhaps suddenly realizing the violence of her reaction. "How can anyone think either Dad or the people running YES! are religious extremists?"

"Good question," Quinn said mildly. "Why don't we see if we can figure that out? Todd, let's go over your involvement in the organization. You told us you began it fifteen years ago to help disadvantaged youth."

He nodded. "Yes. My parish is in a poor neighborhood in Toronto. The children who live there are as bright and capable as their counterparts in wealthier areas of the city, but they lack social skills, not to mention a network of successful adults, to help them advance. I believed that mentoring, along with learning interpersonal skills, would help these young people succeed. I approached the CEOs of several non-profits I worked with and they were enthusiastic. We tested the idea out on a small group of no more than half a dozen high school students. After participation in our program, they all applied to university and each of them was accepted. They all did well, graduating with honors."

"That was fifteen years ago?" Quinn asked, making a note.

"No, no, that first trial was a few years earlier. We did another couple of test groups to refine the idea, before we actually created YES!." Todd stared over Quinn's shoulder, clearly looking into the past. "Odd. Thinking back now, I realize that in the beginning our purpose was more teaching social skills than social activism. Leadership was always there, of course, and networking, because both are instrumental for young people to get ahead. But social activism..." He shook his head. He frowned in a pensive way. "When did that change?"

Quinn consulted notes he'd made from their first night in Ottawa when Todd had come to the condo to speak to them. "Ten years ago, YES! moved its headquarters to Ottawa. Could it have been then?"

Todd rubbed his chin, the pensive expression still fixed in place. "We moved the headquarters a year after Gordon Widdowson was hired as CEO. His wife was offered a job with a rather important lobbying organization working on the climate change file. That meant she would have to relocate to Ottawa. We knew he'd want to move with her, so he would leave us." He shrugged. "Well, we couldn't break up a family, could we?"

"You suggested the headquarters move along with him," Quinn said.

Todd nodded. "We had a small management team, so it made sense, even though some of us who had been active from the beginning had to take a step back. Gradually, over the years, our earlier board members from the Toronto region were replaced by others from the Ottawa area."

"Did that happen with students and mentors as well?" Quinn asked.

Todd wrinkled his nose. "To a degree. You must understand, there are many needy young people in Ottawa as well as Toronto. We were expanding as much as anything."

"The two men I talked to on Saturday night both had family members enrolled in YES!. They also had salaries in the top one percent. When did YES! start bringing in students from well-to-do families?"

"The change was discussed while the headquarters was still in Toronto."

Quinn raised his eyebrows. "Discussed?"

Todd pursed his lips as he nodded. "The board was considering ways to move forward and someone brought up the suggestion. We were in the middle of examining the idea when Gordon came to us with his personal changes. To be quite honest, the thought that we might lose him took precedence over an amendment to our enrollment policies. Gordon was very much in favor of the change, so we approved it at the same time we agreed to move the headquarters to Ottawa."

Quinn could see a pattern forming. If his father were here, listening to Todd's description of events, he'd be formulating a plot about a deliberate and wide-ranging conspiracy to change the social framework of the organization.

Quinn was of a more practical turn of mind. What he saw was a group of earnest, well-meaning people with high ideals, but not a lot of management experience, being swept away by a forceful man of equally strong ideas that were perhaps not completely in sync with their own. Moving the headquarters some distance away had allowed Gordon Widdowson to shift the mandate that YES! worked under in ways that would allow it to become the organization he envisioned. The ideals were close enough to those of the original founders that they didn't notice the modification or didn't think the alterations were important enough to question.

"So YES! moves to Ottawa and at the same time the make-up of the student body changes."

Looking rather pained by Quinn's phrasing, Todd nodded.

"What else changed?"

"What do you mean?" Todd asked, his tone indicating confusion.

Quinn shrugged. "I assume you had a group of mentors you worked with in Toronto. If the student body changed, did the makeup of the mentors change too?"

Todd brightened. "Oh, I see. Yes, they did. We still had a program in Toronto. It was mainly filled by disadvantaged youth who worked with our regular mentors. The Ottawa contingent needed local mentors, as you can imagine. Gordon found them, with the help of his wife, I might add. Such a remarkable woman. Everything was organized smoothly."

Rather grimly, Quinn asked, "Are you the only member of the current board who was there at the founding of YES!?"

"Founding," Todd scoffed, smiling to take the edge off his tone. "Such a pretentious word. But, yes, I'm the only one who was part of the original group who got together to help all young people succeed." He cocked his head and frowned. "What does it matter?"

Quinn didn't answer. "You come up to Ottawa each year for the instructional section of the program, don't you?"

"For part of it. We incorporate the annual general meeting into that time period." He smiled. "I make a point of addressing the students. It's a heart-warming experience, you know. They always—silly children!—they always cheer me after my speech and they're quite wonderfully supportive of me. But, of course, that's what we're trying to teach them, how to embrace change, to be more than what they were before, to bond together to help each other succeed. Of course, they would be supportive." He chuckled. "In fact, they tend to follow me around and hang on my every word. Ridiculous though that is."

Tamara, who had been listening in silence to Quinn and her father, said in a low voice, "Oh, Daddy."

Todd turned to her looking confused. "What's the matter, Tamara?"

She drew in a deep breath. There was affection and concern in her eyes. "When I'm at a workshop, I listen to an important speaker with deference, but I don't follow him about and gush all over him. It's not normal."

Todd shook his head. "Tamara, what are you suggesting?"

Tamara bit her lip, her expression worried. It was Quinn who answered. "A cult doesn't have to be religiously oriented. The word can also be used to indicate a behavior." Hell, he thought, he sounded like his father now, pontificating on word use.

It didn't help that Todd was looking at him like he'd just arrived from another planet. "What exactly are you saying?"

Tamara sighed. "A cult of celebrity, Daddy. When people become obsessive about a person. YES! must have shaped a creation myth around you and you never noticed."

Quinn nodded. "They eased you out of active participation in the running of the organization and put you on a pedestal where you couldn't see the changes they were making."

Todd paled. "They? As in Ralph Sharpe?"

"No. As in Gordon Widdowson and his wife, along with the people he hired. They changed your practical, skills-based curriculum into one designed to encourage young people to embrace progressive causes, and they used you as a figurehead to help get their ideas across."

"What's wrong with progressive causes?" Todd asked, raising his brows skeptically. "Give me an example how this could be a problem."

"The daughter of a Dogwood MP enrolls in YES!. By the time she graduates from the program, she's become a social activist who will no longer talk to her parents," Quinn said.

Todd's lips parted, then he closed them again and wet them nervously. "I would never do anything to separate a child from her parents. This is... I can't believe this."

"Believe it," Quinn said. "The MP told me the story himself on Saturday night. He was the one who called YES! a cult."

"Dear heavens," Todd whispered.

Tamara looked at Quinn. "What do we do?"

"I need an intro to Ralph Sharpe's daughter, Karla. I've talked to her brother. He was the other person who called YES! a cult. He told me Karla was also estranged from her father because of YES!. I need to hear her side of the story."

Shaken, Todd nodded. He pulled out his phone and scrolled through his address book. After a quick conversation with someone at YES!, he was calling Karla Sharpe.

CHAPTER 20

Roy, Sledge, Alice, and Stormy made it back to the condo before anyone else that afternoon. Alice bustled off to check flight schedules and to see if Hammer's plane was on time. Roy read a text from Christy to their group chat noting that she'd ordered several platters and salads from a local caterer for dinner that evening. The food was to be delivered at five and someone needed to be at the condo to receive it.

Roy texted back that he'd be there, so he settled down to do a little work in the community room while Sledge and Alice headed out to the airport to collect Hammer. The cat curled up on the sofa and went to sleep.

The food looked pretty good, Roy thought when it arrived. He had the deliveryman drop it in the community room and when he was alone once more, he peeked inside the boxes. One contained what was described as Tuna Niçoise, and another was clearly a charcuterie platter. There were salads, including one made of ancient grains, and another that was mainly beets. Dessert was included, of course. He didn't think Sledge could cope without it. He closed the boxes again, made sure they were securely latched so the cat couldn't shove his inquisitive nose into them, then went back to work.

The others started arriving about a half an hour later. Christy, her parents, and Noelle were the first. Noelle was bubbling with enthusiasm for the sights she'd seen that day and chattered happily to anyone who would listen. Christy inspected the food, while Rachael and Miles headed up to apartments to gather cutlery, plates, and glassware for dinner.

Ellen and Trevor came in not long after, followed by Quinn, whose expression was grim. That wasn't good, Roy thought. It looked as if whatever he'd learned today, he didn't like the ramifications. Sledge, Alice, and Hammer arrived last and while Sledge took Hammer up to get him settled Alice pitched in to help set the table and lay out their food platters.

Dinner conversation was lively. Noelle described La Machine to Hammer, filling him in on the event that would be capped by the concert he and Sledge would be part of on Sunday evening. Alice outlined the busy schedule he and Sledge would have before the concert. It included promo interviews and practice time with the other bands and the session musicians who'd been hired to back up Sledge and Hammer.

Rachael asked Hammer if he'd ever been to see the Parliament buildings, then, when he said he hadn't, proceeded to describe their visit that morning in great detail. Not to be outdone, Noelle enthusiastically described the aviation museum. Hammer listened with good-natured amusement and asked questions in the right places.

When dessert had been consumed and after dinner coffee was in front of everyone, Noelle headed off to stream a video on the enormous TV on the other side of the room. The adults settled down to discuss the case. The cat, who had enjoyed some of the excellent tuna, settled on Christy's lap.

Hammer started the conversation off.

"Sledge says you're working on a case." He looked around the table, a smile in his eyes, a small one quirking his lips. Hammer approved of their detecting habit. They'd helped prove his brother wasn't guilty when SledgeHammer's former manager, Vince, was murdered and he'd been at the party when they'd spectacularly revealed the killer of Vancouver property developer Clayton Green.

"The murder of a local businessman and philanthropist," Christy said. "A friend of Quinn's asked us to investigate. Her father is the prime suspect and the cops aren't looking much further than him."

Hammer shook his head. "Typical." His tone was gloomy, although amusement still lurked in his eyes. "So, have you figured it out yet?"

"Not yet," Trevor said crisply. "But we do have some leads."

Hammer raised his brows and Sledge laughed. "The prime suspect the cops are looking at is the leader of a cult the victim was busy dismantling. We figure everyone involved in the cult is or should be a suspect. Plus, the victim had some questionable business practices, so we assume there are a bunch of people who've been cheated by him who might want to take their revenge. Add to that, he's been trying to muscle into one of the national political parties. Lots of opportunity there."

Hammer's eyes had widened at the word 'cult'. Now he laughed. "Who is this guy and what kind of cult was he dismantling?"

"His name was Ralph Sharpe," Christy said. She shot a critical look at Sledge. "And the cult isn't really a cult. It's one of those networking associations that teach people leadership roles and then sends them out into the world to make a difference. It's called YES!. You may have heard of it."

"YES!" Hammer appeared to ponder the name, then he shook his head. "No, can't say I have. But I have heard of a company called Sharpe Products. Does it have anything to do with him?"

"That's Ralph Sharpe's company," Quinn said. "What have you heard?"

"My mom bought an electric can opener from them. She saw it advertised in an infomercial and it was supposed to work anywhere. It didn't. It lasted about two months before it broke. My dad fiddled with it, but he couldn't get it working again. Piece of junk."

Rachael leaned forward. "Sharpe Products also makes the Compress-a-Brick trash compactor. Have you heard of that?"

"Oh, yeah. My mom is a sucker for infomercials. When she saw the Compress-a-Brick, and those cute little bricks it forms out of your garbage, she almost bought one. Then she realized it was made by Sharpe Products so she didn't."

"We have one upstairs," Rachael said. "I'll show you. We also have a Compact-a-Brick. It was the original invention the Compress-a-Brick was modeled on. It's much better quality. If your mom's still interested, tell her to buy a Compact-a-Brick."

Hammer laughed. "Will do."

"So where do we go from here?" Sledge asked.

"You and Hammer need to meet with the other bands and work out the structure of the concert. Two of the musicians you worked with on your last tour will be coming into town on Saturday. You need to have a song list by then." As Alice spoke, Jayden Torres, Hammer's assistant, was busy nodding. He was a compact youth, clearly intimidated by the authoritative Alice. At the moment, she was calling the shots and everyone on the Sledgehammer team was falling into line.

Except Sledge. "I'm not walking away from this."

Jayden sat up a little straighter. Alice glowered. "I'm not asking you to. I've been helping with this investigation too, remember? But this concert is important. Justina will be arriving tomorrow evening and we need to be prepared."

"Where does she expect to stay?" Ellen demanded, her voice frosty. All the apartments in the condo had two bedrooms, but with the arrival of Hammer and Jayden, most of those bedrooms were being used. Only Ellen and Trevor had a bedroom available in their units. If Justina were to stay at the condo, Ellen's spare bedroom would have to be allotted to her.

"She booked a room at the Sheridan," Alice said in a matter-of-fact tone.

Something off there, Roy thought.

The cat echoed his thought. *We're not good enough for her?*

Ellen waved her hand. "It doesn't matter. I'm just glad she doesn't expect to stay here."

Alice and Jayden appeared confused. Hammer raised his brows. Sledge laughed.

It didn't take long for Alice to get back on track. "Tomorrow, you and Hammer will work on SledgeHammer issues. After that, we'll see."

Sledge glared at her. Alice glared back.

Roy cleared his throat. "Sledge and Alice and I got some good leads from Sharpe's secretary, Jennie Symmonds."

What about me? I was there too!

Roy ignored the cat's comment and added that Jennie had given them two names and they'd interviewed one, a fired employee by the name of Vernon Platt. "There's also a supplier Sharpe screwed with we didn't have a chance to talk to." He rubbed his chin. "I could talk to him tomorrow."

Quinn shifted uneasily in his chair. "You don't know a lot about business, Dad."

"I know about people," Roy retorted, annoyed.

"I'll go along with you," Trevor said. He didn't look particularly excited by the idea.

"We'll take the cat," Roy said, his eyes gleaming. Trevor brightened.

"Won't a businessman think it odd you're coming to interview him with a cat in tow?" Miles said.

Roy pounced on that. "Exactly! The cat undermines the subject's sense of reality and makes him vulnerable to interrogation."

"How very diabolical," Rachael said, amusement in her voice. Her mother had already told Christy that she enjoyed Roy's theatrical flights and ever-active imagination.

"I'm out of the loop," Christy said. "Noelle and I are going to a splash park in one of the towns east of here."

"And we're joining them," Miles said.

"Yes, it's supposed to be a hot one tomorrow. I'm looking forward to being in the water all day," Rachael said.

"We need to get to the bottom of this cult business," Quinn said. "Todd gave me an introduction to Karla Sharpe. I have an appointment with her at one p.m."

That left Ellen to decide if she wanted to join Trevor and Roy, or perhaps Quinn, and work on the investigation, or if she wanted to take a play day with her niece and family. "I've never been to a splash park. I think I'd enjoy the experience."

The mind boggles.

Ellen pursed her lips in a disapproving response to Frank's cheeky comment and Roy almost laughed.

Trevor wasn't so easily amused. "We have come a long way since we arrived here and began this investigation, but we have a major impediment we need to deal with or all of our work means nothing."

"Fortier," Quinn said.

Trevor nodded. He leaned forward, his expression intense. "We can provide motive. We can even identify if someone has an alibi for the evening Sharpe was killed, but we can't provide definitive proof. If Fortier isn't willing to investigate further, Todd can still be charged and he would go to trial."

"If we find the murderer, he'd be acquitted, wouldn't he?" Rachael said.

Trevor nodded. "With a good lawyer, probably. But trials are tricky things and you can't depend on a certain outcome." He tapped the tabletop. "What's worse, though, is the negative publicity leading up to the trial. People believe that if you're charged, you're guilty. The damage to his reputation will be extensive. The damage to YES! by extension will also be heavy. Then there's the legal cost. A good defense lawyer is expensive. Does Todd Ahern, United Church minister, have the money to pay for his own defense?"

Sledge shrugged. "Doesn't matter. I'll pay for it."

Trevor shot his son a sharp, critical look. "Todd Ahern is a proud man. Do you think he'll let you?"

Chastened, Sledge compressed his lips into an annoyed line.

Quinn said into the silence, "You're saying we need to get Fortier on side."

"Yes, but how?" Trevor said impatiently. "He won't talk to me. You saw him on Saturday. He wants us gone."

"He'd listen to Archie Fleming." Christy added with a laugh, "He was intent on running us out of town, but the moment we said Archie's name, he backed down."

"Archie," Trevor said thoughtfully. He nodded slowly. "It could work. But how do we persuade him to help us?"

Ellen smiled. "We invite him and Marian to dinner tomorrow night."

Wide-eyed, Alice said, "You're going to invite the leader of a national political party to dinner on short notice?"

Christy laughed. "Why not?"

"Oh, I don't know, busy schedule? National figure pre-booked for months in advance? Look," Alice said. "I know you're friends with his wife, but people like them, they have people like me arranging their lives. It's not inviting your next-door neighbor for a last minute potluck."

She clearly doesn't know Marian.

"You're absolutely right," Christy said. Roy figured she was talking more to the cat than to Alice.

Ellen said, "Marian is all about family and friends. If we invite them, I think they will come."

Alice threw up her hands and rolled her eyes in a disbelieving way.

Ellen looked around the table. "Shall we give it a try?" When there were nods all around, she retrieved her phone from her purse, selected a number, and dialed. A few minutes later, she hung up. "They'll be here between five-thirty and six tomorrow for dinner." She smiled at the surprised Alice. "Piece of cake."

CHAPTER 21

Jennie Symmonds was a capable woman and an excellent ally Roy decided when Joel Grogan's secretary announced he was expecting Roy's call and willingly scheduled a meeting with her boss for that morning. Jennie had paved the way and Roy appreciated that.

Impulsively, he ordered flowers sent to her office—after he'd checked to make sure she hadn't left her job as yet.

Joel Grogan was the president and owner of Grogan's Warehousing. The company was located in a large building on the outskirts of Ottawa with easy access to Highway 417, the main transportation corridor in the region. His warehouse was an enormous hive of activity, with boxes stacked to the rafters and people busily either taking them down or building them up.

As he and Trevor crossed through the warehouse, Roy kept Stormy safely in the tote used to carry him. In this scene of bustling activity, it would be easy for a cat to be injured, or to cause injury if someone was surprised by his presence. The cat must have agreed. Though his head was poking out of the bag, he made no attempt to escape its confines.

Grogan's office was at the front of the building and constructed on a shallow mezzanine level. The walls were mostly glass, providing an expansive view of the action on the warehouse floor. Joel Grogan himself was a tall barrel of a man with hefty shoulders and a wide chest. His head was shaved and his features were unremarkable in a soft fleshy face. He was wearing a dark suit with a pale pink dress shirt. That the suit jacket had been hastily donned for their arrival was obvious, for his silver tie wasn't knotted tightly. Roy suspected he'd been working at his desk with jacket off and tie loosened before they'd come. Since he himself was wearing his usual casual shirt and jeans, and Trevor had opted for a golf shirt and chinos, he felt sorry the man had felt the necessity to tidy himself up for their benefit.

Grogan got straight to the point once the introductions were over. "Jennie Symmonds suggested I speak to you, Mr. Armstrong. How can I help you?"

His expression was professionally polite, but his gaze was locked on Roy's tote bag and the cat inside it. Roy had the sense he was not at all comfortable talking to someone who included his pet in business meetings. That suited Roy just fine. "Trevor and I are investigating Ralph Sharpe's murder. Jennie Symmonds thinks you might be able to help us with information on how Ralph did business."

Grogan didn't immediately answer. He dragged his gaze away from the tote bag, looking first at Roy, then Trevor. Finally, he said, "Are you PIs?"

"Neither of us is a private investigator," Trevor said. "I'm a lawyer and I'm researching the information on behalf of an individual the police are viewing as their prime suspect."

Grogan's attention shifted to Trevor. Stormy extricated himself from the tote and hopped down from Roy's lap.

"The do-gooder, you mean," Grogan said.

"That is not how I would describe my client," Trevor said. His dry tone said he didn't really disagree with the description, though.

Grogan nodded. "You're trying to shift the focus of the investigation from the fancy school he runs and push it onto Sharpe's business interests."

"We are trying to find out if the danger in Sharpe's life came from his professional involvement, rather than the volunteer work he did," Trevor said. His voice was even, without a lot of inflection. He wasn't challenging Grogan, but he wasn't letting him get the upper hand either.

The man's mouth tightened. "I didn't like Ralph Sharpe, but I didn't kill him."

Stormy jumped up onto his desk. *Good. Now we've got that out of the way, let's move on to the important stuff.* The cat butted Grogan's hand. Surprised, he began to pet him. He looked from Trevor to Roy with a frown.

"Why didn't you like Ralph Sharpe, Mr. Grogan?" Trevor asked.

Stormy arched under Grogan's stroking hand. *Go ahead. You can tell him. It's okay.*

Grogan looked from the cat to Trevor and Roy again. Roy raised his brows, made his expression questioning. Trevor cleared his throat. Grogan's mouth hardened. "He almost put me out of business, that's why."

Stormy began to purr. Roy did his best to look encouraging. Trevor's expression was inscrutable.

Grogan sighed and said, "Three years ago, Sharpe acquired a company I'd been working with. We had had a long association. I provided warehousing and distribution for their product. I'd won the contract when they first started up, and for six years we simply amended that contract if necessary. Then Sharpe bought the company and everything changed."

"Jennie said you had to rebid to keep the contract," Roy said.

Grogan grimaced. "I have to rebid annually now. And every year Sharpe Products demands a new concession. A point or two off the distribution fee, faster turnaround on shipment. That kind of thing. My margins are so thin I can barely cover my costs."

"Why do you bother working with his company then?" Roy was genuinely interested. It seemed unfathomable to him to continue in a business that was going nowhere.

Grogan waved his hand at the interior window. "I have a large space here and it needs to be filled. Until I can find other contracts, I need to keep Sharpe Products as a client."

Stormy meowed, reminding Grogan that his primary job was to keep patting him. Smiling faintly, Grogan looked down at the cat as he began to pat him again.

How's that going?

"Better than expected," Grogan said, still looking down at the cat. "I hope to have a full list of well-paying clients by the time my current contract with Sharpe Products is over. If I make my target, I won't be rebidding." He appeared unaware he was answering a voice in his head and not Trevor or Roy.

Purring noisily, the cat flopped onto his side. *Good for you. Sharpe sounds like an unpleasant sort to do business with.*

"Sharpe by name, sharp by nature." Still focused on the cat, Grogan switched from Stormy's back to his now accessible side.

"Are you suggesting Sharpe engages in underhanded business practices?" Trevor asked.

Grogan looked up, frowning. He looked down at the cat, then up at Trevor again, before he glanced at Roy. He cleared his throat.

"You can tell us," Roy said in a reassuring way.

Grogan looked from one to the other, his eyes narrowed. Then he shrugged. "Why not? Sharpe has—had—a nose for the next big thing. It's no secret he was a marketing genius. Take the company I worked with. They made a handy little can opener that was battery powered and fit in a drawer. You could use it anywhere. In your kitchen, on your deck, camping. Anywhere. It was a great idea and the people who bought it, loved it. The problem was, it was more expensive than bigger, clunkier plug-in electric can openers, so its market share wasn't great. Sharpe acquired the company, took the production offshore, and cut the price. In the first year under Sharpe Products, sales went up. They skyrocketed the second year, then tanked last year."

"Why?" Roy asked. He thought he knew the answer. This must be the can opener Hammer told them about last night.

"Quality," Trevor said.

Grogan nodded. "Yup, that's it. The previous owners had the product made here, across the river in Quebec, actually. Like me, when Sharpe Products took over, that company had to rebid on their manufacturing contract and they didn't make the cut. Sharpe gave the contract to a bidder in the Far East. The items the new manufacturer produced were not as durable and tended to break after a few usages. People started to complain, but before they did, he sold a ton of product."

Even more puzzled than before, Roy said, "It doesn't sound like a good business model to purchase a company for the product it makes, then allow that product to fail. How do you make a profit? How do you stay in business?"

"You don't," Grogan said. "At least the company you bought doesn't. You make a big profit, then when the company fails, you write the loss off against the profit and take a tax write off."

Roy considered himself a bright guy, but he was even more confused than before. "Okay, but I'm still not seeing a profit here."

Trevor sent Grogan a knowing look. "You don't pay full value for the company you acquire. You pay a portion in cash to secure the deal, and the rest in shares or options. Am I close?"

Grogan nodded. "In the case of my can opener company, the owners told me he provided a base payment of twenty percent of evaluation. They had a lifetime percentage of the revenue from all units sold. Sharpe told them a pretty story about intensive marketing, growing market share, sending the product international. He described revenue in the billions, with their annual share in the millions." He shrugged. "They were blown away. Are you surprised?"

"What kind of a lifetime was he projecting for the product?" Trevor asked, somewhat grimly.

"Twenty-five years."

"Wow," Roy said, understanding at last. "And they got, what three?"

What a bastard.

"He was that." Grogan shook his head. After a moment, probably when he realized that neither Roy's nor Trevor's lips had moved, he cleared his throat uneasily. "He hasn't dumped the product yet, but I can see it coming."

Trevor's gaze was level. "He's done it before."

Grogan nodded. "Many times. He's a quick in-and-out man."

"Why would anyone believe his sales pitch and make a deal with him, then?" Roy asked.

"Ralph Sharpe was a salesman, and a very good one. He was also ruthless. If he wanted your company, he'd sweet talk you into selling it, or he'd force you into it."

"Hostile takeovers," Trevor said.

Grogan nodded. "He doesn't just buy up local firms who might know his reputation, either. It's a big country. Lots of small businesses are looking for investors. They may not know much about Sharpe Products beyond the fact they've seen them on an Internet advertisement or an infomercial on late night TV."

Trevor shook his head. "Trust is an amazing thing."

"It is that. Now, gentlemen, is there anything else I can tell you?"

"Have the police spoken to you at all?" Trevor asked.

Grogan shook his head.

Have to ask, then. Where were you when Sharpe was killed?

Grogan looked from Roy to Trevor. He cleared his throat again, in that uneasy way. "I suppose you want to know if I have an alibi for the night Sharpe was killed."

Roy nodded in an encouraging way. Grogan's mouth narrowed.

"Is that really necessary?"

Yup.

Trevor raised a brow. Grogan sighed. "I was at home with my family. Okay?"

You have our thanks.

"You really do," Roy said. "Come on, Cat. Back in your bag."

Must I?

"Yes."

Grogan's eyes widened as Stormy got up lazily. He butted Grogan's hand, then licked it gently, before trotting to the edge of the desk. From there he jumped onto Roy's lap, and with great dignity, submitted to being stuffed into the tote.

Trevor and Roy rose. Trevor reached out his hand as Roy slung the bag's straps over his shoulder. "Thank you for your time and assistance today. We appreciate it."

Staring at the tote bag, with the cat's head now sticking out of the opening, Grogan nodded. He seemed to be frozen into his chair.

We'll be in touch if we need anything more.

Grogan nodded again. Sweat beaded his brow.

"Time to go," Trevor said gently. "Good luck, Mr. Grogan."

Roy looked back as they began their descent to the warehouse floor. Grogan was still sitting stiffly, staring at the big windows, watching them leave. Roy had a feeling he'd be there for a while after they were gone, trying to make sense of the impossible.

CHAPTER 22

As his interview with Karla Sharpe was not until one o'clock, Quinn decided to contact his father before he set out. He was curious about how the meeting with the disgruntled supplier had gone. His call caught Roy at the right moment. He and Trevor had recently finished talking to their target and were looking for something to do.

Roy invited himself, Trevor, and the cat along to Quinn's interview with Karla Sharpe. It wasn't exactly what Quinn had had in mind, but he could live with it. He knew his father and the cat were likely to cause some kind of disruption, but he had Trevor to help keep them both in line.

He hoped.

Karla Sharpe was an attractive young woman with short dark hair, big, blue eyes and a soft, pretty face. She was wearing a summer dress with a medium-length skirt that flared when she moved. Though her clothes didn't advertise family wealth, Quinn recognized an expert hand in the simple style and also in her leather heels, which he was certain were hand stitched. Her employer was one of the many educational institutions in Ottawa, located in an area called Centrepoint, which was some distance away from the condo. She worked in the fundraising department.

Karla met them inside one of the college's buildings, at a bustling cafeteria. Recognizing her was an easy task. She was as tall as her brother and had similar features. When he introduced himself and the others, she nodded briskly. "You'll have to excuse me if I eat while we talk. I only have a half an hour for lunch."

"How's the food here?" Roy asked amiably, ignoring the questioning look she'd given him and Trevor as Quinn made the introductions. "We haven't had lunch either, so I'm a bit peckish."

As Roy spoke, the cat popped his head out of the tote bag. Karla frowned. "The food's fine. It's a cafeteria." She looked from the cat to Quinn, then back to Roy. "You can't take a cat in there."

Resigned, Quinn said, "What would you like, Dad? I'll pick it up for you." So far, things were on a steady downward slope and he wasn't doing much of a job keeping them under control.

"Whatever," Roy said. A second later, he blinked and his features twisted into an expression of innocence—if a middle-aged man with long hair tied back in a queue wearing a plaid shirt and jeans could ever look innocent. He said affably, "How about some shrimp, hold the mayo and seasonings. Or maybe some plain tuna?"

"A chicken leg," Trevor said helpfully. "Cold, if possible."

Roy beamed. "That's the idea."

Karla's expression was becoming more and more critical.

Quinn knew exactly what had caused this food freak show. The damned cat was talking again. If he didn't stop this ridiculous circus now this interview was going to turn into an out-of-control disaster. "Why don't you come with us, Trevor? You seem to have a handle on what Dad wants."

Trevor's eyes twinkled. "My pleasure." He turned to Karla with a smile. "Is there a place we might sit outside to eat our meal? Where we could, er, let the cat out of the bag, so to speak?"

Karla stared at him for a moment, then she laughed. "Yeah, there's a small courtyard that's accessed at the end of the corridor over there."

"Great!" Roy said. "I'll go ahead and find us somewhere to sit. I'll meet you there."

With Roy and the cat safely out of the way, things settled down a bit. Between them, he and Trevor found meals for both Roy and the cat—not shrimp, but some kind of fish destined to be used in a taco but cooked plain at their request. Together with Karla, they made their way out to the courtyard, which turned out to be a grassy lawn dotted with picnic tables enclosed by the college's buildings. Roy had found them a table near an enclosure made with snow fencing that appeared to be the home of a family of ducks. He'd released the cat from the tote bag and Stormy now stood with his nose pressed between the slats of the storm fencing, eyes glued on what must be almost a dozen ducklings.

"Is the fence high enough to keep your cat out? Can he jump it?" Karla cast a worried look at Stormy, then followed it up with a disapproving one for Roy.

"The cat's not going to hurt the baby ducks," Roy said. He followed that up with a pointed, "Are you, Stormy?"

The cat turned his head at the sound of his name and his tail lashed ominously. Trevor cleared his throat and shared a concerned glance with Roy.

"The cat must be hungry," Quinn said, gritting his teeth. Karla was giving every indication that if the damned cat hopped into the duck pen and ate one of the ducklings, she'd raise a ruckus so big they'd have to slink out without getting a thing from her, just to save themselves.

"Stormy!" Roy said, snapping his fingers. "Get over here. Trevor's got you fresh fish."

Quinn realized the cat was glaring at him. Evidently, the beast wasn't pleased by Trevor's choice of protein and had decided to blame Quinn. Fair enough. If this interview went south, he was going to blame the cat.

Karla set her tray on the table and settled in while Roy broke the fish into small pieces and put the plate onto the ground for Stormy, who condescended to come over to the picnic table to sample his fish. They all took bites of their lunch.

Karla opened the conversation. "Look, I don't have a lot of time, so let's get started. Todd told me there's some rumor going around that YES! is a cult. Is that correct?"

Relieved to begin and pleased they weren't going to have to struggle through a thicket of small talk to get to the heart of the matter, Quinn nodded. "Your brother and another man both referred to it that way."

Karla shook her head. "Idiot. If Dad was still alive, I'd probably say Hunter was trying to suck up to him, but since he's gone..."

"We're very sorry for your loss," Trevor said, sounding sincere.

She shook her head. "Thank you, but I haven't had a relationship with my dad for years, ever since I decided that a man who was all smiles when he was in public, but shouted at his family and treated his workers like dirt, wasn't much of a father." She sighed. "At one point, I believed Hunter and I could take over Sharpe Products and make everything right. I was naïve."

Roy raised his brows. He glanced at Trevor, then they both looked down at Stormy, munching away at his fish lunch. Roy said in a musing way, "It's never easy for a kid to step into his father's shoes."

Was his father repeating something the cat had said? So far, it didn't appear that Karla heard him anymore than Quinn did. He was relieved. There was no telling what would happen when their interviewees were aware of the cat's voice. "What were you naïve about?"

Karla shrugged. "What my role in the company would be. Dad told me that when I graduated from university, he wanted me to run the Compress-a-Brick product line. It looked to be our biggest product yet and I was excited. We agreed that while I was in school, I'd spend some time at the office, getting to know the staff and letting them get to know me."

"Sounds like a sensible plan," Trevor said.

She nodded. "It worked too. I'd enrolled in YES! and taken their leadership courses. I was keen to get involved. The problem was, when I did, I found out how angry the people who worked for Sharpe Products were, how they felt cheated by the way my dad treated them. I went to him with their complaints and he said they were just whiners. He wanted to know their names so he could fire them. Can you imagine? I wouldn't rat any of them out to him and he was furious. He blamed YES! for what he called my betrayal and said they'd brainwashed me."

"That's where the cult stuff comes from, then?" Roy asked.

"Probably." She shrugged, then leaned forward, her expression suddenly earnest. "Look. YES! is a place that encourages learning and discussion and self-realization. They cap that off with internships in decent organizations that enhance those qualities. Some people—like me!—come away with a new set of goals and a better understanding of where they fit in the world. Others realize they like where they were planning to go and understand why they wanted to go there. It's all a matter of personal growth. YES! doesn't care where you end up, just that you do it to the best of your abilities."

"Did the argument about how YES! influenced your decisions finish your relationship with your father?" Quinn asked.

She nodded, looking miserable. "I told him I wouldn't work for the company unless he gave me free rein to make changes. He refused. That was the last time we talked. Now that he's gone, I wish it could have ended differently."

She sighed and chewed her sandwich. Quinn could see that her eyes were suspiciously moist. "Must be tough," he said sympathetically.

She nodded. "I second guess myself, you know? If I'd been more accommodating, could I have helped those poor people who worked for him? Could I have changed him?" She made a face. "Probably no to both. Dad was Dad. He did things his way and if you didn't like it you had to move on." She sighed again, her expression gloomy, and took another bite.

"Have you any idea who might have wanted to kill your father?" Trevor asked, deep in lawyer mode.

She must have caught his tone because she said sharply, "Not me! Besides, as I told that police detective, Fortier, I was at a fundraising event the night Dad was killed. I have a hundred people who saw me there. I was the MC and I was on and off the stage all evening." Calming down a bit, she added, "I didn't like my dad, but he was my dad. I wouldn't hurt him."

Trevor nodded. Roy glanced down at the cat, now licking his chops after consuming all of the fish. He hopped up onto Roy's lap and started to clean his face with one paw. Quinn decided the wretched beast must have made another comment, and wondered what it was.

The answer came in the form of a question from Trevor. "From what you've told us, your father could have had many enemies," Trevor said. "Are there any possibilities you can think of?"

Karla stared at her sandwich. The silence hung heavily. Finally, she looked up. "If you're talking about someone who might be mad enough to harm my father, you should talk to Elias Keane."

"Who's he?" Roy asked.

She hesitated, then said, "He created the Compress-a-Brick, and boy, does he have a story to tell."

The decision to provide them with a name had clearly been a struggle. That raised questions in Quinn's mind. "He's one of the ones you championed to your father?"

She didn't reply immediately. When she finally spoke, her tone was defensive. "Yeah."

He shot up his brows and let his expression turn skeptical. "Why tell us now when you refused to out him to your father?"

Anger painted her cheeks red and she glared at him. "Because my father was a jerk, but he didn't deserve to be murdered. I know the cops are going after Reverend Ahern, but that's a crock. Someone killed Dad and I want to know who." Her mouth turned down in an unhappy way. After a moment, she stood and gathered the remains of her lunch in quick, jerky movements.

Quinn stood as well. He held out his hand. "Thank you for your time, Karla. One last request."

Shooting him a wary, sideways look as she shook his hand, she said, "What?"

"Elias Keane is more likely to talk to us if you give us an introduction."

She studied him for a moment, then she reached into her purse for her phone. Her expression was hard and angry as she dialed. "Elias? It's Karla Sharpe. Yes. Thank you, I appreciate it. Listen, there are some people I'd like you to talk to about the development of the Compress-a-Brick. Yes, it's important. This afternoon? Great."

Punching the disconnect button, she dropped the phone back in her purse. "You have an appointment in an hour. You'd better hurry. You don't want to be late. Elias is a stickler for punctuality."

CHAPTER 23

Trevor parked his car in the lot at the Sharpe Products office building. They all piled out and paused to look at their surroundings. Traffic whizzed down March Road, a dull roar behind them. Ahead was the concrete mid-rise headquarters building, honeycombed with windows.

"Good thing you have the car, Three," Roy said, using his long-time nickname for Trevor. "Sledge let the taxi go when we came to see Jennie Symmonds the other day and we had to hoof it to find another."

The cat's head popped out of the tote. *You let the cab go and Sledge backed you up. Alice was the sensible one who said we should keep it.*

Trevor raised his brows and didn't respond. Quinn, of course, didn't hear the cat's comment.

Roy shot the cat a dirty look as they all tromped into the building. This time, the pretty young receptionist, who looked disappointed to see Sledge wasn't with them, called to announce them. Elias Keane came out to the lobby to greet them.

He was a youngish man, somewhere around Quinn's age, Roy thought. A little rumpled, as might be expected of an inventor, he was dressed in a white shirt, blue tie, and black suit trousers. He hadn't bothered to put on the suit jacket that must match the pants and the tie was only loosely knotted. After they'd introduced themselves, he said, "There are benches behind the building. Let's go there to talk."

They followed him back outside, then around the building where a grassy and surprisingly well-landscaped area had been laid out. If the front of the building was a concrete wasteland, the back was a secret garden, quiet, soothing, welcoming. The area included sturdy picnic tables, a couple of round, wrought iron ones, along with dainty chairs, all painted a pristine white, and several traditional park benches. Elias sat on one of the park benches. Quinn sat at the other end. Roy and Trevor each pulled up one of the wrought iron chairs. Roy put the tote on the grass and undid the zipper so the bag opened completely. Stormy stepped out, stretched, then sat on his haunches to clean a paw.

Elias looked at him in puzzlement. "You come to meetings with a cat?"

"He likes road trips and he was with us when we talked to Karla Sharpe," Roy said, leaning down to stroke Stormy. The cat rose to rub lazily against his leg.

"Right," said Elias, clearly dubious about traveling with a cat. He shook off the distraction and turned to Quinn. "Karla said you wanted to talk to me about the Compress-a-Brick. What did she tell you?"

"Not much," Quinn said. "She told us you had issues with how her father treated you and though she championed you to him, he wouldn't help you."

"True enough." Keane looked skyward, saying in a musing way, "Where to start? There's so much I could tell you." He brought his gaze back to Quinn's. "Okay. Here's the basics. The Compress-a-Brick is a cheap knockoff of the better quality, better engineered, Compact-a-Brick." He shook his head. "Ralph Sharpe was such a cheapskate he even copied the name."

"We bought one of each," Roy said. "Nice to know we weren't imagining the quality difference."

Keane nodded. "If you put them together and do a test, you can really see the difference, but, you know, I didn't do a bad job creating a much less expensive product. The brick the Compress-a-Brick creates might be less dense and easier to deconstruct than the Compact-a-Brick product, but if all you want to do is put a smaller amount of trash out for your weekly garbage pickup, the Compress-a-Brick is your best bet." He shrugged. "Just don't try to build your garden path with the bricks it produces."

"Do people do that?" Roy asked, fascinated.

Of course not. Duh.

Keane nodded again. "It's one of the suggested uses for the product on our website. We get people sending us testimonials about how great it is to recycle their garbage that way."

Yuck. Stormy wandered over to Keane's legs and rubbed against them. *You seem like an interesting man. I want to talk to you. Will you listen?*

Roy looked at Trevor with raised brows. Quinn glanced from one to the other with a frown. He must know the cat was talking and resent it. "You sound pretty high on the product."

"Why not? True, I didn't create the idea and my product brief was to change it only as much as was needed so the new product didn't violate patent law. Which I did, but I also tweaked the specs to do some redesigning of it. So, this product is mine and I'm proud of it. I have a stake in it. Not as much as the original inventor, but some."

Stormy flopped down on Keane's feet and rolled onto his back. *You're not going to listen, are you?* There was a sigh in the voice.

"Who is the original inventor?" Trevor asked.

"His name is Stanley Crawford. He lives here in Ottawa." A cloud passed over Keane's features. "He's a nice guy."

"Is he the owner of the Compact-a-Brick company? Or did he lease the patent for the product to them?" Trevor asked.

"Owner," Keane said as he carefully moved his feet out from under the cat.

"Isn't copying a patented product then selling it as your own a little risky?" Roy asked. He waved his hands. "Couldn't Crawford have sued Sharpe Products?"

Elias laughed. "Ralph would have loved that. More publicity for the Compress-a-Brick. Bigger and better sales numbers. Seriously, I'm good at redesign. I figured out what elements were those of a standard compactor and what was specific to the Compact-a-Brick. Then I created new parts to replace the ones Stanley used to make the bricks. So, if he had sued—which he hasn't so far—we could truthfully say we didn't use any of the patented elements in his machine."

"And you can't patent or copyright ideas," Trevor said.

Keane pointed at him with his forefinger. "Exactly."

"Karla told us you were upset with her father," Quinn said. "I don't quite see that in what you're telling us."

Keane's jaw hardened, then slowly jutted forward. "Yeah. Well, you see Ralph considered the work I did part of my job. So, no bonus, no royalty, no special thank you. Not even a raise! And that's a big deal with the product selling in the hundreds of thousands."

"Wow," said Roy.

Keane nodded. "Ralph wasn't the kind of guy who was interested in beginning from nothing. He liked to buy companies with good ideas. Then he'd get me to figure out how the product could be manufactured more cheaply. Once we had that in place, he'd advertise the hell out of it, until the market was saturated, then he'd dump it and go on to the next one."

Wagging his finger, Keane continued, "But Stanley wouldn't sell to him, so we had to redesign. A much bigger job. I didn't care about those other products. All I was doing was replacing quality materials with more flimsy ones. Not a big deal. But the Compact-a-Brick? I worked hard on that baby. It was mine. I deserved more than what I got."

"You mentioned Crawford was here in Ottawa. Did he ever approach you? Or do you know if he ever approached Ralph Sharpe about the Compress-a-Brick?"

"Yeah. I think he came to the office here one day to ask Ralph to cease and desist. Ralph came down to R & D after his visit to crow. He said Stanley begged him to stop selling the Compress-a-Brick, but like, why would he?"

"I suppose Crawford's sales were down," Roy suggested.

Keane snorted. "Down? They're practically nonexistent. Compact-a-Brick is going bankrupt, for sure."

"That's unfortunate," Roy said.

"For Stanley Crawford, not for Sharpe Products," Keane said with a shrug.

"Have the cops talked to you about this?" Trevor asked.

Keane shook his head.

"Can you tell us your whereabouts, then, on the night Ralph Sharpe was killed?" Trevor asked.

Keane shot him one of his defiant looks and for a moment Quinn thought he wouldn't answer, then he shrugged. "I was at home, here in Kanata. Alone, because my damned wife divorced me two years ago for being a dumbass and not demanding royalty rights for the Compress-a-Brick. No one in the house but me and the TV, because she took our son with her." His jaw jutted again. "That satisfy you?"

Trevor simply raised his brows and smiled. "Thank you for your candor."

Keane looked at his watch and stood. "Look, I've got to get back. Is there anything else you want to ask me?"

Quinn looked at the others. Roy and Trevor both shook their heads. Quinn put out his hand and said, "I think we're good for now. I'll be in touch if I need anything more."

Keane nodded and shook.

They watched him stride away.

"Well, that was interesting," Roy said.

Quinn nodded. "A wealth of information."

Trevor laughed. "Fortier is going to be annoyed."

∽

"Ralph Sharpe had some questionable business practices," Roy said, shaking his head as he helped Christy spread a new linen tablecloth over the large boardroom table. They were in the community room setting up for the dinner with Archie and Marian, who were due to arrive in about an hour. Roy had no idea why a tablecloth was necessary, since the table surface was a gleaming walnut finished with some kind of polish that made wiping away food stains a breeze. Ellen had apparently made a special effort to purchase the cloth, though, so it was going on the table, needed or not.

Noelle was watching TV while Ellen fussed and the others followed her instructions. As they tidied up, laid the table, and otherwise made the room look more elegant, Roy, Trevor and Quinn were filling Christy, Ellen, and the Yeagers in on what they'd discovered that afternoon. Sledge, Hammer, and Alice were still out working on concert details. They weren't expected back for the dinner.

Trevor nodded, but said, "From what we were told, none of what he did was illegal, though."

"Were these dubious business practices enough to make someone murder him?" Ellen asked. She looked skeptical as she carefully folded a linen napkin that matched the tablecloth.

Quinn deposited his load of plates onto the table. Christy started laying them out. "Yes. Elias Keane, the man who re-engineered the Compact-a-Brick for Sharpe Products, has no alibi and a lot of resentment because the product he created has been a big success and he isn't getting any part of the windfall."

Trevor nodded agreement. "Not only isn't he getting any financial bonus, but he lost his family because of it. He's laying blame, and it's not on himself."

Holding a plate, Christy paused to think about that. "So, we have someone who worked for Ralph Sharpe as a possible suspect. What about the supplier Jennie Symmonds mentioned? What was his name? Joel something? You and Trevor went to see him today, didn't you, Roy?"

He nodded. His job was cutlery, so he was waiting until Christy had the dishes laid out. "His last name is Grogan. He's not a suspect, though." He paused and thought, then shook his head. "Unless he lied about his whereabouts at the time of the murder, that is."

He didn't. I made him nervous. He was too busy trying to figure out if I was the voice or not to lie.

"Agreed," Roy said, nodding.

"Translate, please," Quinn said crisply. He was following Christy, putting wine goblets at each setting as she finished laying out the plates.

Roy's eyes gleamed with amusement. "Frank spooked him. He doesn't think Grogan would be able to lie."

Quinn grunted and shot the cat a scowling look. The cat stared back, green eyes wide. Roy stifled amusement. The competitive hostility between Frank, Christy's late husband, and Quinn, her current boyfriend, was always more obvious when she was in the room.

"Grogan didn't have a lot of motivation, anyway," Trevor said, ignoring the exchange. "Sharpe forced him to cut his fees to the bare minimum, but he was still paid for his work and he's been able to find new clients that are better paying. He may not be making a lot of money, but he's not going bankrupt either."

"What about Sharpe's daughter, Karla?" Christy asked. "Is YES! really a cult, Quinn?"

He shook his head. "It sounds like YES! uses some pretty heavy group bonding strategies, but Todd Ahern was adamant that it is a learning institution, nothing more. Karla Sharpe agreed in her own way. She scoffed at the idea and was particularly caustic about her brother Hunter. She claims she was already questioning how her father managed his business before she became involved with YES!. Her participation in their program merely helped her clarify her thoughts and identify how she wanted to live her life."

He described Karla's argument with Ralph Sharpe and her distress that there had never been any reconciliation between them before his death.

Christy grimaced. "Poor woman." She paused for a moment, thinking. "She was at work when you talked to her, you said."

Quinn nodded.

Rachael, who had been over by the cabinets unwrapping one of the packages Ellen had arrived with, joined them at the table. In her hands were two large pillar candles. "And she worked at a college?" Rachael asked. She sounded quite surprised.

Christy nodded at her mother. "Yeah, that was my thought too, Mom."

Ellen raised her eyebrows as she looked from one to the other. "Would you care to explain?"

Christy laughed and Rachael shrugged apologetically. "Educational institutions tend to be fairly generous with time off for personal problems like bereavement. Why was Karla Sharpe at work when her father died only a few days ago?"

"At a guess," Quinn said, "it was because of the estrangement."

"Suspicious though," Christy said.

"Unfortunately, she has an alibi." Roy said gloomily, then told them about the fundraising event.

Trevor rubbed his chin thoughtfully. "I didn't think about this at the time, but what if her event was downtown? At a location near the place where her father was killed? She could have ducked out, done the deed, then gone back to the event."

"Wasn't he hit on the head before he was dumped into the water?" Miles asked. He was carrying another two candles, twins to the ones his wife had brought over. When the others nodded, he said, "Wouldn't there have been blood spatter on her clothes?"

Trevor rubbed his chin again. "Maybe."

"I don't think Karla did it," Quinn said suddenly. "Elias Keane is a good option, but what about this other guy, Stanley Crawford?"

Roy said, "An interesting thought." Quinn had been standing back, reviewing the table with a faraway look in his eyes before he spoke. Did that mean he was starting to see a pattern developing in his mind's eye?

Trevor nodded in agreement, seeming to be on the same page Quinn was.

When the others appeared uncomprehending, Quinn lifted his hands expressively. "Stanley Crawford invented the Compact-a-Brick. He refused to sell his company to Sharpe Products, forcing Ralph to get his own in-house engineer to recreate the product."

Christy looked at him with a frown. "You think he should be a suspect?"

Quinn shrugged. "Why not?"

Maybe because he still has his company and the other people Sharpe fleeced don't?

Roy frowned and Trevor did more chin rubbing.

Christy frowned at the cat, but she didn't repeat Frank's comment. Instead, she said, "You think we should concentrate on the business side of Ralph's life."

Quinn nodded. "Look, we've narrowed the field, and we have some suspects we can put in front of Fortier, but he's not going to go searching for hard evidence unless we have someone who is a pretty tight lock. We need to dig deeper and I think this Compact-a-Brick inventor is the next level we need to explore."

"Well, why not?" She looked around the table. They all nodded.

Quinn glanced at his watch. "We've got a half an hour or so before the Flemings arrive. I'll see what I can dig up on him. That way we can include him in our list of suspects tonight. I'll interview him tomorrow and get more information from him."

The cat yawned. *Waste of time.*

Fortunately, Quinn didn't hear.

CHAPTER 24

After Quinn left, they finished setting the table and the room. Then Trevor, who had already changed for the evening, promised to stay in the community room in case Marian and Archie arrived early while Christy and Ellen went up to their apartments to change. Rachael, Miles, and Noelle followed. Roy settled onto the couch to keep the cat and Trevor company.

In her apartment, Christy made sure Noelle had a shower and washed the chlorine out of her hair before she got ready for the evening. She'd asked her daughter last night if she wanted to stay, but Noelle preferred to go out to dinner with her grandparents. They'd chosen the pizza restaurant Sledge had found in the ByWard Market. Rachael sweetened the deal with the promise of a movie after they ate, a schedule Christy thought wistfully would be rather fun. By the time Christy had finished her own shower, Noelle was dressed in jeans and a fresh T-shirt and she'd brushed out her wet hair. There was no need to use a dryer on it. The day was still hot and her hair would dry quickly in the late afternoon warmth.

Christy did dry her hair, though, before she dressed in her nicest pair of trousers and a silk blouse, then went to see her daughter and her parents off for their evening out. That done, she took a deep breath, then headed for the community room. There, she found the others assembled in the comfortable seating area. The cat was perched on the back of the sofa, waiting for his cue.

To make the evening fancier than a simple potluck with the family, Christy had suggested dinner be catered by a high-end restaurant she'd read about that offered gourmet meals, including wine pairings, delivered to your door. She'd ordered the meal for six-thirty, giving them time to enjoy drinks beforehand.

Archie and Marian arrived at five forty-five. Christy opened the front entry for them and Marian breezed inside, with Archie following more sedately.

"Darling!" she said, exchanging air kisses with Christy. "You're staying in an unfinished condo. How fascinating."

Christy was relieved to see that Marian's outfit was similar to hers—stovepipe trousers, a silk top, fitted at the waist and bloused above it, with long-sleeves that flowed as she moved. She smiled at Marian. "Sledge's personal assistant found it for us. We were looking for a house, but we're a big group, so it was challenging. Hello, Archie. How are you?"

He shook her hand. Like his wife he was casually dressed in slacks and an open-necked shirt. "I'm well." He cast her an assessing glance.

He was probably wondering why they'd been invited, Christy thought. She gestured toward the common room. "Our dining room is this way. Would you like to go in?"

"It's good of you to have us over for dinner," Archie said to Christy as they neared the community room.

"It's our pleasure," she replied, smiling.

They reached the door. Marian flitted inside. Archie followed, still talking. "But I'm not sure what we can do for you."

You can help us solve a murder.

Frank had been carefully coached on his role that evening. He was to try to get through to Marian, because, they all agreed, she was the one who'd be most open to participating in their detection endeavors. Christy also thought Marian, like Kim Crosier, one of their Vancouver friends, was flexible enough to welcome the idea of having an unknown voice speaking in her mind. Since not everyone heard him immediately, Frank was to start the conversation as soon as the couple arrived.

"Darling!" Marian said, focusing on Ellen. "How lovely to see you tonight. We are delighted to be here."

Archie froze.

While Ellen and Marian exchanged air kisses, the cat hopped off the couch and trotted across the room to where Archie was standing immobile in the doorway. Stormy sat down in front of him in his tidy way, tail curled around his paws, back straight, and looked up. *That's me who's talking.*

His eyes a little wild, Archie looked at Christy.

She smiled and pointed to the cat.

He looked down, then back to Christy. His eyes narrowed into a rather fierce frown.

Don't attack her. I'm the one doing the talking. We know who killed Ralph Sharpe, but Fortier is stuck on Todd Ahern as his prime suspect. He won't listen to us, but we think he'll pay attention if you're involved.

Frank's statement didn't lessen the hostility in Archie's expression. Christy said, "It's true. Fortier thinks this is a political killing because of Ralph's association with your party."

"Are you suggesting—"

"That I can hear the voice too?" Christy smiled as she nodded. She gestured to the cat. "Archie Fleming, meet my late husband, Frank Jamieson, who is currently rooming with our family cat Stormy."

Archie cast her a disbelieving look. "Mrs. Jamieson, Christy! You don't honestly expect me to believe a ghost is communicating with me through your cat?"

Roy had sauntered over from his place by the sofa. He held out his hand. "Roy Armstrong. Nice to meet you."

Hijacked by social niceties, Archie wiped the skepticism from his face as he shook Roy's hand and said, "A pleasure." His gaze sharpened. "You're Roy Armstrong, the author, aren't you?"

Roy nodded, smiling amicably. "Yup. And I can hear the cat too." He gestured to the others in the room. "We all can."

Frowning again, Archie said, "Marian can't." Marian was currently chatting with Ellen and Trevor, oblivious to the cat's conversation. Quinn was by the drinks counter, fixing a cocktail for Marian.

A surprising failure. The voice sighed. *I thought Marian would hear me and you wouldn't. Maybe she'll come round before the evening's over.*

"Interesting," Archie said. "Usually, it's Marian who is open to, er, odd experiences." Archie appeared to be warming to the idea of talking to a ghost. Or at least he wasn't rejecting it out of hand.

He crossed the room to his wife. "Marian!"

Quinn, holding the cocktail he'd poured for Marian, came over to his father and Christy. "Did the cat talk? Marian doesn't seem to be affected."

Roy chuckled. "She isn't. It's Archie who can hear him."

Quinn's brows rose. "Really? I wonder why."

"That strange relationship between Marian, Fred Jarvis, and Archie came through Marian," Christy said thoughtfully. "He's used to accepting weird situations."

Quinn laughed and said, "He's the leader of a major political party. This is a little scary."

Noticing her husband, Marian said, "Darling, come and say hello to Ellen and Trevor."

Archie said, "Say something, Frank."

Marian looked from Ellen to Trevor, puzzled. "Frank?"

I'm not sure he fully believes yet. He's testing us, Aunt Ellen.

"My late nephew, Frank Jamieson," Ellen said.

"He lives in the cat, Marian."

Marian looked at her husband. "But Frank Jamieson is dead." Her confused expression turned to one of pleasurable fascination. "Are you saying he's a ghost? That you can hear his ghost?"

"They all can." Archie gestured to the others in the room.

"I can't." Quinn handed Marian her cocktail. "It appears you and I are the only ones immune to his dubious charms."

Yeah, yeah. Brag about it like you're something special.

The cat had followed Quinn over to Marian. He now rubbed against her ankles, twining around her in that particularly affectionate cat way.

"Oh," Marian said. She handed her glass back to Quinn, then bent to pick up the cat. She held him so she could look into his face, apparently searching for evidence of Frank Jamieson in his eyes. "I would so like to talk to a ghost."

Open your mind and let it happen.

"The cat says you can't be uptight," her husband said helpfully.

"When am I ever uptight, Archie Fleming?"

"Good point." Archie stroked the cat's back. Stormy began to purr.

"Oh, is that Frank Jamieson talking again?"

Christy came up, holding a glass of wine. "No, that's Stormy the Cat. He's Frank's landlord."

"So to speak," Trevor said, as both Marian and Archie looked amazed.

He's not my landlord! He's my roommate. We're pals.

"Are you saying Frank and the cat can talk to each other? Oh, my heavens, this is so thrilling," Marian said.

Quinn, who handed Trevor Marian's drink to hold, had gone back to the drinks counter to prepare one for Archie. He came back now and handed Archie a Scotch.

Archie accepted it with a nod. "Thanks." He immediately downed a considerable portion.

Marian snuggled Stormy against her chest. "You must talk to me!" she said in a sultry voice.

Trevor, looking rather uncomfortable at this display, cleared his throat.

I'm trying!

Archie shook his head. "He is talking, Marian. Maybe if you don't worry about it, he'll start coming through."

Marian pouted. "You're right of course, darling." She sighed, then put Stormy back onto the floor. The cat rubbed his cheek against her leg, then wandered over to the couch, which he hopped up onto, before jumping up to perch on the back where he had a good view of the room and the people in it.

Marian took back her cocktail from Trevor and sipped. "How lovely of you to want to introduce us to your ghost and his cat. An unusual reason for a dinner invitation, but most welcome."

"Actually, they want our help solving Ralph Sharpe's murder," Archie said.

His glass was empty. Quinn asked if he'd like another. Archie nodded so Quinn went off to fetch it.

Marian opened her eyes wide and looked around at the rest. "Why don't you just ask Frank?"

Christy stared blankly at Marian. "Ask Frank?" Trust the woman to come up with a completely unreasonable, but sensible, idea given the circumstances.

"Surely, he can talk to other ghosts. Don't you think Ralph would want to have his murderer punished?" She wrinkled her nose. "He was always such a judgmental man. If you crossed him, he'd go out of his way to get you."

"He wasn't that bad," Archie protested. "Sure, he was aggressive and maybe too controlling, but you're talking cold-blooded revenge, Marian."

"Whether he would be vengeful or not, isn't the issue. He'd want the person who killed him caught." She fixed her husband with a determined expression. "Don't you agree?"

Archie had been married to Marian for a long time, Christy thought. She had a sense that he didn't actually agree, but he wasn't going to make a big deal of this and have a disagreement with Marian over it. Moments later, she was proved correct.

"Could be," he said.

Marian nodded briskly. She looked at the couch. "Well, Frank. Ask your friends. Who did it?"

It doesn't work that way. I'm not a ghost. I'm not haunting the cat. He invited me in when I died. The essence of me, the best of me. He's not interested in rooming with a ghost. And he isn't because I'm not!

Marian looked around the room. "Well? Did he say something? Who did it?"

Archie sighed. "He said he doesn't talk to other ghosts."

From the gleam in Marian's eyes and the determined expression on her face, Christy was certain she intended to encourage Frank to move out of his comfort zone and seek out the ghost of Ralph Sharpe. Stormy was now hunched on the sofa back, his legs tucked beneath him, his tail curled protectively around him. He looked the picture of an upset cat. Whether it was Frank or Stormy who was feeling put upon, Christy didn't know, but she was certain being pressured by Marian wouldn't help.

"We have several people with excellent motives and no one to vouch for them at the time of the murder. Now we need to explain to Inspector Fortier why we suspect these people and convince him to dig deeper into their movements and backgrounds. But he won't talk to us."

Archie frowned. "You want me to contact him?"

"That's what we were hoping," Ellen said.

Quinn returned with Archie's freshened glass. He accepted it with a smile and a nod. "What makes you think he'll listen to me?" Archie's tone was incisive, his gaze sharp. He was back in business mode, the offbeat husband no longer in evidence.

Trevor responded, very much the legal professional. "Fortier believes the reason for Sharpe's murder is politically motivated. Todd Ahern's connection with both Sharpe's daughter and Randy Dowell's proves the point to him. Dowell is an MP of course, and Sharpe was a strong supporter of your party."

Archie raised his brows. "As painful as it is for Randy, the situation with his daughter is a family matter. I suppose the people at YES! might have been deliberately trying to recruit his daughter so she could turn him, but, if so, it clearly didn't work. All that happened was a complete separation from the girl. They don't even speak to each other anymore. How could she influence him to change his political views?"

"Exactly," Roy said.

Christy heard the buzz of the lobby intercom and hurried to answer. As she expected, it was the delivery of the evening's curated dinner. She accepted the packages then brought them back into the community room.

They were still talking about Fortier and how best to gain his cooperation.

"All right," Archie was saying. "Suppose I convince him to come to my office. How am I going to persuade him to check out these new suspects?"

"Frank will tell him," Marian said cheerfully.

Not going to happen. Fortier won't listen to me.

With the help of Ellen, Christy was unpacking the bags at the drinks counter.

Ellen whispered, "This is not going well."

Christy nodded. "We need to make Marian understand she can't tell anyone about Frank and Stormy."

"Yes, indeed." Ellen sounded fervent, as if she was suppressing a shudder at the thought of Marian broadcasting their secret to the world.

"That won't work, love," Archie said. "First, he apparently can't hear Jamieson, but more importantly, Fortier's a cop. He needs concrete evidence." He raised his brows and looked at Trevor and the others. "What evidence do you have?"

"Unfortunately, nothing solid," Trevor said. "That's why we need Fortier's help. But we do have strong circumstantial cases for each suspect."

Archie thought about that as Christy called them to the table for the first course. As he sat down, he said, "You should be at the meeting, Trevor. You too, Quinn."

They both nodded. Archie had just agreed to be their go-between.

"We should all be there," Roy said.

Archie shot him a demanding look. "Why?"

With a grin that bordered on mischievous, Roy said, "As a group, we make a big impact."

Archie narrowed his eyes. "Fortier deals with crimes involving politicians and diplomats. He's used to people who speak in subtext and innuendo." He impaled a delicately spiced shrimp with his fork. "Big impact will not work with him."

"I agree," Ellen said. "Consider how the wretched man reacted when I called the local police to complain about him when he came to arrest Tamara Ahern for Fred Jarvis' death." She sat straighter and threw back her head. Her expression was insulted. "He accused me of being a mad woman. Imagine that!"

"He's a narrow-minded fellow," Marian said. "I don't much like him."

"That's neither here nor there, Marian," Archie said.

She sniffed in a disapproving way.

Christy said hastily, "I think Archie's right. Trevor should be there for his legal skills and Quinn for his investigative ones. The rest of us can wait for our assignments after you three have secured Fortier's help."

Quinn nodded agreement and the discussion turned to what information would be needed to convince Fortier to help and when the meeting should take place.

The last was an easy one to decide. Archie had a busy schedule with limited openings. The only time was eleven o'clock the next morning.

"What if Fortier won't agree to the time?" Christy asked.

Archie winked at her. "If I tell Fortier I want to talk to him in my office, he'll come. Fortier believes in chain of command, and I outrank him. He'll be there."

Christy hoped he was right.

CHAPTER 25

The Compact-a-Brick Company offices and warehouse were located in a busy industrial area in Ottawa's east end. The building was low-rise and pedestrian. No fancy architectural flourishes embellished the practical façade, but the grounds around it were nicely landscaped and there were benches and picnic tables for staff to sit at and enjoy the outdoors when on their breaks.

After researching him prior to the dinner with Archie and Marian, Quinn called Stanley Crawford to set up an interview. The man had been open to talking to him, but he'd asked that Quinn come early in the day while it was relatively quiet. Quinn agreed.

So now it was eight in the morning and he was parking the van and scrutinizing the building on his way to find out if Stanley Crawford could be their killer.

He laughed a little at himself for that over-the-top thought. He was clearly spending too much time with his dad and his wide-ranging flights of fancy. Who knew? Maybe Stanley Crawford had a watertight alibi for the evening in question. Time to find out.

The inside of the Compact-a-Brick building was as tidy and comfortable as the outside was. The receptionist was still opening up her station for the day, but she smiled as he entered and told him Stanley was ready for him. Instead of calling her boss to collect him, or leading him to Crawford's office herself, she simply gave him directions and said he couldn't miss it.

As he walked down a long corridor to the back of the building, he passed offices with doors open and the people who used them getting settled for their day. Several looked up as he passed and smiled in a friendly way. There was a sense of warmth—no, community—in the building and he wondered if that came from the boss. He'd soon find out.

Stanley Crawford's door was open and he was standing, waiting to greet Quinn when he arrived.

Quinn tried not to envision the people he was interviewing prior to meeting them, but the Compact-a-Brick was such a nerdy idea that he'd formed a mental image of a short, hunched man with stringy brown hair who wore black-framed glasses with thick lenses. Instead, he saw a tall man, lean but not thin, whose narrow face held a warm, welcoming smile. In his forties, Crawford's hair had once been red-brown, but he was balding now and there wasn't much left of it. He wore a white shirt, open at the neck and dark suit trousers. He hadn't donned a tie or the matching jacket for the meeting.

Crawford held out his hand. "Mr. Armstrong, good to meet you."

"Thank you for agreeing to talk to me," Quinn replied. Like Crawford, he was wearing a shirt without a tie, and chinos. He also hadn't bothered with a jacket.

They shook. Crawford gestured for Quinn to enter the office. He saw a discussion area with a sofa and two padded chairs by the windows. The view was of a grassy area that must be behind the building.

"Take a seat, why don't you?" Crawford gestured to the seating area, then to a coffee maker on a table against one wall. "Would you like a coffee?"

"Thanks, I would." While Crawford was busy making each of them a cup, Quinn scrutinized the office. It was large, but that was the only concession to a typical CEO's space. The room was compartmentalized into areas—desk for paperwork, the discussion area for informal talks, a drafting table for design work. Each space was decorated a bit differently, giving it its own character. To Quinn, that suggested a complex, but organized, mind. He settled with his back to the windows so he'd have the light on Stanley Crawford's face while he interviewed him.

Handing Quinn a cup emblazoned with the Compact-a-Brick name and company logo, Crawford said, "I looked you up after you called, Mr. Armstrong. You have a formidable reputation."

"Please, call me Quinn, and thank you." He took a sip of the coffee. It was his first of the day and it went down well.

Crawford nodded, then grinned. "It's Stan for me. So, shall we get started? I'm always open to talk to the press about my compactor, but given your reputation, I'm sure you're not here to do a product review of the Compact-a-Brick."

Stan got right to the point. Quinn liked that about him. "I'm not and I am." When the other man raised his brows skeptically, Quinn laughed. "I'm working on the murder of Ralph Sharpe, though I'm also here because a friend of mine bought a Compact-a-Brick. She's totally impressed by it." His grin widened. "She's already planning craft projects using your bricks. I think you've forever altered how she perceives garbage."

Stan's eyes brightened. It was clear he liked his product praised. "I'm delighted to hear that. The trash compactor isn't a new idea, but how we deal with our household garbage has changed considerably from the 1980s when the concept first became popular. When I designed the Compact-a-Brick, I had people like your friend in mind. People who care about the environment and who want to find a way to recycle or reuse everything they discard. It's always a pleasure to know I've connected with someone."

"You certainly did in Rachael's case." Quinn paused to take a sip of coffee. Over the rim of the cup, he watched Stan as he continued. "Ralph Sharpe created a product called the Compress-a-Brick. It competes with yours." He gave a low laugh. "Rachael tested it out. She says it's not as good as the Compact-a-Brick."

Stan had stiffened when Quinn mentioned the Compress-a-Brick, but he relaxed again when Quinn added Rachael's conclusion about the two products. Smiling, he said, "I have to admit that I wish Sharpe Products had never come out with the Compress-a-Brick, but whenever anyone compares the two products, as your friend Rachael did, they come to the same conclusion she did. The Compact-a-Brick does the job better. Over time, they'll also discover that it will outlast the Compress-a-Brick as well."

Quinn nodded. "The clerk in the store she bought it from said the same thing. The price can be a problem for many people, though, can't it?"

Stan's mouth pursed. "It can and that's the main thing the Compress-a-Brick has going for it. Sharpe Products sells it at rock bottom prices." He shrugged. "I suppose that's because they get it made cheaply offshore, while I have mine manufactured here in Canada and insist on using the highest quality materials. The Compact-a-Brick is designed to be an integral appliance in every kitchen and is manufactured to last."

His pride in the product he made was evident. Quinn eyed him thoughtfully. "The Compact-a-Brick Company only manufactures the one product, correct?"

"At the moment," Stan said, perhaps a little defensively. "We're working on new ideas, but we don't have any ready to market as yet."

Quinn looked over at the drafting table. "You design them yourself?"

Once again, the man relaxed. "I have an R and D team, of course, but I'm an engineer by trade, so I also work on the new concepts."

"It must take a lot of time, energy, and money to take a product from concept to market," Quinn said.

Stan laughed. "You bet. I nursed the idea for the Compact-a-Brick for years before I perfected the design, then I had to find seed money. Once I had that, I could start designing the manufacturing method. The last to be developed was the sales and marketing component. It was quite a long process."

Like his office, Crawford had compartmentalized the way he'd created the Compact-a-Brick and the company that produced it. Sales and marketing came last. Was that because it was the final stage in creating a retail product? Or was it because it was the process he was least interested in?

Any company that neglected sales of their product was bound to have trouble, if not to fail. And The Compact-a-Brick Company had stiff competition in the Compress-a-Brick, which was a promotional powerhouse. "I'm told that Sharpe Products tends to find new products through acquisition. Yet, they reverse engineered the Compact-a-Brick to make the Compress-a-Brick. That's a bit odd, don't you think?"

There was knowledge and amusement in Stan's expression. He was quite aware what Quinn was asking by implication. "Ralph Sharpe approached me about buying The Compact-a-Brick Company. His offer was interesting, but not particularly enticing. At the time, we'd had some excellent press that resulted in an uptick in sales. People were buying our product and liking it, I might add. I thanked Sharpe for the offer but said no thanks. Nine months later, the Compress-a-Brick hit the market and I started to get complaints about its quality."

"*You* got complaints?"

Stan nodded. "Similar name, similar product. People seemed to think we'd put out a cheaper, low-end version ourselves. They asked why we'd abandoned our core values to make a quick profit."

He stopped, was quiet for a moment, before he began again. "Social media was full of unhappy people seeking redress from us. Occasionally, someone would post that the Compress-a-Brick was manufactured by a different company, but that didn't seem to make much difference. Our sales have been going down steadily over the last three years."

"That's tough," Quinn said, and meant it. "Have you tried getting some social media influencers on your side?"

Crawford's jaw hardened. "We've tried everything. Though I'm not happy about it, the Compact and Compress-a-Brick are apparently irrevocably linked together."

"Do you regret not accepting Sharpe's acquisition deal?"

"No." Crawford's eyes narrowed fractionally and the look in them hardened. "Never. When Ralph Sharpe made me the offer, I looked into him, into what happened to the companies he acquired after the transition to new ownership was complete." He shook his head. There was disgust in his voice as he said, "People were fired, long-term staff who'd developed the product and cared about its future. The products themselves would be degraded in the same way the Compress-a-Brick is a cheap knockoff of the Compact-a-Brick. Quinn, I didn't build this company, or the Compact-a-Brick itself. My staff did. We created this wonderful product together and I wasn't going to betray them for a wad of cash and future royalties."

"When Sharpe Products came out with the Compress-a-Brick, did you consider suing them for patent violation?" Quinn asked.

If anything, Crawford's expression became even stormier. "My lawyers suggested I make sure that the product was similar enough to be a violation first. When we took it apart, we discovered Sharpe had done a good job. It was just different enough to be considered a separate product. Admittedly, within the same family as the Compact-a-Brick, but not a complete copy. The lawyers told me not to waste my money."

Quinn raised a brow. "Your marketing department didn't suggest that it might help differentiate your product from Sharpe's?"

Crawford frowned. "How so?"

"You sue Sharpe Products for creating a poorly designed and manufactured copy of your much higher quality one. Make sure the media gets the press release. Put it up on your website so people can see it. Tweet about it, put it on your Facebook page. Let people know the Compact-a-Brick is made by a completely different company than the Compress-a-Brick and isn't responsible for the imperfections in the Compress-a-Brick."

After a minute of frowning silence, Stan shook his head. "That wouldn't have worked. Ralph Sharpe was a marketing genius. He'd have turned those arguments on their head, somehow. There was no truth for Ralph Sharpe, only implications and layers of lies. He had no conscience and he'd do whatever it took to make money."

"You didn't like the man."

"No, I didn't. Should I have? His company office is in Kanata, west of Ottawa, but he arranged for the Compress-a-Brick mailing address to be here on the east side of town, close to The Compact-a-Brick Company's headquarters. It's a mail drop only, but the address is on the same street as ours. The name of his product is only a few letters different. How can people not think the two versions are made by the same company?"

"How desperate are you?"

"What do you mean?" Crawford sounded honestly confused, but was there also a hint of relief in his voice?

"Is The Compact-a-Brick Company going to fold?"

"I'm not going to tell you about my company's financial situation." The statement was made evenly, without heat.

Quinn smiled easily. "Fair enough. How about this, then. Where were you the evening Ralph Sharpe was killed?"

This time Stanley Crawford raised his brows. "Again, I don't think that is a relevant question."

"It is though," Quinn said, watching him carefully. "You've given me a number of reasons for disliking Ralph Sharpe. If you don't have an alibi for the night of his death, you're a potential suspect in his murder."

Crawford stared at him for a full minute, then he surprised Quinn by laughing. "I realize that finding Ralph Sharpe's killer would be a great scoop for you, Quinn, but I didn't kill him. You need to look elsewhere for the person who did him in." He stood. "Now, my day is about to get busy, so we're done here."

Quinn stood as well. "Thank you for seeing me, Stan." He moved toward the office door. There he paused. "By the way, have the police interviewed you about your business dealings with Sharpe Products?"

Stan shook his head. "The cops aren't interested in me, Quinn, because they don't need to be. I refused to do business with Ralph Sharpe. That it."

But was it? As Quinn left the building, he wondered.

CHAPTER 26

When Quinn got back to the condo, he discovered a meltdown in effect. It wasn't what he'd planned for his return. During the drive back to New Edinburgh, he'd thought about likely suspects and he was ready to put his ideas to the others over coffee in Christy's suite.

That was not to be. Christy's door was propped open and he could hear raised voices as soon as he exited the elevator.

"I'm not leaving this location." That was Sledge, and from the hardness in his voice, he was angry and trying to hold on to his temper.

"There is no way to protect you if the paparazzi find you." Was that Justina? It had been a couple of months since they'd met at a barbeque put on by Kim Crosier, so he wasn't completely sure. But he did know the voice didn't belong to any of the regular residents of the condo and Justina had arrived in Ottawa yesterday. What was she doing in Christy's kitchen, though? She was staying in one of the downtown hotels.

"So? No one knows I'm living in an empty condo complex in New Edinburgh. Why would they look for me here? I'm not worried." Sledge again.

Quinn walked into the apartment at that point. Halfway into the living room, Christy saw him from her spot in the kitchen and hurried over to him.

She took his hand and pulled him deeper into the suite, away from the view of those in the kitchen. "Thank God you're back."

He took a moment to draw her close and tilt up her chin so he could kiss her. She closed her eyes, wrapped her arms around his neck, and kissed him back.

"Okay," he said when they'd ended the kiss a satisfying time later. "Fill me in. Is that Justina Sledge is fighting with?"

"Yes." Christy sighed. "She arrived ten minutes ago and Alice brought her up. She started criticizing everything as soon as she arrived. It didn't help that Frank's been taunting her, trying to make her admit she can hear him. Alice is in a state, because Justina thinks our condo commune is the dumbest idea on record and it's all Alice's fault. Hammer is still asleep, but Sledge is up and he's grumpy. I'm not sure if it's because of Justina's attitude or if he's just overtired. Ellen doesn't like hostilities before breakfast, so she's assumed her icy society queen demeanor. Trevor is trying to calm her down and your father is helping Frank annoy Justina. My mom tried to be nice to Justina, who snapped at her in response, so my dad's now mad at her, too."

Noelle chose that moment to come out of her bedroom. Dressed in her pajamas, her hair unbrushed, she yawned. "Hey, Mom. What's for breakfast?" Now ten, she'd begun to sleep a little later in the mornings. She blinked and frowned. "Hi, Quinn. What's going on?"

"Arguments in the kitchen," he said, not sure how the girl would react to seeing her mother still cradled in his arms.

Though Noelle scrutinized Christy and Quinn, she didn't comment. "Between who?"

Christy sighed again. "Justina, Sledge's new manager has arrived. She's mad at Alice for putting us in this condo building instead of a hotel."

"Well, that's just dumb," Noelle said. "This is an awesome place." She headed into the bathroom.

Christy relaxed a little and laughed as she looked up at Quinn.

He shook his head. "Let's go see if we can sort this thing out."

As they walked into the kitchen, Sledge, who was sitting at the table wearing a SledgeHammer T-shirt and frayed jeans, was saying, "And I'm here with my family and friends. A hotel with rooms for all of us together wouldn't have worked. This was a brilliant solution by Alice."

Standing on the opposite side of the table, her dark hair carefully styled and dressed in a beautifully cut silk blouse with linen trousers, Justina said firmly, "I see no reason for these other people to be here with you. You're in Ottawa to do a concert, not to have a family get-together."

"Are you serious?" Sledge's voice rose. Temper was climbing very close to the surface.

"Who is this person?" Ellen said, her tone imperious, her voice icy. She was perched on one of the bar stools at the kitchen island. Her back was against the wall. A plate with the remnants of bacon and eggs was at her elbow. She glared at Justina. "Yes, I know. She thinks she's important. Unfortunately for her, she's not."

The damned cat was talking again, and if Alice and the Yeagers hadn't been here, it wouldn't have mattered that Ellen's temper was so frayed that she was talking back to him. Fortunately, everyone was focused on Justina, whose face had reddened before Ellen spoke. Justina, of course, knew exactly what the cat had said. Quinn wondered what she thought about Ellen obviously hearing the cat as well.

No matter. Time to wrestle the focus from Justina and her complaints and back to the reason they were all camped out in the condo. "Morning, everyone."

They all looked at him, including Justina and the cat. The expression on different faces was fascinating. Alice was relieved. The Yeagers both greeted him with welcoming smiles, which gave him a good feeling. Sledge was frowning grimly and Ellen's expression was colder than he'd ever seen it. His father winked. Trevor nodded, his expression saying he'd like to sort this out, but he needed help.

Christy handed Quinn a cup of coffee. "I'm making scrambled eggs and bacon. Would you like some?"

"Absolutely." He'd had a few sips of the cup Stan Crawford had given him, but he needed more. He took a deep drink of coffee before he glanced around the group. "Okay, everyone. We need to make plans."

"You found out something interesting from the inventor?" Trevor asked from his position at the island beside Ellen. Like her he had a plate scraped clean of a recent breakfast before him.

Quinn nodded. "Stanley Crawford's got motive and no alibi."

"Ralph Sharpe stole his idea, didn't he? Then he made a crummy copy he sells for peanuts," Rachael Yeager said with considerable satisfaction. She and Miles were at the table, just finishing off their food. "I knew the Compact-a-Brick man would be angry about it."

"Pretty much," Quinn said. "Sharpe made it worse by promoting the Compress-a-Brick in ways that implied Crawford's company was behind it. The Compact-a-Brick's reputation suffered as a result. He won't admit it, but I think his company's in financial difficulties."

Rachael shook her head, looking somber. "Poor man."

"Are you people trying to solve a murder, again?" Justina shot a disapproving look at Sledge. "Rock stars should not be involved in tracking down killers. I told you that last time."

Sledge tensed even more, if that was possible, then Justina went bright red and he laughed.

"It's true Sledge's profile went up when he helped bring down Clayton Green's killers," Roy said. "That was a fun evening." He, too, was perched on a stool at the island and like Ellen and Trevor he'd finished his food. He was holding a mug between his hands that must have recently been refilled, for he was blowing on the beverage inside, cooling it for consumption.

Smiling wickedly, Sledge said, "SledgeHammer sold more records that month than we did all of the previous year. And our sales that year were pretty robust."

Still red, Justina said, "All the same..."

Quinn cut her off. "We have three suspects the cops haven't even interviewed. None of them has an alibi for the time Ralph Sharpe was killed." He ticked them off on his fingers. "Elias Keane, the man who re-engineered the Compact-a-Brick, thinks Sharpe shortchanged him for the work he did to make the Compress-a-Brick possible. Stanley Crawford invented the original Compact-a-Brick, an idea Sharpe stole from him and made a big success, freezing Crawford out and tanking his profits and maybe his company. Sharpe's daughter, Karla, hated everything her father stood for and she was angry that he was in the middle of a hostile takeover of YES!, an organization she loved."

"Don't forget the two women we uncovered earlier," Roy said. "Like Karla Sharpe, Cassandra Weldon was a former participant and a big supporter of YES!. Then there's Mia Goodwin, the soon-to-be-former Director of Curriculum at YES!. She lost her job and her future because of Ralph Sharpe."

Quinn nodded. "Good point, Dad. We can't ignore the YES! involvement, but I have a hunch we should focus on Sharpe Products and Ralph Sharpe's business connections."

"The eggs are ready. Find yourself a place at the table, Quinn." Christy put four plates on the island between the stove and the table, along with cutlery. Sledge, who was the closest, passed the plates and cutlery down the table to Quinn, Justina, and Alice. Keeping one for himself, he settled in to eat.

"Thanks," Quinn said. He glanced at his watch. "We've got about an hour or so to thrash out how to present our list of suspects to Fortier when we meet with him. After breakfast, I'll see what I can find out about The Compact-a-Brick Company's finances. If they're as bad as I think, that's certainly a good reason to take a closer look at Stanley Crawford."

"Great eggs, Christy," Sledge said as Quinn paused to eat.

"Thanks. I made them with cheese and cream. Keeps them moist." She smiled as Noelle, still in her pajamas, drifted in, yawning. "Hi, kiddo. Ready for breakfast?"

Noelle nodded. There were no seats at the table at the moment, so she said, "I'll watch some TV until breakfast is ready."

Christy went to her and gave her a kiss on the cheek. "Thanks, kiddo. I'll call you."

Noelle nodded and wandered off.

Trevor rubbed the bristles on his chin. He was dressed casually, ready for breakfast, but not the meeting at Archie's office. "Fortier is convinced that Ralph Sharpe was murdered because of his links to the Dogwood Party."

"Links to the Dogwoods?" Miles repeated. Of all of them, he'd done the least detecting and was consequently not as up to speed as the rest. "Does that mean he's found a main suspect other than Todd Ahern?"

Trevor shook his head. "No. Because of the link to that Dogwood MP, Randy Dowell, he believes that YES! is a politically motivated subversive group, with Todd as its mastermind. He thinks it has to be stopped."

"YES!?" Justina said. "There's nothing wrong with YES!. It's an organization designed to help young people succeed. I am where I am because I was able to attend one of their programs."

"Really?" Sledge said, examining her.

She looked around the table. There was pink in her cheeks as she nodded. "The network of friends and colleagues you meet is amazing. I didn't go into nonprofit work as many others did, but I learned so much from my time with them."

"Then you'll understand why we're all here," Sledge said. He stared fixedly at Justina. "We're trying to keep Todd Ahern from being arrested for a murder he didn't do."

She stared back at him, biting her lower lip. "I didn't know…"

There was a pause, during which Justina's cheeks flamed and everybody else except the Yeagers and Alice raised their eyebrows or cleared their throats.

"All right! Yes, I've been hyper critical and I shouldn't have been."

Rachael raised her brows as she glanced at her husband in a questioning way, while Alice frowned at Justina's statement. The rest merely looked impatient. Quinn realized the cat was talking again.

"Fortier may be resistant to investigating the suspects we've found. We need to push him to act," Quinn said. "How?"

Sledge shrugged. "Fortier thinks the murder was political. You're meeting him in Archie Fleming's office. Let Archie put pressure on him." He looked over to where the cat was sitting on Rachael's lap watching the action, and grinned. "Yes, I know I'm brilliant. Thank you."

Justina narrowed her eyes at him and Alice frowned in a confused way.

Quinn said dryly, "It's an idea. I'm not sure how brilliant it is."

Sledge made a rude gesture with his finger.

Quinn laughed. He glanced around the table. "Other options?"

Flipping the bacon she was frying for Noelle's breakfast, Christy said, "Fortier is by-the-book, methodical. He'll respond to information that's detailed and presented clearly."

"The man needs to be shaken out of his comfort zone." Ellen's tone wasn't quite as frosty as it had been when he walked in, but Quinn judged she was still annoyed. She glanced at Stormy. "He's intimidated by the cat. You should take him to your meeting."

Justina choked on her coffee.

CHAPTER 27

Not long after breakfast was finished, Trevor and Quinn headed off to Archie's office on Parliament Hill. Both agreed it would be wise to arrive at the meeting early so that they would already be present when Fortier arrived.

Since they had to pass through security to enter the Parliament Buildings, they factored in extra time to deal with that, too. Traffic moved steadily and as security wasn't backed up, they had time to soak in the ambiance of the old stone building that housed Canada's parliament as they made their way to Archie's office.

As the leader of a party, he had a suite of offices, including one for his chief of staff and another for his political staff. There was also a waiting area. That was where Quinn and Trevor languished until he was ready for them.

An inner room, it was a simple space, with white plastered walls, crown molding, a clunky wooden desk from the early twentieth century occupied by an efficient woman working on a massive desktop computer. A sofa and two padded chairs that looked like something out of an old-fashioned London men's club provided seating. A quick look through the open doors of the other offices showed a similar decorative style.

When they were finally admitted, they discovered Archie's personal office was a complete contrast to those of his staff. The room was spacious, the walls paneled in dark wood with a gleaming patina. Three windows, not quite floor to ceiling, but close, bathed the room in warm light. His enormous mahogany desk, a fine example of a cabinetmaker's skill, was positioned in front of the windows. Two chairs, much like the club chairs in the outer office, were arranged in front of it, but there was also a conversation area near a stone fireplace to the left of the desk. The room oozed power, old and well used. In spite of himself, Quinn was impressed.

Archie was scratching a comment onto a printed document when they were shown into the room. Not looking up, he said, "I'll be just a moment, gentlemen."

Quinn looked at Trevor, who raised his brows and shrugged.

When he was satisfied with whatever note he was making, Archie buzzed for a staff member. A young man, looking harried, rushed into the office. Archie handed him the document and said, "See that this goes out immediately."

"Yes, sir." The young man's eyes were scanning the document even as he turned away to follow through on his orders.

Archie gestured to the comfortable looking chairs in front of his desk. "Please, sit down." He didn't offer a beverage.

They sat.

Fortier arrived seven minutes after he was expected to. As the young man from earlier ushered him into the office, Archie looked at his watch. He didn't have to speak or tap the timepiece to make his point. His raised brows and the significant look he shot the inspector were enough.

Fortier's jaw hardened. Like Archie, he was wearing a dark suit, a white shirt, and a tie. Unlike Archie, his suit was off the rack from a chain menswear store. The suit needed to be pressed and the fabric had a bit of a shine, suggesting he'd been wearing the garment for a number of years. Archie's suit, on the other hand, was handmade by an expert and the fabric was of the finest quality. He looked both elegant and in command.

"My apologies, *Monsieur*," Fortier said. His tone sounded more annoyed than apologetic. "I was unavoidably detained at a crime scene."

Archie's assistant left the room, quietly closing the door behind him.

Archie's expression didn't become any warmer as he continued to stare at Fortier. He didn't indicate the inspector should be seated. After a lengthy silence, he finally said, "Indeed? Then I suppose I should be relieved you found time to attend this meeting."

Temper flashed in Fortier's eyes but was quickly suppressed. He glanced from Archie to Quinn, to Trevor, then back to Archie. "It was my understanding that you wished for an update on the status of the Sharpe murder investigation." He paused while Archie nodded. Then, his mouth pursing into a hard line, that flash of temper again in his eyes, he gestured to Quinn and Trevor. "Why are these two gentlemen also here? They are not involved in this case."

Unintimidated, Archie leaned back in his chair. He tapped the arm with one finger as he studied the cop, his expression cool. "I disagree, Fortier. Now..." He sat forward quickly, clasping his hands together on his desk. "Where are you at with this case?"

Fortier schooled his face into an expressionless mask, but his body was tense. The man was furious, Quinn thought. Not the best way to begin the meeting.

Fortier put his hands behind his back and stood stiffly. "We continue to follow leads, but we are not prepared to make an arrest at this time."

"Are you investigating any other suspects, or are you still fixated on Todd Ahern?" Archie asked.

"Fixated? Ahern is our prime suspect, it is true, but—"

Archie waved a hand dismissively. "So, you haven't been interviewing other suspects."

"Should our investigation lead to other suspects, we will speak to them, of course," Fortier said, unaware he was falling neatly into Archie's trap.

"Excellent!" Archie indicated Trevor and Quinn. "Mr. McCullagh and Mr. Armstrong have unearthed several suspects with strong motives and no alibis for the night in question."

"With all due respect, Monsieur, these men are not the police. They may believe they have viable suspects, but it is unlikely that they do. I am busy—"

"I'd like you to hear them out," Archie said. The snap in his voice told everyone in the room that this was a directive, not a request.

Fortier flushed and temper leapt into his eyes again. His mouth set in a hard line, he looked to be on the verge of refusing.

Archie took note and pressed his point in an even, but not conciliatory tone. "Mr. McCullagh is a renowned defense lawyer who has convinced many, many juries that a defendant is not guilty. He's done that by refusing to accept that the obvious was the actual. Mr. Armstrong is an investigative journalist who has uncovered the hidden truth behind numerous scandals that on the surface appeared to be something quite different. Both men are worth listening to."

Fortier's jaw was now rigid. He looked as if he wanted to stomp out of the room and slam the door with a flourish but was holding himself back through an extreme act of will. Quinn thought that they were going to have a hard time getting through to the inspector, no matter how persuasive they were.

Archie gestured toward Trevor. "Mr. McCullagh, Trevor. Will you begin?"

Trevor cleared his throat. "Inspector, we accept that the police have resources we cannot hope to replicate and that you have been working tirelessly to find Ralph Sharpe's murderer. You and I have discussed this case in the past and as you know, I don't believe Todd Ahern perpetrated this crime."

Fortier nodded, acknowledging Trevor's statement, but in no way softened by it.

"However, we are concerned that you have been searching on the surface of Sharpe's life, looking for the killer in places where there was obvious conflict."

"We go where the evidence leads, *Monsieur* McCullagh, and that is straight to Todd Ahern," Fortier ground out.

"Then why haven't you charged him?" Trevor snapped, his demand as sharp and incisive as if he were in a courtroom questioning a witness on the stand.

Fortier wasn't easily intimidated. "We will when the evidence supports it."

Trevor pointed an accusatory finger at him. "You can't, because the evidence isn't there to find."

To Quinn's surprise, Fortier drew in a deep breath, then let it out slowly. His jaw worked, then he said, "You may be right, *Monsieur*. Ralph Sharpe was killed on an overcast, dark evening, when the area was all but abandoned. We have one witness who claims she saw two men, one of whom could have been Ralph Sharpe, beside the locks near the Bytown Museum. When she noticed them, they were speaking to each other. She did not see the unknown person attack Sharpe, but she thought they were arguing. She hurried on her way, thinking that a dispute between two strangers was none of her concern."

Incredulous, Quinn said, "That's all you've got?"

Fortier shot him a resentful look. "She said one of the men wore a black or very dark blue suit. Todd Ahern owns a black suit and wears it frequently."

Trevor raised his brows. "So do thousands of other men, including you and Archie, here. Did this witness see anything else? Did you find this dark-suited man on any security footage from cameras in the area?"

Fortier drew another deep breath, then said, "No."

"If you arrested Todd Ahern with that amount of evidence under my watch, I'd ensure the charges were dropped before he ever saw a jail cell."

"And that is why we have not requested an arrest warrant be issued for him!" Fortier said, pushed to his limits.

Quinn leaned forward. "If you don't find out who really killed Ralph Sharpe, if Todd Ahern isn't arrested and given his day in court, but remains the prime suspect, he will always have to live with the stigma of being a killer. His life will be ruined."

Fortier shrugged. "Then he should not have killed Ralph Sharpe."

"And what if he didn't?" Quinn said quietly. "What if Elias Keane or Stanley Crawford killed Sharpe? Or even Sharpe's daughter, Karla." He didn't mention the other two women they suspected, Mia Goodwin and Cassandra Weldon. They didn't fit the physical profile Fortier had just described. Even dressed in a trouser suit that mimicked a man's business suit, they'd both have been clearly identified as women.

"Karla Sharpe did not kill him." Fortier waved his hand dismissively.

"Karla Sharpe is a tall woman with a slender build, who could easily own a dark jacket and trousers. Her hair is short. From a distance, and from the back she might be mistaken for a man," Trevor said.

"Why would she murder her father?" Fortier retorted.

"She hated everything he stood for and how he ran his business," Quinn said. "She also resented his assumption that she would be part of that business. Talk to her. She has a weak alibi."

Trevor added, "More often than not, murders are committed by a family member. We both know that, Inspector."

Fortier frowned. He hadn't agreed to interview Karla Sharpe, but Quinn thought he could detect a softening.

"These other two men you mentioned, *Monsieur* Armstrong. I have not heard of them. Who are they?"

That was a major concession on Fortier's part, and Quinn was quick to offer information untainted by criticism of the inspector's oversight. "They're individuals from the business side of Sharpe's life. Elias Keane is a disgruntled employee with a senior position at Sharpe Products. Stanley Crawford is a competitor who believes Sharpe pirated his invention and in doing so has forced his company to the verge of bankruptcy."

"And how did you discover these people?" There was a touch of interest in Fortier's voice.

"We dug into Sharpe's life. Not just his public persona and his political and volunteer activities, but his family life and the people he worked with and did business with. I can send you a file with the background information we discovered, if you'd like."

Fortier's expression said he wouldn't like that at all, but he was a professional to his starchy, rules-oriented soul, so he said, "Yes, please do. All right, I will question these people, but with little evidence, I do not have much hope that this crime will be solved, even if one of these people, and not *Monsieur* Ahern, is the guilty party."

Archie drummed his fingers on his desk. "You don't have the murder weapon?"

Fortier shook his head. "None was found at the scene."

Still drumming his fingers, Archie's expression turned thoughtful. "I didn't know. I assumed it was perfectly clear how he was killed."

"*Monsieur* Sharpe drowned. We know he suffered a blow to the back of the head prior to being pushed into the canal. The weapon was most likely a piece of piping, probably metal. Nothing resembling that was found at the scene, however."

"What about other evidence? Blood spatter, that kind of thing," Quinn asked.

"The amount of blood his head wound produced was limited, with most of the bleeding being internal. As I mentioned, the evening was overcast. Between the time *Monsieur* Sharpe was killed and when he was found floating in the lock, a thunderstorm occurred. It included a heavy rain shower, which washed away most evidence of the incident. We did find a small patch of blood residue, enough to confirm that the head injury was received there, but that was all."

Quinn's gaze was steady on Fortier. "So, all you have is the witness statement, which is far from specific."

"Exactly," the inspector said with a nod.

Quinn glanced at Trevor, who nodded. He turned back to Fortier. "Then we'll just have to find some way to get the killer to confess."

Fortier snorted and raised his brows. "How?"

Archie sighed, shrugged, then amusement crept into his eyes. "There's a cat. And I know Marian will want to be involved."

Startled, Fortier stared at him.

Archie gestured toward Quinn and Trevor. "Let these two arrange the scenario. They're good at that kind of thing. They'll get the confession, then you can make your arrest." When Fortier opened his mouth to protest, Archie held up his hand. "We need to find the killer, Fortier. Do you have a better idea?"

The inspector closed his mouth. His narrowed eyes and set jaw indicated he didn't. Slowly, he shook his head.

"It's decided, then," Archie said briskly. He glanced at his watch. "Gentlemen, I have a meeting in five minutes, so I'll leave you to work out the details at your leisure. Keep me informed."

Quinn and Trevor stood. The meeting was over. Archie had done as they asked and prodded Fortier into working with them to unmask the killer. While the inspector wasn't precisely on side, he was at least listening.

Now they had to put it all together and construct a plan that would unmask the killer. Time to get down to work.

Fortier's phone rang as they were leaving Archie's office. He answered by stating his name abruptly, then listened, casting Quinn and Trevor wary glances from time to time. They were out in the hallway, finding their way to the main foyer so they could exit the building when he said something quickly in French, listened again, nodded, then disconnected.

Quinn raised his brows. "Problems, Inspector?"

Fortier nodded. "I am afraid I will have to leave you gentlemen to create your little fantasy on your own. Contact me when you have something useful." After another quick, short nod, he strode off, rapidly putting distance between himself and Trevor and Quinn.

Quinn watched him go with a jaundiced eye. "It didn't take long for him to abandon ship."

Gazing at Fortier's rapidly retreating back, Trevor frowned. "He may not show up at any gathering we organize. We'll have to make contingency plans for that."

Quinn nodded. "We'll video and record the meeting. Could that be used in court, if necessary?"

Watching as Fortier disappeared around a corner, Trevor rubbed his chin. "Audio is permissible if one person knows the conversation is being recorded. Video is trickier, but if we state at the beginning of the meeting that it's being videotaped, anything we capture should be admissible." He rubbed his chin thoughtfully, still staring at Fortier's retreating back. "It doesn't really matter, though, does it?"

He glanced at Quinn, who raised his eyebrows.

Trevor grinned rather wolfishly. "We don't have to do Fortier's job for him, do we?"

"Our goal is to exonerate Todd Ahern," Quinn said slowly as he watched Trevor's grin turn devilish.

"Precisely," Trevor said. "Without being properly advised of his or her rights, the confession may not be admissible in court, even if it was witnessed by several people and captured on video. However, it's proof that Todd isn't the perpetrator. Fortier may have to go back to doing solid police work to get the proof he needs for a conviction of the real killer, but that is not our problem. It's his."

Quinn laughed. "Ever the defense attorney."

Trevor chuckled as well. "It's second nature."

They had reached the exit doors and made their way out to the open air. Quinn looked across the courtyard to Wellington Street, not really seeing the broad expanse of grass intersected by paths and bordered by a wrought iron fence. "We'll need a meeting place that has an audiovisual capacity."

Trevor nodded. "And a secondary room where Fortier can view the action if he shows up."

"The condo has Internet, but it isn't set up to record a meeting. I suppose we could put Alice onto it. She's worked miracles before, but…"

Their steps had brought them to the path that bisected the lawns. As they walked along it toward a circular stone monument holding an eternal flame commemorating Canada's centennial, Trevor shook his head. "We also need a reason to bring our suspects together. Why would Elias Keane and Stanley Crawford agree to meet in an unfinished condo?"

"Not the condo then. What about a meeting room at a hotel?"

"Same problem. What's the excuse we use to gather our key players together?"

Just past the eternal flame, they paused at the iron gate that opened onto Wellington Street. Quinn grimaced. "This exhibition Noelle has been talking about, La Machine, is happening this weekend. There may not be any hotel space to be had at short notice, anyway."

Trevor nodded bleakly. They both stared at the traffic slowly making its way along the crowded street.

"AV capabilities," Quinn muttered. "Who has AV—" He brightened and said, "TV stations! I'll bet Bryant Matthews would be willing to arrange a studio for us—"

Trevor interrupted before he'd even finished his thought. "If we secured a confession, the station would want to broadcast it immediately. Remember the fuss that happened after we convinced Clayton Green's killer to confess and someone filmed it then uploaded the confession onto social media."

Quinn laughed. "Sledge got a lot of sales out of the notoriety. But, yes, I get your point. Better to keep the confession private until we know how Fortier plans to proceed."

"Exactly," Trevor said.

Quinn stared moodily at the passing cars. "Which leaves us with the same problem. Where do we hold our meeting?"

CHAPTER 28

They began walking again, passing through the iron gates onto the sidewalk, then heading for the parking garage where they'd left their car. As they walked, they discussed, but they hadn't reached a conclusion by the time they found the car and they were out of ideas when they arrived at the condo.

There they found Roy and the cat settled in the community room. Roy was working on his laptop. The cat was sleeping.

Roy looked up as they entered. "Well? Did you have success?"

"We did," Trevor said, nodding.

"I'm sending Fortier the material I put together on each of the suspects. He's agreed to review it and to interview them." Quinn sat at the table, opposite his father.

Trevor nodded agreement as he pulled out the chair beside Quinn. "Fortier doesn't have much forensic evidence, so it looks like the only way to solve this case is for the killer to confess."

Roy sat a little straighter. His eyes gleamed. "That's our job."

He said it as a statement, not a question, but Quinn nodded anyway. "The trouble is, we can't figure out a reason to bring our suspects together, or a venue to meet. Trevor and I both think we'll only get a confession if Fortier isn't in the room. But unless he hears it himself, he won't believe it, so we need to videotape the meeting. That narrows our options."

Roy looked from one to the other. "Putting aside a venue for the moment, what do they all have in common?"

Quinn knew what he was doing. He was in Dad-mode, using this as a teaching moment to force him to use his creative brain to come up with an innovative solution. He had the uncomfortable feeling Roy already knew the answer to the question he'd asked.

He sent a glare his father's way. "They may have murdered Ralph Sharpe."

Trevor snorted. Roy grinned. "Getting warmer."

"Come on, Dad! This isn't a game."

Roy didn't bend. "It's a start. But there's more that links them than the victim."

Fuming, Quinn stared at his father until suddenly inspiration saved him. "They're all involved with Sharpe Products."

Roy pointed his index finger at him and said, "Bingo."

"Sharpe Products," Quinn muttered. "Elias Keane works for the company. Stanley Crawford had his product stolen by them. Karla Sharpe was supposed to become an executive there." He looked from his father to Trevor. "I'll bet Sharpe Products has a boardroom. And I'll bet that that boardroom has audiovisual capacity."

Roy smirked as he nodded.

Trevor said, "We need to talk to Hunter Sharpe about hosting a meeting."

First though, they had to figure out why Hunter would want to host the meeting and then decide who should approach him. That didn't happen until they were deep into a dinner that was a wide selection of Thai and Vietnamese dishes.

Pretty much everyone was there—including Marian Fleming, who'd called Christy to ask for an update on behalf of Archie, who had a dinner meeting with Ezra Gaynor to deal with some party issues. Christy didn't have an answer and Marian was at loose ends, so Christy invited her to dinner.

Quinn had sent his notes on their interviews with Karla Sharpe, Elias Keane, and Stanley Crawford to Fortier shortly after the discussion with his father in the community room. The inspector acknowledged receipt, but nothing more. At least, Quinn thought at the time, he knew the man had the data. How he used it would, of course, be up to him—not Quinn.

Still, he hoped Fortier would show professional courtesy and inform him if or when he interviewed the new suspects. By dinnertime, he hadn't, reinforcing the need to plan a way to coax a confession from one of their prime suspects.

The trouble with designing an important scheme like this one was that everyone wanted to add their bit. That led to considerable confusion and a lot of dead ends, but, eventually, to a workable outline. By the end of the meal, it had been decided that Archie would approach Hunter Sharpe with a request that he invite his sister and the two inventors to a meeting. The ostensible purpose would be discussions on the restructuring of Sharpe Products. Archie would also inform Fortier of the meeting. That was Quinn's idea. He figured Fortier would ignore any requests to meet that came from himself or Trevor. The group also agreed that Todd Ahern should be there, since he remained a prime suspect in Fortier's mind. Quinn would be the one to invite him, though. Hunter didn't need to be involved with that.

Hunter would also have to know that Quinn and Trevor would be at the meeting and that it would be video conferenced to a breakout room somewhere nearby, and taped as well. That would allow Fortier, and anyone else interested, to watch the proceedings. The recording was to ensure Todd's innocence would never again be doubted.

Quinn quickly realized that anyone else included almost everyone at the table, including Marian, who had enthusiastically supported Quinn's suggestion that Archie be the go-between.

It was a good plan until the cat asked what his role would be. That necessitated some adjustment, which resulted in Roy joining Quinn and Trevor at the meeting.

The next step was timing. By now, everyone wanted the case solved as quickly as possible. Today was Wednesday, so Quinn suggested the next afternoon, subject to all of the players being available to meet.

For the plan to work, all the dominoes would have to fall neatly into place, including Archie. Quinn expected problems to divert the scheme, starting with Archie, but to Quinn's surprise, he accepted his role without a quibble when Marian called him (on speaker) once the plans were agreed upon. His one veto was the date. His schedule was full on Thursday afternoon, but open late on Friday. The extra day would also give him more opportunity to convince Hunter, then Hunter to convince the others, to attend the meeting.

At the time of Marian's call, Archie was still with Ezra. He drew the man into the plan without a moment's hesitation, announcing that if Hunter proved difficult, Ezra, who was much closer to him, would convince him. He promised to be in touch once the plans were in place.

The next day, with nothing to do but wait for news, everyone was ready for an outing. They decided to visit the Omega Safari Park in Gatineau, on the Quebec side of the Ottawa River. Sledge and Hammer were both keen to go, but Justina had scheduled a series of interviews promoting the concert. With La Machine already setting up in the city, interest was high. She wanted to take advantage of it. Disappointed, they both requested to be kept in the loop about the results of Archie's intervention. Like virtually everyone in the group, they intended to be in on the final action.

The park included drive-through paddocks where guests could view the wildlife from the comfort and security of their cars, but it also included walking trails and picnic areas. It was when they had stopped at one of the picnic sites to enjoy the sandwiches they'd brought with them that Archie phoned with news.

It had taken the combined effort of Archie and Ezra to convince Hunter to agree to the meeting, but once he had, he'd become an energetic accomplice. He'd secured the participation of the three suspects. The meeting was set for five o'clock the next day. Ralph's former assistant, Jennie Symmonds, would be setting up the audiovisual equipment and organizing the feed into the supplementary room where the observers would be stationed. It was her last day, and she was enthusiastic about being involved. Fortier had proved more difficult, but he'd also bowed to Archie's pressure. He would be there, though reluctantly.

Jennie had asked how many people would be involved, so they did a quick count there at the picnic table with the sun shining down on them and the rustle of leaves in the breeze. As it turned out, only Christy and her parents opted out. Friday was the first day for La Machine and Noelle was excited about seeing the giant machines in action, so they would be downtown all day. Quinn understood her reasoning—she had no role to play and her presence wasn't necessary. Her focus was Noelle and he was okay with that.

～

The boardroom at Sharpe Products was a fine example of minimalist chic. The long oval table was highly polished teak, the padded chairs upholstered in royal blue to accent the pale blue walls. A thick carpet covered the floor, but it was beige and not meant to draw the eye. Stocked with coffee and other beverages, a credenza, also gleaming teak, ran along the wall behind the head chair. Above it was a huge screen for video conferencing or to project presentation slides.

Hunter Sharpe, wearing a dark suit, mauve shirt, and silver tie, was already seated at the head of the table when Jennie Symmonds showed Quinn, Trevor, and Roy—who was carrying the cat in Christy's tote bag—into the room. Quinn and Trevor wore chinos and tieless dress shirts. Roy was garbed in his usual jeans and a checked shirt.

Frowning, Hunter rose to greet them. "I expected only Quinn Armstrong and Trevor McCullagh."

Before he could ask who their third was, Roy held up his hand in a wave. "Roy Armstrong. I'm the cat wrangler." He smiled in a way that might mean he was many cents short of a dollar, or that he was a really annoying person, depending on how his viewer chose to interpret it. He lowered the tote bag to the beautiful teak table and allowed the cat to step daintily out.

Hunter's gaze was riveted on the cat. "The cat wran—why is a cat even here?"

"The cat was with us when we talked to all three of our suspects about your dad. They won't be surprised to see him, but it's unusual. It will unsettle them, you know? Distract them," Roy said, with a perfectly straight face.

Hunter stared at him for a few more moments, then shook his head. He frowned at Quinn. "My sister and I don't agree on a lot of things, but I can't believe she killed our father."

"She doesn't have an alibi," Quinn said. He stopped when Hunter stiffened, his eyes widening. Quinn looked at Trevor, then Roy. The faces of both had identical expressions of pleasurable surprise.

Roy caught his eye and grinned. "Hunter can hear the cat."

Hunter's gaze darted from the cat to Roy, then to Trevor, and finally in with an almost pleading look, to Quinn. "Wh... what?"

Quinn shook his head and sat down. He wasn't sure if this was a good development or not.

Roy sat down too. He was still grinning. "Like the cat said, his job is to try to get through to the suspects and shake them up."

"You can't give any indication that you can hear him, though, once we're video conferencing," Trevor said. "Not everyone can, so you don't want to appear crazy to those who can't."

Hunter fell into his chair. He stared at the cat. "Who are you? What are you?"

Crouched on the table, the cat's tail swished gently from side to side. Hunter stared intently at him, apparently listening to whatever he was saying.

Finally, he muttered, "This is just weird," which Quinn thought was quite true.

Jennie Symmonds appeared in the doorway. "Todd and Tamara Ahern here for the meeting, Mr. Sharpe."

Hunter dragged his gaze from the cat. "Who?"

As Todd and Tamara crowded through the door, Quinn said, "I asked Reverend Ahern to come. He's Inspector Fortier's main suspect. He should be here." He frowned. "I'm not sure why you're here, Tamara."

She colored. "When Daddy told me about this meeting, I thought he should have someone to advise him. I wasn't going to let him come alone."

"Advising him is my job." Trevor raised his brows and sent her a quelling look.

She lifted her chin. "You're going to be doing the questioning. I'm not sure you'll be unbiased."

Trevor's eyes narrowed.

He was annoyed, Quinn thought, not surprised. Tamara had just impugned his professional integrity. "This is actually my show, Tamara. I'll be the one asking the questions—"

Hunter rolled his eyes and Roy choked back a laugh.

The damned cat was talking again. As usual, he was probably saying something rude. Quinn cleared his throat. "Tamara, why don't you join the others in Ralph Sharpe's office? It's just down the hall. We're video conferencing the meeting. You can see and hear everything there."

Todd nodded, kissed her on the top of her head. "Good idea. I'll be fine, Tamara."

"Daddy…" she said, and didn't move.

"Go, now." He gave her a gentle shove.

Her expression grimly annoyed, she glanced around the table. Quinn nodded his agreement with her father, and Roy winked. Hunter's expression was blank, while Trevor was still clearly annoyed.

Tamara shook her head, but she turned and marched out of the room.

Todd sat down beside Roy. "She worries about me." The cat turned to look at him and he reddened.

"Not another one!" From Hunter's expression, he didn't approve.

"Another one?" Todd repeated, frowning.

"Who can hear the talking cat," Hunter replied. "Everyone here can."

"Except me," Quinn retorted briskly. "Todd, we're taping this, so if the cat says something, you can't acknowledge it. We don't want Fortier thinking we're all nuts."

"No, indeed," Todd murmured. He shot the cat a sideways look that was part disapproval, part dismay.

"And remember," Trevor said. "The other three people at this meeting can't hear the cat."

"You mean we're part of a select few?" Hunter grinned. He must be getting used to the idea he was tuning into a cat's voice in his mind.

Trevor nodded. "Precisely."

Ignoring Hunter's rather smug expression, Quinn said, "Okay, this is the way we are handling—"

"Here are Karla and Elias Keane," Jennie Symmonds said, arriving in the doorway and cutting Quinn off. No more time to give directions. He could only hope that the two new additions to the cat's audience would mind their tongues and not give away the secret.

Elias had apparently wandered down the corridor from his office, because he was wearing dark suit trousers and a pale blue dress shirt. He'd loosened his tie and unbuttoned his collar. His shirtsleeves had been rolled up his forearms, completing the look of a man who saw himself as off duty, but who hadn't quite made it out of the office yet.

Karla must have come straight from work, as she was wearing a business-like straight skirt and a short-sleeved summer blouse patterned with small flowers, but plainly styled. Her expression revealed nothing of her thoughts as she walked into the boardroom. Nothing, that is, until she saw Todd Ahern seated at the table. Then she stopped, frowning. "Reverend Ahern. How nice to see you, though I am surprised you're at this meeting."

"Nice to see you, too, sis," Hunter said, arching a brow.

There was snark in his tone. Karla waved her hand in casual dismissal. "Hi, Hunter."

Smiling, Todd stood, his hand out to shake. "Karla! Meeting you today is unexpected, but most welcome. I understand from Mia Goodwin that you're doing well. You're in the fundraising department of one of the local colleges, I believe."

Karla took his hand in both of hers and smiled warmly. "I am and I'm enjoying the work immensely. It feels wonderful to be part of an institution that shapes young minds."

"It's a worthwhile vocation and one I understand completely," Ahern said.

Hunter frowned in an irritated way and his tone was biting. "Karla, can you please sit down? Elias, thank you for coming. Have a seat."

Before Elias could reply, Karla squeezed Todd's hand. "We'll talk later, I hope."

Todd agreed and they both sat down. With a nod to Hunter, Elias sat as well.

"We're waiting on one more person, then we can begin," Hunter said.

Karla jutted out her chin and said, "Why don't we start with your accusation that YES! is a cult and I've been taken in by it."

"Karla..." There was impatience in Hunter's voice.

"Yeah, and while you're at it, explain what these three guys are doing here." Elias gestured toward Quinn, Roy, and Trevor. "I thought this meeting was to be about restructuring the company and new innovations."

"Well..." Clearly floundering, Hunter stopped abruptly.

"I'm here as Reverend Ahern's legal counsel," Trevor said. His voice was cool, his expression haughty.

Elias looked confused. "What does Ahern have to do with the Compress-a-Brick? When you came to interview me, I thought it was because you were trying to help Karla."

"They were, Elias," Karla said. She flicked a look at her brother, then more directly at Todd. "Hunter, along with my father, thought Reverend Ahern was some kind of cult leader and when my father was killed, Hunter directed that bias to the cops."

"Come on, Karla—"

She curled her lip. "No, Hunter, don't pretend to sound all reasonable in that condescending way of yours. I know what Dad tried to do to YES!. I know you wanted it to be the focus of the investigation, but Dad was a jerk. He screwed people in business all the time. Look at Elias here. He's the perfect example."

Elias raised his eyebrows but didn't comment.

Jennie Symmonds appeared in the doorway again. "Stanley Crawford is here for the meeting." She stepped to one side.

"Come in, Mr. Crawford," Hunter said. Jennie nodded and slipped away. Stanley stepped into the room.

"What's he doing here?" Elias demanded.

CHAPTER 29

Trouble ahead, Roy thought. From his narrowed eyes and pursed mouth, Elias Keane was the picture of a man prepared to do battle.

"He's here because I asked him," Hunter said. "Sit down, Mr. Crawford. Do you know everyone?"

Crawford shook his head. Like Hunter, he was formally dressed in a business suit. His was black, his tie was dark blue, and his shirt was a paler sky blue. And, Roy noted, as the man moved to the chair beside him, his shoes were polished to a shiny hue. Stanley Crawford was in the enemy's boardroom for negotiations and his choice of outfit was like protective armor.

Hunter gestured as he introduced each person. "My sister, Karla Sharpe. Elias Keane, the head of Sharpe Products' R&D department. Quinn Armstrong. Todd Ahern and Trevor McCullagh. And, ah, Roy Armstrong."

Crawford's eyes narrowed when he heard Elias's job title. Roy doubted any of the names that came after actually registered with him.

The man's hand shot out, forefinger extended, pointing to Elias. "Are you the guy who copied my Compact-a-Brick?"

Elias didn't pretend to misunderstand him. He grinned in a competitive way and nodded. "I took it apart then put it back together again, better."

"It's not better!" Crawford said. "I bought a Compress-a-Brick. I tested it. The brick it produces isn't as strong. It breaks down quickly—"

"It's garbage!" Elias retorted. "No one wants it to last forever."

Exactly what I said.

"Of course they do!" Crawford retorted, stung by this statement.

Hunter rubbed his forehead as he shot a baffled look at the cat, who had retreated to Roy's lap when Karla and Elias arrived. He drew a deep breath as he pulled himself up a little straighter. "Now that we're all here, we'll begin." He paused, looking around the table. "As the result of my father's death, I am now the CEO of Sharpe Products."

That statement was met with stony expressions from Karla, Elias, and Stanley. The cat yawned.

Hunter plowed on. "As my sister has already said, some of my father's business practices were questionable."

Karla snorted. "You think?"

Hunter ignored her. "I want to retool the company as we move forward into the future."

"How?" Karla's tone was aggressive, her expression demanding.

Hunter glared at her. "More focus on R&D."

"Really?" There was a hopeful look on Elias's face, but he shook his head. "Your father said stuff like that, but what he really meant was that he was going to buy some stooge's company out from under him—"

Stan banged his clenched fist onto the tabletop. "I am not a stooge!"

Roy jumped, almost spilling the cat onto the floor.

Watch it!

Elias shot Crawford a pointed look. "Did I say you were? You refused to sell to him, which allowed me the opportunity to re-engineer your product. The way the Compress-a-Brick has been selling, it also should have helped make me a ton of money, but Ralph said the redesign was part of my job description, and my work belonged to the company." He turned to Hunter. Wagging his finger at him, he said, "In the future, R&D work comes with royalties and patent protection. I've got dozens of great ideas, but I won't give them to you unless I've got a guarantee I'll be properly compensated."

Hunter stared at Elias. Roy had a feeling he wasn't prepared for the demands his head of R&D was making. Or maybe he wasn't prepared that their elaborate staging designed to catch a killer was turning into an honest to goodness business negotiation.

When Elias finished, Hunter waited a second or two before replying. His tone was even, though his expression had tightened. "You have one of the highest salaries in the company and I happen to know my father gave you a raise after the Compress-a-Brick was a success."

"Yeah, and that salary and the perks that go with it are okay for day-to-day stuff, but if you want really innovative ideas, I need more."

The two men glared at each other. Finally, Hunter said, "Fair enough. Take three of your best ideas and work up a proposal for each of them. Then we can discuss next steps."

After jerking his head in a short nod, Elias said, "I can do that."

"Did you ever put the same proposal to Ralph Sharpe?" Quinn asked into the short pause that followed.

Elias laughed. "Are you kidding? Ralph generated ideas. He didn't ask for ours. He created what he called the R&D department and hired me to run it because poor old Stan here refused to sell him his company. I was a few years out of university with a young family and he was offering a big salary with benefits included and four weeks vacation right off the bat. I thought I'd hit the jackpot. It wasn't until I realized how much money the company was making off my intellectual property that I started to resent the deal I'd been given." He grinned cockily and winked at Crawford. "If Stan had been more of a pushover, I don't think I'd have a job now."

Karla waved her hand. "Okay, Hunter. You've made a deal with Elias. I hope you mean it honestly and stick to it. Now, dear brother, why did you want me here?"

Hunter slid a sideways look at Quinn and Trevor. Karla picked up on it immediately. Her eyes narrowed and her face scrunched up into a frown. "I know that look. You're plotting something. With these two guys, I bet." Her eyes snapped with temper as she pointed aggressively at Quinn and Trevor.

Both stared blandly back, confirming nothing. Hunter reddened.

The cat hopped from Roy's lap onto the table. *Siblings. When I was a kid, I wished I had a brother or sister. Now, not so much.* Taking up a position in the middle of the table, he began to clean his paw.

Quinn, of course, didn't hear, but Trevor looked startled and Hunter's expression turned grim. Roy rolled his eyes. Frank, he thought, was getting bored because none of the suspects could hear him.

"Karla..." Hunter said in a long-suffering voice.

"Oh, stuff it," she snapped. "When you said you wanted to bring me into the business, I thought there was a possibility it would work. Five minutes into this meeting, I know how stupid I was to waste my afternoon coming here. I've got better things to do with my time than to stick around and trade insults with you." She pushed her chair back. "I'm out of here."

∼

In Ralph Sharpe's office the multitude of people gathered to watch the meeting glanced uneasily at each other.

"That was not supposed to happen," Archie said mildly.

He'd taken the leadership role ever since he'd arrived in the room. Jennie Symmonds obeyed him without a thought, and Marian took it for granted. Sledge, always the happy observer of idiosyncratic human behavior, found both Archie and Marian fascinating. Other people in the room, though, were not quite so charmed.

Fortier, for one. Sledge had the sense that if Archie hadn't been here, the detective would already have bolted, as Karla Sharpe seemed ready to do.

"This is a pointless exercise," Fortier said with a sniff.

On the screen, Stormy bounded to the edge of the table and into Karla's lap before she could stand up. Karla shrieked. "What is this creature doing?"

Roy raised his eyebrows and said, "He's a cat. He does what he wants to do." He cocked his head and smiled. "I think he likes you."

On cue, Stormy rubbed his cheek against her chest and began to purr. Looking baffled, Karla reached up to stroke him.

"Stormy has bought us some time," Ellen said. "We need to do something."

She looked directly at him. Sledge blinked. He supposed it was a compliment, but Ellen had always intimidated him with her proper Jamieson ways. He cleared his throat and said weakly, "What do you suggest?"

She narrowed her eyes. "They all think they're there because Hunter is reorganizing Sharpe Products. They want something. What can we give them?"

Fortier threw up his hands. "*Mon Dieu!* I am not here to waste my time at a self-serving business meeting."

Tamara grabbed his arm. "No! You can't go! This is my father's only opportunity to be cleared. I won't let you leave."

Fortier glared at her. "Unhand me, *Madam*."

Ellen and Sledge ignored them. "What do they all have in common?" Ellen said.

"The Compact-a-Brick," Alice said, her gaze darted from one to the other.

"Alice!" Justina said. "This isn't our fight. We're only here because Sledge and Hammer insisted they wanted to be part of this. We should be working with the other bands on staging for Sunday night."

Sledge ignored Justina, but once again, Alice had come through in a crisis. "Quinn said Stanley Crawford's company is almost broke." He pointed his forefinger at Ellen, then back toward himself. "He needs investment capital."

Ellen's eyes widened, then gleamed with delight. "And we can provide it."

Sledge nodded. "This is what we're going to do…"

∽

Back in the boardroom, Todd Ahern tentatively reached out to stroke the cat. The purring intensified. "It seems like a nice cat."

Duh. And I'm a he, not an it.

Todd snatched his hand away as if burned.

Hunter cleared his throat. Karla glared at him, while continuing to pat the cat.

The door to the conference room opened, refocusing everyone's attention. Standing there, deliberately pausing to make an entrance, was Sledge. As usual, he was dressed casual cool—ripped jeans, scuffed leather boots, and a black T-shirt logoed with his band's name. His appearance was in stark contrast with the carefully dressed suspects and Hunter Sharpe. After a moment to ensure all eyes were on him, he sauntered into the room. Alice, whose pantsuit was closer to Karla's business attire than Sledge's rock world style, hurried after him. Excitement brightened her eyes and infused her features. Justina, in tight black pants, a form fitting top, and a short jacket, was somewhere in between Sledge's style and Alice's. She followed more slowly and her expression said she was annoyed and didn't approve of what was about to happen.

Irritation at the interruption had Stan Crawford frowning. "Who are you people?"

Alice clucked disapprovingly. Justina shook her head and said, "I told you this was pointless."

Sledge ignored them both as he shot Crawford an amused look. "I could ask the same of you." He extended a hand. "I'm Rob McCullagh, by the way."

Looking confused, Stan shook it. "Stan Crawford. Are you related to the lawyer?"

"I'm Sledge." He sat down at the foot of the table where he lounged with casual cool in the swivel chair.

Clearly, Stan had no idea what the name meant, but Karla's eyes brightened and she stopped stroking the cat. "Sledge of SledgeHammer? Oh, my gosh!" Stormy batted her hand to convince her to restart. She patted him again, but in an absentminded way.

Hunter also appeared to be a fan, though he affected an air of sophisticated *savoir faire* to hide his glee. "Sledge of SledgeHammer, what are you doing in my boardroom?"

Sledge smiled faintly. "I heard a restructuring was going on and I wanted in on it."

At that, everyone stared at him in amazement except Justina who rolled her eyes, and Alice, who nodded. "I'm Sledge's personal assistant and I've been researching investment opportunities for him. We're quite impressed with the potential of the compacting machine."

Hunter's eyes widened. "You want to invest in the Compress-a-Brick?"

Elias pumped his fist in the air. "Yes!"

Stan's expression was gloomy. "Typical. The Compact-a-Brick is the real thing, but whoever you are, Mr. Sledge of SledgeHammer, you've been seduced by the knockoff."

Sledge pitched his voice low and somehow made it dangerous. "What makes you think I'd be satisfied with a copycat?"

Hunter opened his mouth, probably to protest, but the cat scooped him. *Hey, watch it! That's an intolerant slur against cats. We don't copy anyone. We're all originals.*

Sledge laughed. Roy saw Hunter's expression morph from dismay to surprise, then delight. Apparently, the idea that Sledge of SledgeHammer might also hear the cat brought him considerable pleasure.

Stan said hesitantly, "It's the Compact-a-Brick you want to invest in?"

Sledge nodded.

Alice aimed a haughty look at Stan as she said in a bored voice, "We will, of course, be investigating the company thoroughly. The financial records must be in perfect condition and there can be no dodgy practices in how the company is run."

"Of course," Stan said. His eyes were wide and there was dawning comprehension on his features that there might be a way out of his looming bankruptcy.

Alice nodded. "Excellent. We'll also be scrutinizing you personally."

And with that, Stan seemed to deflate. The little flicker of hope died in his eyes, his face fell, and his shoulders sagged. Then he pulled himself together. Straightening, he said, "Why? My company is more than just me."

Alice waved her hand airily. "Of course, but—"

Justina assumed a bored look and inspected her nails. The pose said what she was about to say was so obvious, she could be doing nineteen other things and still get her point across. "Sledge is an international celebrity. He can't be involved with people who aren't completely reputable."

"Now, just a minute—" Stan began.

She looked up at that, skewering him with her gaze. "For instance, he couldn't be involved with Sharpe Products since it's quite obvious Ralph Sharpe, the late CEO, was not what he seemed. He wouldn't have been murdered if he didn't have something to hide."

Karla slapped the table with her open hand to get everyone's attention. "Who are you? And why are you bad mouthing my dad?"

Sledge straightened. A crisp, compelling tone replaced his usually lazy manner. "She's my agent and her specialty is PR. She can spin a positive review out of nothing at all, but she can't work with poisonous threads." He leaned forward. His demanding gaze swept the table. "Someone in this room killed Ralph Sharpe. Which one of you did it?"

CHAPTER 30

Karla was the first to react. She reared back, her eyes wide. "Are you suggesting I killed my dad? What kind of person do you think I am?"

Sledge shrugged. Trevor said in his best courtroom manner, "Your relationship with your father was strained due to your participation in and support of YES!."

She shrugged. "So what?"

"You have no alibi for the time of the murder," Roy said. "That gives you motive and opportunity."

Her eyes flashed. Roy thought that if Karla was the killer, she wasn't going to admit it easily. "A motive so weak it's ridiculous. I didn't kill him. I couldn't."

"There," Hunter said. "My sister wouldn't hurt our dad and neither would I."

Elias nodded. "Yeah, and I'm out too."

Quinn raised his brows. "Are you sure? You don't have an alibi for the time of the murder, either. You were furious at Sharpe. You thought he cheated you out of your rightful rewards for an extremely successful product." He jerked his head, indicating the table and those around it. "You confirmed that earlier today in front of all of us."

"I also said I'd lucked into a great job at Sharpe Products. Sure, I'd like to have had royalties on top of my salary, but I'm not suffering. When I'm ready to leave, I'll go. I won't kill the guy who owns the company."

Hunter nodded. He gestured to Elias as he said to Sledge, "So no one at Sharpe Products killed my father. Now you can see that this company is worth investing in." He waved at Stan Crawford. "I can't say the same about Compact-a-Brick—"

"What do you mean?" Crawford shouted. "I have nothing to hide!"

"Great." Sledge shot him a pointed look. "Why don't you tell me all about Stanley Crawford, then."

"Compact-a-Brick is an innovative way to deal with common household waste—"

Sledge held up his hand, palm forward. He shook his head. "I don't want the corporate sales pitch. I want to know why you ran a thriving company into the ground."

Crawford gasped. "I didn't! That bastard Ralph Sharpe did that with his cheap knockoff of my Compact-a-Brick. My invention was brilliant and he stole it. He priced it so low we couldn't hope to compete with it. Then he used fraudulent marketing to drag the Compact-a-Brick into the dirt. The man was slime."

"Hey!" Karla said.

"I think you're exaggerating—" Hunter began.

The cat cut him off. *Keep quiet! And make sure your sister shuts up.*

Hunter's expression turned horrified, but when Karla opened her mouth to speak again, he squeezed her arm. She looked at him, her eyebrows raised in question. He shook his head. On her other side, Todd Ahern did the same thing. She frowned, but she didn't speak.

Karla's interruption had given Stan enough time to realize what he was saying, take a deep breath, and change directions. "Five years ago, when Ralph Sharpe offered to buy my company, the Compact-a-Brick had been on the market for three years. It was selling fifty thousand units a year and was receiving good reviews. We were essentially a regional company, with our product sales mainly in Eastern Ontario and Toronto. Then one of the national TV networks did a news piece on us and our sales went up. I thought the company was ready to break out into the national market. That was when Ralph contacted me with an offer to buy the company. I turned him down."

Sledge tapped the table with his fingertip as he studied Crawford. "You're not open to new investment, then?"

Crawford's mouth twisted. "His offer benefited me alone."

Raising his eyebrows, his expression skeptical, Sledge said, "You own the company. You're the inventor of the product. Who else would he compensate?"

Stan leaned forward. "My team. The people who took a great idea and got it off the ground, from drawing up the original blueprints, to finding a great local manufacturer, to warehousing and distribution, to marketing it. The ones who run the office, take orders, make sure the customers are happy. Without them, the Compact-a-Brick wouldn't exist. They needed compensation too."

Nodding, Sledge said, "I get it. You're loyal to your team. So, you turned him down. What happened next?"

"He told me I'd better accept his offer or I'd regret it."

Hunter winced. Karla opened her mouth to make some kind of rejoinder. The cat tapped her hand with his paw, claws in. She looked down at him, smiled, then began to stroke him. Todd and Hunter exchanged a look. They both appeared to be relieved.

Sledge rubbed his jaw, then he grinned. "Fighting words."

Stan sighed. "Prophetic words. The sales rise from the news clip was a spike, not the new normal, and sales leveled off. Still, we were doing well, even though we hadn't broken into the larger national market. Then, just over a year after I turned down his offer, the Compress-a-Brick launched. It took off immediately. Ralph sent me an email…" His voice trailed off.

"Must have been unpleasant," Sledge said sympathetically.

Stan's jaw hardened and his eyes narrowed. "It was nasty. He was gloating."

"Really? You were probably being oversensitive. Ralph was a businessman. Why would he bother gloating over a merger that didn't happen?" Roy asked, congratulating himself on the skeptical tone in his voice. Karla's impulsive interruption had allowed Crawford to get control of his emotions and, so far, Sledge hadn't been able to push him back into a dangerous venting mode. Roy hoped his jibe would be just what was needed to get the man back on track.

It worked. "The email said, and I quote, I told you so, and if you think you're losing sales now, just wait. I'm going to drive you into the dirt." His gaze burned with a hot blaze of fury. "You think I was oversensitive? If you do, well, think again."

"Made you mad, did he?" Quinn said.

Stan slapped his hand on the table. "Yes!"

"And it did get worse, didn't it?" Trevor said.

Stan gritted his teeth. "As his sales went up, mine went down. Profits stalled, but that was okay. I could still pay my employees and my suppliers, all the people who relied on Compact-a-Brick." He drew a deep shuddering breath. "Then the lies started. The bad reviews naming my product when it was really the Compress-a-Brick they were talking about. Reviews written by his marketing team, not real purchasers."

Justina chose that moment to weigh-in. "This is a sad story and does not reflect well on Ralph Sharpe, but what we, that is Sledge, need to know is how you responded to that challenge."

Crawford stared at her, silent.

Sledge smiled faintly. "What kind of man are you, Stan? Did you fight or did you flee?"

Crawford didn't answer.

"You turned turtle and did nothing, didn't you?" Pushing back his chair, Sledge sighed. "Pity. The Compact-a-Brick is a great idea, but I can't do business with a coward."

"I confronted him!"

Half risen from his chair, Sledge sank back down. "When?"

Stan hesitated, but when Sledge raised his brows, he muttered, "A while ago."

Sledge shook his head. "Not good enough, Stan. A year ago? A month ago?" He paused for a second, then added demand to his voice as he said, "The night he died?"

Stan's eyes were locked with Sledge's. "He kept sending me those taunting emails. It wasn't enough for him that he was killing my business.

He wanted to destroy me, personally. I asked to meet him. Not here, but privately, where we could be alone. I just wanted him to stop."

Sledge nodded in an encouraging way.

"He said he'd meet me down at the Rideau locks, near the Bytown Museum. Why, I don't know. Maybe because he liked the theatrics of it?" He shrugged. "Whatever his reason, when we were finally face-to-face, he laughed at me. He said it was fun watching me regret I'd ever crossed him. I couldn't believe it, that any man could be so cruel! I asked him if he was ever going to end the harassment. He just laughed and said when you're done, when The Compact-a-Brick Company was corporate history." He drew a deep, shuddering, breath, shaking his head at the same time.

"How did you kill him?" Quinn asked in a calm, dispassionate voice.

Crawford's eyes flashed as he looked at Quinn. "I didn't kill him! It was an accident. I admit, I was angry. I gave him a shove and told him to get out of my life. He stumbled and almost went down. He was the one who was furious then. He shouted, 'No one pushes me around,' before he came at me. He swung, but he was old and fat and his punch didn't connect. I pushed him again and he lost his balance and fell against one of the narrow bridges that cross the locks. He knocked his head on the edge of the hand railing, but even that didn't stop him. He righted himself, then swung at me again. The knock on his head slowed him down, though, and I backed away."

When Crawford ground to a stop, Trevor gave him another push, using his authoritative courtroom voice. "What happened next?"

Stan sighed. His gaze roamed from face to face, finally fixing on Trevor's. "Sharpe swung again, then staggered when his punch didn't connect. By this time, we were on the edge of the path beside the canal. There was a big black iron bollard sticking out of the concrete. As he tried to regain his balance he tripped over it and toppled into the water. He came up sputtering, absolutely furious. I stood there and laughed." Crawford put the heels of his hands over his eyes in a futile attempt to hide from the image in his mind. He shook his head. "Then I walked away."

He was alive when you split?

For the benefit of those who couldn't hear the cat, Roy repeated the question. He thought his tone caught the shocked skepticism that had been in the original.

Crawford slowly lowered his hands. He nodded.

"You didn't try to help him?" Karla demanded, her voice rising with anger.

Stan shook his head.

"Why not? How could you?" Emotion darkened her voice. The anger remained, but it was colored with anguish, tinted with despair.

Crawford colored in response to her tone, but he shouted, "Because he was such a vile man, I figured he deserved the dunking!"

"You killed my dad!"

"Not on purpose!"

Silence followed the words as everyone absorbed the impact of Crawford's confession. It was broken by Trevor.

"I'm not your legal counsel, but I suggest you consider employing a lawyer before you say anything further," he said mildly, just as Inspector Fortier burst through the door.

Tamara was right behind him. She pushed past Fortier as she rushed over to Todd Ahern and threw her arms around him in a hug. "Daddy! I knew you were innocent." She looked up and over to Quinn. Her eyes were shining. "Thank you, thank you, so very much."

He smiled. "You're welcome, Tamara."

Roy noticed Quinn push back his chair, apparently ready to leave. He was the only one, however. The cat remained cradled in Karla's arms and Trevor had what Roy liked to think of as his lawyer face on. Eyes alert, expression sober, but somehow cautionary. Stan Crawford might not have hired him as his lawyer, but Trevor wasn't going to allow Fortier to trample over the man's rights.

"*Monsieur* Crawford," Fortier began. He was ready to begin official business, but the rest of the audience who had been watching the event in Ralph Sharpe's office bustled into the boardroom.

In the lead, Marian brushed past Fortier. Archie, his expression bright with enjoyment, followed close behind. She breezed up to Sledge and wrapped him in a hug. "You were magnificent!"

Sledge's eyes bugged out. "Um..."

Frowning, but respectful, Fortier said, "*Madame* Fleming, if you please."

Marian gave Sledge's shoulders another squeeze, then straightened and waved her hand in a grand gesture. "Of course. Carry on, Inspector."

When Archie shook his hand, and murmured, "Well done," Sledge grinned.

Looking pained at this interruption, Fortier said, "*Monsieur* Crawford, you will come to the Ottawa Police station with me."

His eyes wide, Stan stared at the inspector. "Am I under arrest?"

"You are not being charged at this moment. I will need to question you formally." Fortier looked around the boardroom and all the extraneous people it contained. "In the appropriate location."

Trevor pointed an admonishing finger at Crawford. "Tell him you won't answer any questions until you have your lawyer present."

Fortier winced. "*Monsieur l'acovat*, please do not interfere."

Trevor simply raised his brows.

"I want my lawyer with me before I'll talk to you," Crawford said.

Trevor smiled at him. Fortier sighed.

Hammer, a bigger, heftier, version of rock star cool, punched Sledge on the shoulder. "Hey, man, that was some performance. Is Sledge-Hammer going to lose you to the movies?"

"He's not ready yet," Justina said briskly. Her expression and tone said she wasn't ruling it out in the future.

Sledge laughed. "No way."

Fortier, with his hand around Crawford's arm, was urging him to leave the boardroom. At Hammer's comment, Crawford stopped short. He stared at Sledge. "That was a performance? You mean, you're not interested in investing in Compact-a-Brick?"

"Of course not," Hunter said disdainfully. "If Sledge wants to invest in either product, he should back a winner, Sharpe Products' Compress-a-Brick."

Karla rolled her eyes. "Honestly, Hunter. Give the man a break. He's about to be charged with murder. You don't need to pile on."

Hunter reddened.

Alice tapped her finger against her cheek. "With better sales and marketing, Compact-a-Brick might be an excellent investment. The company is undervalued at the moment, but the product is a quality item that has an audience waiting for it. It might be something we should discuss, Sledge."

Standing near the doorway, on the edge of the group, Ellen was an elegant contrast to Hammer and Sledge's rock star look, and Marian's dramatically flowing summer dress. "The Jamiesons may also be interested." She stared disapprovingly at Hunter as she spoke.

Karla laughed. "Brother, dear, looks like you might be starting your tenure as the CEO of Sharpe Products backing a loser."

"Thank you," Stan said fervently. His eyes glistened. He seemed to be much more emotionally invested in the future of his product than he was in his own immediate problems. "Compact-a-Brick and all the people who love it and have nurtured the company all these years welcome your interest. If you invest, you won't be disappointed."

Fortier tugged at the beleaguered inventor's elbow. "*Monsieur* Crawford, come."

After one last look at Sledge, Alice, and Ellen, Crawford allowed himself to be led from the room.

Quinn caught his father's eye and Roy nodded. This was as good a time as any to gather up their little band and depart the scene. He stood up. The cat unwound himself from Karla's arms, hopped onto the table and stretched. Sledge pushed his chair back and stood as well.

Jennie Symmonds appeared in the doorway. "We recorded the whole meeting. What should I do with the tape?"

"Send it to McCullagh," Hunter said abruptly. He seemed to still be smarting over his sister's criticism.

"I'll come out and give you my contact info," Trevor said.

Jennie nodded and they left the boardroom together.

"This has been enthralling," Archie said, looking around the room. "Thank you, all, for involving me."

The cat yawned and ambled over to Roy, who had the tote bag open, ready to receive him.

"And me," Marian said, beaming at the world in general. She turned her high wattage smile on first Sledge, then Hammer. "And we'll be at your concert on Sunday. I'm so excited!"

Hammer grinned, clearly entertained by her. Sledge smiled more thinly. Roy thought he was wary of receiving another hug and kiss from Marian.

He needn't have worried. She smiled generally, gave a cheerful wave then said, "Come, Archie. We must prepare."

He looked interested. "Really, dear? What do you have in mind?"

The look she sent him was coyly seductive. "You have to ask?"

Archie brightened. "In that case... Good-bye everyone. Until Sunday!" He gave a little wave as they departed.

Ellen shook her head. "That man wants to be our prime minister."

"Amazing," Justina said.

"What will happen to Stan?" Alice asked as Trevor returned to the boardroom.

"Most likely he'll be charged with manslaughter," Trevor said. "Whether he'll be convicted at trial or not is up to the jury. A good lawyer could argue that Sharpe had willingly participated in the fight and was conscious when Crawford walked away. The prosecution would counter that leaving a man who had recently hit his head alone in a body of water was dangerous and irresponsible." Trevor shrugged. "The decision could go either way."

The cat settled into the tote. *Not our problem.*

Roy pulled up the sides and closed the zipper half way. He nodded. "Totally agree."

Quinn looked around the room. "Come on, everyone. Let's go home."

The cat's head popped out of the opening and Stormy meowed loudly. *I hate to say this, but I agree with the reporter. We're done here.*

DEATH OF A CROOKED CAT

THE 9 LIVES COZY MYSTERY SERIES, BOOK 10

Christy stared at the email. The instructions were blunt, to the point, unforgiving.

Deposit $50,000 to the following offshore account within 72 hours. If you do not comply, the attached picture, and others like it, will go viral over social media. The caption will include your name and contact details.

She clicked on the image. It was a picture of a much younger her having sex with her late husband's best friend Aaron DeBolt. The mere idea of that was ridiculous, of course. She and Aaron had been at odds from the time she married Frank and neither of them would ever consider being together in a bedroom, let alone having sex with each other. But the worst thing about the photo was the third person in the image—her daughter, Noelle. She was standing by the bed and very obviously watching her mother engage in what appeared to be very physical and very active sex, and completely unaware of her presence. Or perhaps worse, aware and uncaring.

Cold shivered through Christy, as panic grabbed her by the throat, making it difficult to breathe. She swallowed hard, took a deep breath, and forced herself to focus. Panic was what the snake who sent this photo wanted her to feel. He'd blackmailed many people, she knew, and they usually paid up. Not surprising if they received targeted threats like this one. He was adept at figuring out and taking advantage of a person's weak spot. All in all, he was very good at his job.

The scene depicted in the image had never happened, so the photograph had to have been doctored. She blew the picture up to look for the flaws she knew must be there.

The woman on the bed appeared to have much the same body shape she did, so any changes done to make the individual appear to be her would be in the head area. She scrutinized the face—her face—looking for the joins that must be there. After a couple of minutes of peering carefully, it dawned on her that the expression was wrong. It was calm, almost thoughtful, the way she looked if she was listening to something interesting. Her head was slightly turned, too, again, probably because it was taken from a photo where she was looking over at the speaker. Aaron was positioned beside and above her, making the slight head turn look realistic, but the expression was definitely not that of a woman lost in physical pleasure.

She looked past the expression, searching for more evidence. She could detect no telltale breaks where skin color was slightly different or points where a join wasn't perfect, but there was one place... yes there, where her hair was darker than it should have been as it flowed over her shoulder. She'd been dying her red-brown hair golden blond in those days, yet here the long hair was dark, almost a chocolate color, which was as far from her natural color as the blond was.

She scanned further down the picture and found a mole on the woman's hip where she didn't have one.

Sitting back, she rubbed her temples in a vain attempt to eliminate the headache that had begun to throb there. Whoever had manipulated this image had done excellent work. Two little mistakes and the wrong expression were not enough to provide deniability in the perilous arena of social media.

She moved down to the place where a child's image had been pasted into the photo. At least, she hoped it had been pasted in. The thought of a child actually being part of the original photo shoot that had created this picture turned her stomach.

Whether pasted in or not, the child looked about four or five years old. Her age was of course what this picture was all about. These days, the scandal of a married woman having an affair with a man not her husband was of little interest to those outside their personal circle. But a woman lost in the throws of active sex, oblivious to her small child, was quite another issue.

And if that woman was Christy Jamieson and her child was the heir to the vast Jamieson fortune, there were plenty of people who would be quick to decide that Christy was an unfit mother who must be removed from her daughter's life before she truly scarred the child's young mind.

Well, that wasn't going to happen. She was Noelle's mom and her child would stay with her until Noelle herself decided she was ready to move out. Her jaw hardened and her eyes turned cold.

Time to take this blackmailer down.

Available at your favorite online retailer or through your local bookstore.

ABOUT THE AUTHOR

The author of the 9 Lives Cozy Mystery Series, Louise Clark has been the adopted mom of a number of cats with big personalities. The feline who inspired Stormy, the cat in the 9 Lives books, dominated her household for twenty loving years. During that time he created a family pecking order that left Louise on top and her youngest child on the bottom (just below the guinea pig), regularly tried to eat all his sister's food (he was a very large cat), and learned the joys of travel through a cross continent road trip.

The 9 Lives Cozy Mystery Series—*The Cat Came Back, The Cat's Paw, Cat Got Your Tongue, Let Sleeping Cats Lie, Cat Among the Fishes, Cat in the Limelight, Fleece the Cat,* and *Listen To the Cat!*—as well as the single title mystery, *A Recipe For Trouble*, are all set in Louise's home town of Vancouver, British Columbia. For more information please sign up for her newsletter at http://eepurl.com/bomHNb. Or follow her below.

www.louiseclarkauthor.com

facebook.com/LouiseClarkAuthor